Sixth Grade

Also by Susie Morgenstern

Secret Letters from 0 to 10

A Book of Coupons

Three Days Off

Princesses Are People, Too

Sixth Grade

SUSIE MORGENSTERN

Translated by
GILL ROSNER

VIKING

Viking
Published by Penguin Group
Penguin Young Readers Group
345 Hudson Street, New York, New York 10014
Penguin Books Ltd, 80 Strand, London WC2R 0RL, England
Penguin Books Australia Ltd, 250 Camberwell Road, Camberwell, Victoria 3124, Australia
Penguin Books Canada Ltd, 10 Alcorn Avenue, Toronto, Ontario, Canada M4V 3B2
Penguin Books (N.Z.) Ltd, 182-190 Wairau Road, Auckland 10, New Zealand

Published in 2004 by Viking, a division of Penguin Young Readers Group.

1 3 5 7 9 10 8 6 4 2

Library of Congress Cataloging-in-Publication Data is available
ISBN: 0-670-03680-3

Printed in the U.S.A.
Set in Bulmer
Book design by Kelley McIntyre

For my daughter Mayah
who always tells me about
the things in her life

Chapter

1

*M*argot had read the letter at least seventy times. She had folded and unfolded it so much that the paper was beginning to tear. Although the envelope was addressed to Monsieur and Madame Melo, Margot had opened it, and she knew what it said by heart. Every hour, like a cuckoo clock, she took out this official-looking letter, smoothed it out lovingly, and read it aloud to her family:

```
Dear Parents,
Your child is on the list of students
who will be entering sixth grade at
Pine Tree Junior High School with
English/German/Russian as the foreign
language to be studied.
```

"Anyone would think you were the only kid in the

world going into sixth grade!" snarled her older sister Anne. Anne had completely forgotten what it felt like to leave elementary school and go to junior high. Even if everybody eventually does make it, Margot did feel like she was the *only* one.

So for Margot, this letter felt like winning the lottery. After all of her own doubts, and the painful nagging and those threats from her elementary school teachers, she had finally been promoted—to sixth grade.

Her sense of relief amplified her happiness. Even though she had always been a good student, the fear of having to repeat fifth grade had hung over her like a permanent black cloud all last year. Their fifth-grade teacher was always chiding them: "Come on all of you, wake up, or you'll never get into sixth grade!"

Sixth grade meant another world, the *real* world! You leave elementary school. You enter junior high. For Margot this meant *paradise*.

Maybe he was only trying to terrify us to keep us on our toes, thought Margot. *And he was right. It worked.* Her letter was proof of that.

"Any idiot can get into sixth grade!" was her sister's comment.

Please note that students wishing to specialize in Russian or German lan-

guage should begin in sixth grade,
since class size for these subjects is,
for the present, limited.

Margot wanted to cross out that part. It annoyed her to
think that English was being treated as the language for
cowards and idiots who didn't dare look dragons like
German and Russian in the eye. As far as she was con-
cerned, she was looking forward to finally understanding
American and British song lyrics, which were all over the
radio and in movies and on television. Her mother, who
longed for her to become some kind of scientist, had
encouraged her to take English. "You have to be able to
read English to understand computers or anything tech-
nical or scientific." Her father just shook his head,
shrugged his shoulders, and muttered, "Sure! Shakespeare is a piece of cake!"

"If you want to be in a class with smart kids, you
should take German," Anne recommended, "or Russian."

But Margot didn't like the way German sounded,
and she knew no Russians. She would have been
happy to take Italian, but they didn't offer it at Pine
Tree. To Margot, the challenge of learning a new language seemed impossibly difficult. Just one more thing
to worry about for someone who had enough worries
already.

"Anyway, then it says, '*1.) <u>You are asked</u>*' (Margot told herself that the underlining was certainly a special sign of politeness) '*to send a photocopy of all vaccination records to the above address as soon as possible.*'"

There was nothing inherently difficult in such a request, but in the Melo family, it was the kind of thing that didn't get done without major upheaval. Margot had seen her friends' vaccination record books at school medical visits, but she had never stopped to wonder why hers wasn't like theirs: clean and tidy. In fact, Margot noticed that her mother behaved oddly every time Margot was asked to produce her health booklet.

"Sure, sure, right away, don't worry. I'll find the records. No problem!"

After saying this, Madame Melo would throw open all the drawers, scattering panties and bras over the floor, emptying socks and tights onto the bed, hurling nightgowns onto the chairs and sweaters and T-shirts anywhere she could. Finally, she would lay her hands on a crumpled envelope containing the vital documents. Ever since her daughter's birth, Madame Melo had sworn she would get an official folder to keep her vaccination records in, but with one thing or the other (or more like another thousand things), she had never got around to it.

Eleven years later, here she was face-to-face with a horrible official imperative. "I'll make a photocopy," she decided, realizing that between whooping cough and polio, tetanus and diptheria, she would need thirteen photocopies.

It must be said that Margot's mother was hardly a model of organization. She was always losing important documents and forgetting appointments. The worst thing for Margot was the way her mother pretended to listen without actually hearing a word. Margot often found herself having to repeat the same story three times, or else shouting desperately, "But I already told you!"

Suddenly, Madame Melo changed her mind. "I won't just copy them. This is our golden opportunity to get the real bona fide folder and get all your medical records put in one place!"

The next morning, a fine sunny Wednesday, Madame Melo set off first thing for the municipal office of vaccination records. On the door was a sign with good news: "Open Tuesday mornings from 10 o'clock to 12 o'clock." She spent the next two days wondering whether she should just make photocopies of the records or wait for the following Tuesday to get the folder. Finally, she decided on the photocopies. Margot was relieved, because it could have taken much longer! She had even worried that it might stop her from going into sixth grade. But the first hurdle was cleared.

```
2.) Your presence is requested on
September 2 or 3 at Pine Tree Junior
High School in order that you may
receive your carnet de correspondence.
This must be read carefully and the
relevant pages filled in. You will also
receive a form, five copies of which
must be filled in with accompanying
signatures and photos (regulation pass-
port size).
    Only pupils in possession of all
the correct completed documents can be
allowed into class the first day of
school.
```

This was the ambitious project that Margot tried to get off the ground the very day she returned from her vacation in the country. She couldn't possibly wait till the next day, because she had spent the whole summer thinking about it. She unpacked her suitcase and made for the door.

"Wait!" cried Madame Melo. "Have you got money?"

"Money? No, what for?"

"You probably have to pay for this *carnet* thing."

"What is it?" asked Margot.

"It's a little notebook that the school and the teachers use to communicate with parents."

"Ah," sighed Margot, thinking this was the most important thing in the world. This was new to her. They hadn't used these in elementary school.

Margot went around the family trying to ascertain the price of a *carnet de correspondence*.

"Three francs," called out her aunt, who was spending a few days with them.

"Five francs," suggested her cousin.

"Between five and ten francs," estimated her father.

Her mother handed her twenty francs just to be sure. Margot reappeared an hour later, the time it had taken to get to school, line up, and rush back home.

"It's thirty-five francs. I need fifteen more!" she panted.

"You'll never have time to get back today, dear. It closes at lunchtime and you're tied up this afternoon."

"I'll run," promised the determined Margot.

"Tomorrow!" announced her mother categorically.

Margot went to bed that night disappointed not to have the *carnet* in her hands . . . but at least she knew how much it cost!

3.) Sixth Grade begins Tuesday, September 7, at 1:50 p.m.

Margot lived for nothing but that Tuesday, September 7, at 1:50 p.m. She proudly held up her *carnet de correspondence* for the family to inspect.

"Thirty-five francs! Highway robbery," grumbled her aunt.

"It's a disgrace," sighed her cousin. "That would be enough to buy two lipsticks and an eye shadow."

"I can hardly believe it," declared her mother.

"They use the money for something else," stated her sister. "Maybe to buy champagne to drink when all you brats go home!"

Her father weighed the book in his hands, trying to find some hidden justification for this price. He shrugged his shoulders and kept his opinion to himself!

*   *   *

As for Margot, she thought it was the bargain of her life. The book took up residence as the guest of honor in her room. First, she tidied her desk, then took a sponge and scoured her table clean with Ajax. While it was drying, she tidied up her drawers, the closet, the bedside table and the bookshelves. She threw out toys, books, clothes, and other bits and pieces that she considered too juvenile for her new life.

In this cleanliness and unaccustomed order, she started to fill in her *carnet*. She wanted it to be spotless, an example of perfection in an imperfect world.

Handing the book to her father, she begged him to write a proper signature instead of his usual scribble. She also asked her mother to write neatly. Inspired by their daughter, they tried hard.

Margot needed six photos: five for the five copies of the form and one for the *carnet de correspondence*, and she had only two. She needed these photos right away. She worried that her parents would tell her to wait until the next day, but sometimes her mother understood that a situation could be urgent. Realizing that her baby was in distress, Madame Melo drove her to the automatic photo booth at the train station.

Alas, they were not the only ones who needed photos just before the new school year started. Resignedly, they trooped to the end of the long line: photo booths were few and far between in this town.

After waiting forty minutes in line for the brightly colored booth, Margot tried out several poses in front of the blank screen. She smiled at it so hard that her jaws ached.

The effort was worth it! She finally had her six photos in place. Now all she had to do was decide what to wear for her first day at school. She was seriously considering putting on something totally amazing to mark the occasion. In front of the long mirror in her sister's room, she tried on a multicolored striped skirt. Anne, fully armed with her superior knowledge of sixth grade (she had already been there), stared at her in horror.

"What on earth! You can't go dressed up like a complete nerd, you weirdo!"

"Well then, what should I wear?"

"Just a pair of jeans and a T-shirt!" was the scathing reply.

"In that case, I'll wear my denim skirt."

"Not a skirt! No one wears skirts in sixth grade. Just listen to your sister and put on a pair of jeans."

Margot figured her sister must be right. It would never even have occurred to her that she could perfectly well walk around in a skirt even if everyone else wore jeans. She didn't want to draw attention to herself, especially not on the first day.

The eve of the great day arrived. Wanting to be at her best, Margot went to bed at eight o'clock, even though the sixth graders didn't have to be at school until 1:50 in the afternoon. Her mother came to kiss her good night.

"Mom, I'm scared of sixth grade."

"Scared of what exactly?"

"Everything."

"Everything! What's everything?" insisted her mother.

"I don't know."

"So you're just scared of the unknown. Don't worry, in

a few days you'll be an old sixth grader, and you'll know everything."

"But what if my old friends aren't in my class?"

"You'll make new ones. You've never been short on friends."

"And if the teachers are horrible?"

"You'll survive!" declared her mother, who was losing her patience.

"And what if I don't understand anything?"

"You'll understand!" said Madame Melo reassuringly as she left the room.

It's easy to say, thought Margot. She tossed and turned in bed. She counted sheep. She counted elephants. Then she switched on the light and started to read *Diary of a Frantic Kid Sister* by Hila Colman.

What if I can't find the bathroom? she worried. She rushed to the bathroom as if it were for the last time. She checked her pencil case to make sure she had something to write with. In the end, despite this revolutionary change in her life, she fell asleep after counting to 1776.

Although her sister was starting tenth grade, Margot knew that *she* was the real star of the family today. And of course Anne drove her crazy, dishing out advice. The worst fight began just as they were about to leave. Margot was hitching her schoolbag onto her back.

"Don't tell me that you're actually taking that school-bag to sixth grade?" yelled Anne.

"How am I supposed to pack all this stuff without one?" whined Margot.

"Just take a pencil and paper and that's enough! No one takes a schoolbag the first day of sixth grade."

Margot stuck to her guns. "Well *I* am taking one."

Madame Melo intervened. "Anne, you took a school-bag in sixth grade."

"Maybe I did," came the bitter reply, "but only because you forced me to, and I spent the whole day feeling ridiculous because I was the only one with a stupid schoolbag."

"But it was a brand-new schoolbag, real leather. You chose it yourself, and everyone had bags on their backs," recalled Madame Melo.

"Okay, but we didn't need them the first day."

"So where will I put my books?" asked Margot.

"They don't give you books on the first day."

"Let her do what she likes," interceded their mother.

"Do you want everyone to make fun of her?"

"Don't worry!"

Don't worry! thought Margot, *That's what you always say.*

Chapter

$\mathcal{M}$argot finally left the house, anxious about looking nerdy with her schoolbag, terrified that she might have strict teachers, and sick with the thought that they might have made a mistake and have no room for her in sixth grade after all. She looked neat and scrubbed with her cleanly washed and brushed brown hair, her jeans and brand-new blue T-shirt. What was missing was a smile. Her mother went with her.

Parents and children were standing around in the school courtyard. Margot searched for familiar faces. She caught sight of two friends from her old school and walked toward them.

Suddenly, people started moving toward the large covered area near the classrooms. A stern voice ordered all parents to keep well away from the area and told the children to stop talking and gather under the roof, but the parents remained glued to their children, and the result was complete chaos.

A fat little man with a mustache read out the names of class 6A.

"If you don't keep quiet, you'll have to leave now and start all over again tomorrow or the day after. It's all the same to me."

"Class 6B. If you don't hear your name because of the racket, you'll be removed from the list!"

Margot concentrated with all her might. She was scared to miss her name, scared that they wouldn't call her name, scared that she might even forget it, so she kept repeating it to herself.

"Class 6C. If you go on like this, you might as well all go home!"

"Class 6D. If you don't stop shouting, you'll make yourselves hoarse."

"Class 6E. I'll have to start giving out punishments at this rate."

Margot grew more and more terrified that she had been forgotten. Her name was not on any list. Everyone she knew had already been called.

"Class 6F. Come on kids, please behave." He called fourteen boys and then, miracle of miracles, Margot heard her name.

"Present!" she shouted, and joined the others. When

the class had all been called, everyone followed the home-room teacher into the classroom. Margot, relieved, felt at home right away. Phew! She did exist after all!

The teacher had a motorbike helmet and a crew cut. He seemed nice enough, but he wasn't her type. She preferred men with beards. Still, she hung on his every word. First she copied out the timetable in her *carnet de correspondence.*

	Monday	Tuesday	Thursday	Friday	Saturday
8 a.m.	P.E.: gymnasium	Room 219: Math	Room 106: Physics	Room 230: History	Room 10: Music
9 a.m.	P.E.: gymnasium	Room 212: French	Room 319: English	Room 219: Math	Room 222: Art
10 a.m.	Room 212: French	Room 212: French	Room 219: Math	Room 319: English	
11 a.m.	Room 319: English	Room 319: English	Room 219: Math	Room 212: French	
12-2 p.m.	Lunch	Lunch	Lunch		
2 p.m.	Room 106: Physics	Room 230: History	P.E.: gymnasium		
3 p.m.	Room 324: Biology	Room 6: Industrial Arts	Room 212: French		
4 p.m.		Room 6: Industrial Arts	Room 230: History		

It wasn't too bad. She was free all day Wednesday and Sunday and on Friday afternoons.

The teacher asked two students to volunteer as temporary class representatives until the permanent ones were elected. "Who wants to volunteer?"

No one moved. Not one hand was raised.

"There isn't much to do, just take the attendance report from one classroom to another and hand it in to the school office at the end of the day every day. And you will go to parent-teacher meetings and report back to your classmates. You will be the link between your classmates and the administration."

Not a soul. An embarrassed silence reigned in the classroom. Margot thought it was disgraceful that not one single person was willing to take on this civic duty. So who would do it?

That evening at the dinner table, she told everyone the short history of her first day in junior high school. She started by announcing, "I am the temporary class representative!"

"How come?" asked her father.

"The teacher asked for volunteers, and not one person put their hand up. The poor guy just stood there waiting and waiting. I felt so sorry for him that finally I put my hand up."

"That was nice of you," was her mother's comment. "What are the other kids like?"

"Not exactly brilliant. Can you imagine, one boy didn't even bring anything to write with: no paper, no pencil, no pen. The teacher told him he made a great first impression.

"But," cried Margot for her sister's benefit, "everyone had a schoolbag, and lots of girls were wearing skirts."

"Losers!" sneered Anne. "Did you see any of the other teachers?"

"Yes, one for each subject."

"So, is the building nice?" asked her sister, who had been to a different school.

"Pretty ugly actually. I was disappointed. I don't get it. You know that big building that looks like a palace? Well, I thought our classrooms were there, but no such luck. The palace is just for the administration. We get cement boxes that look like barracks."

"It's always the same," grumbled her mother. "They always put the children last."

"It's not that bad," said Margot consolingly. "Okay, the classrooms are bare—no one decorated and there are no pictures on the walls. The halls are narrow and so full of kids that it's hard not to get squashed, but at least there's atmosphere!"

"And what about the teachers? Are they men or women?"

Margot did a quick calculation. "Five men and five women. It's exactly equal. The art teacher seems a bit weird—she even wants to take us to the museum."

"Good idea," her father agreed. "Have you made any friends?"

"Everyone spoke to everyone else. There are too many boys! I think I'll be friends with a girl named Denise. She seems nice and normal. But she doesn't eat lunch at school. This guy Jean already told me he couldn't stand teacher's pets when I volunteered to be the representative. Too bad!"

"*I* can't stand them either!" Anne interjected, but Margot ignored the remark.

"The trouble is, we have all this stuff to buy for Thursday. Each teacher gave us a list. I think we may have to buy up a whole stationery store. Listen to this! I have a list of everything I need: three files—one green, one pink, and one blue, with paper to match, and three hundred sheets of white paper. One dictionary, one thesaurus, two composition books (not the spiral kind) with one hundred pages each, a compass, a protractor, a T square, a ruler. Then we have special stuff for each subject:

"History: two large notebooks with alternate pages for writing and drawing.

"Physics: two large notebooks with squares.

"Biology: loose-leaf double pages, file dividers, folders, tracing paper, graph paper, drawing paper.

"Art: paints, pencils, a rag, a palette, felt tip pens, and a plastic bag.

"Industrial Arts: one large notebook with small squares.

"Music: A notebook with music paper, a notebook with normal paper."

"In my day, it was enough to have a pencil and paper," said her father.

"And I haven't even read you what we have to have for all the other subjects."

"Well, maybe you can see what you have left from last year," suggested her mother.

"I'll go with you tomorrow afternoon," offered her sister. "Anyway, I have things to get, too."

"Don't forget all those files piled up in your room."

"But Mom, I need a blue one, a pink one, and a green one. Those others with pictures on the covers are no good to me now."

"Do what you like, but try not to throw all your money away!" That was another of her mother's classic remarks.

"Don't worry Mom, I won't!"

Chapter

3

That Wednesday was the annual free-for-all in the back-to-school departments at all the stores. Scrap paper, graph paper, lined paper, and a thousand other items were being tracked down by a crowd of children and parents on the hunt for ballpoint pens, notebooks of every kind, dividers, erasers, and the rest.

Margot was furious to see that the whole population of the town had chosen the same day to descend on the stationery department. If there hadn't been all those people, it could have been fun, but all of the stores were total chaos, and you had to line up forever to pay. She spotted a few faces from her class waiting their turns like she was. Margot's head was spinning. When she finally got home, exhausted, she checked that her purchases actually corresponded to the items on the list. She was amazed to find that about a dozen little things were missing. She started searching in her cabinets and in old bags, and after begging a few things from Anne, she managed to get just about everything.

She emptied out her schoolbag. Then, studying her purchases and her schedule, she ceremoniously and methodically filled her bag for the next day. In bed, she tried to learn the room numbers of the classrooms by heart. French, 212; English, 319; History, 230; Biology, 324. She was sure she would get lost. That night, she dreamed she was trapped in a terrifying labyrinth with no way out.

*   *   *

In the morning, she managed to find room 212, and just for that, she gave herself a pat on the back. The French teacher, a squat, morose little man with a suit and tie, gave a test to find out the class's level. Denise gritted her teeth to show Margot her disgust. Then the teacher announced unenthusiastically that they would be reading *Le Medecin malgré lui (The Doctor in Spite of Himself)* by Molière, and dictated their first homework: an essay entitled "Fifteen Minutes in My Life."

In English class, Margot learned to say *the cat, the dog, the book, the blackboard, the chalk, the teacher, the table.* The kids were in hysterics and felt like babies who were just learning how to speak. One short, round boy named Dan seemed unusually boisterous and couldn't stop shouting out, "Speak English?" and "How do you do?" through the whole class.

After the first two hours, Margot didn't think she could face the next two. It was her most dreaded subject: math. She couldn't help thinking that life would be a much better experience without this subject, though Annick thought the teacher seemed "cool."

"Well I don't!" was Margot's verdict.

The only good thing about this lesson was that the teacher didn't give them any homework.

By lunchtime, she was starving and joined the crowds rushing to the cafeteria. At last, here was something that she could look forward to. Margot was always glad to eat. But she didn't expect the total stampede: a thundering horde of kids swinging their schoolbags threatened to crush her! Gradually, her panic grew. She felt suffocated, prisoner to the pushing, shoving crowd. Carried along by this human wave, Margot arrived at the cafeteria door only to be told that there was no more room for the first lunch period.

Panic stricken, she searched for a phone booth. There was one in the middle of the schoolyard. She dialed the number, and on the brink of tears, poured out the whole tragic story to her mother. "Mom, I nearly got trampled to death. It's horrible. And I'm starving."

"So come home."

Margot needed home like someone in the desert needs water. "Can I?"

"Why not?"

"I don't know if I'm allowed to. Oh, who cares! I'm on my way."

She ran all the way home.

"Well, if that's what sixth grade is like, they can keep it." She told her mother about her dreary morning, and about her dangerous trip to the cafeteria.

"Don't worry, you'll get used to it!" The more her mother consoled her, the more nervous she became.

*   *   *

The afternoon went more quickly, with physical education, more French, and history. In gym they were going to do jazz dancing, and in history, the beginning of civilization. The future was looking brighter.

On the way home with her head full of projects, homework, and dreams of good grades, Margot suddenly jumped out of her skin. She felt a heavy, threatening hand on her shoulders, and a voice whispered, "Tonight you're coming home with me!" She didn't know what was happening. She pulled away and started to run. It was one of the seventh- or eighth-grade boys. For the second time that day she arrived home shaken and breathless. Junior high school was dangerous.

"I was attacked in the street," she cried, wondering whether this qualified as rape.

"I got raped!" she yelled to see what would happen. Her mother and sister rushed to her side.

"What happened?"

She explained about the heavy hand, the boy, the sinister "Tonight you're coming home with me!"

"Is that all?" asked her sister, who had been hoping for something juicier.

"It's nothing," soothed her mother. "You'll get used to it. Maybe he likes the way you look. It's not such a crime."

She was hardly reassured. Nevertheless Margot decided to start on her homework. But first, she had an irresistible longing. She stole into her sister's room and tried on a bra. The two lacy cups sagged sadly on her flat chest. With a sock for a substitute breast in each cup, she pranced in front of the mirror practicing her powers of seduction. Just then, her sister walked in and declared, "Wowee! What a babe!"

Margot, dead with embarrassment, muttered, "Not exactly!"

She closed her bedroom door and sat with her elbows on her desk and her face in her hands trying to stimulate ideas. She wanted to write her essay, but she didn't know which fifteen minutes in her life to choose, there were so many! She went to ask her sister.

"Do the fifteen minutes before sixth grade."

"No, everyone will do that."

"You can do the fifteen minutes before you were born."

"I don't remember anything about that."

"So make it up."

"I don't feel like it."

"Do your violin competition at the music school."

"That's not a bad idea. Thanks!"

In her room again, Margot found herself in front of the terrifyingly blank page of double-spaced lines. She listened to the sounds of the city: the traffic roaring, dogs barking, a screaming jackhammer, children shouting. She couldn't hear herself think. To top it off, the phone rang.

She sighed irritably. Who could get anything done in this house?

Her sister started singing, as if she were purposely trying to make matters even worse. Margot put cotton balls in her ears and a ski hat on her head. She tried to control her mind by writing the first words on the page: "Do You Know What It Is Like to Have Stage Fright?" She thought it was a good title, but she wasn't sure of herself. This was her first sixth-grade essay. She went to see her mother, who found the title adorable.

"What can I say now?"

"Well, just go on."

"Easier said than done! How can I work in this racket? Couldn't you put in soundproof windows? How do you expect me to get anything done with one person singing, a dog barking, and the telephone ringing nonstop?"

"Don't worry! You'll get used to it," repeated her mother like a prerecorded message.

Margot slammed the door and thought about her title. "Stage fright, stage fright, stage fright." After the burst of creativity that had produced her brilliant title, there was none left for the essay itself. Then the telephone rang yet again.

"Margot, it's for you! Estelle!"

Estelle had been her best friend in fifth grade. She lived in a different neighborhood, so she was going to a different junior high school.

"So how are things?"

"Fine."

"Is your class nice?"

"Great!"

"Do you have homework?"

By the time they had described the teachers and the students, and told a few stories, it was already time for dinner. Margot had not started on her essay.

"I don't know how I'm supposed to get anything done when I get disturbed all the time. I can't concentrate."

"Oh, what a prima donna! It's the same for me, and *I* manage," was her sister's scathing comment.

"Your room is twice as big."

"Don't worry," interrupted their mother. Margot and her sister smiled at each other and chanted in unison, "You'll get used to it."

*   *   *

Margot looked again at her homework notebook:

Essay number one: free expression. In a text of 150 to 300 words, write about a short episode in your life. It should describe something exciting, which happened in a maximum of fifteen minutes.

Margot sounded out her friends.

"What are you going to write about, Catherine?"

"My first quarter of an hour in kindergarten."

"What about you, Denise?"

"The first time I went skiing."

"And you Nicole?"

"When my grandfather died."

Margot decided that their ideas were a hundred times better than hers. Where would she find 150 to 300 words to say about her stupid violin competition? She had two more weeks to think of something, but already it felt like a dead weight. If only her room weren't so noisy.

During these first few weeks, she worried nonstop. She tried her best to concentrate, but it was hard. After the honeymoon back-to-school period, all of Margot's classmates had become champion chatterboxes. Chatting was contagious for Margot, who couldn't resist providing commentary to Denise or Catherine or Philippe on the stupidity of various teachers.

In English, everyone would chatter. Camille would whisper to her neighbor, while Nicole and Dan compared notes on the latest gossip. The teacher would calmly announce, "Quiet please. We're going to listen to a tape." And the noise would continue as if he had not spoken. Camille, feeling sorry for him, suddenly shouted out, "Oh, just shut up!" but the teacher thought the remark was meant for him. Camille got a zero for the day, and the class got to copy out the first three chapters of the book by hand.

Margot's head began to fill up with worry about assignments she had to do for the next month, the next week, or the next day. From lesson to lesson, homework just piled up. Every day she went home and started to work, but it was a bottomless pit. The more she did, the more she had to do. With so much noise from the street and from the house, how would she ever get perfect grades? She would often complain at the table: "How am

I supposed to work? Catherine's parents have bought her an anti-noise helmet. It's fantastic. She isn't disturbed by noise, and her grades have really improved." Margot sounded like a TV commercial.

"I never had any anti-noise helmet, and I manage okay," retorted her sister.

"In my day, we managed without these things," muttered her father.

"In your day, there was no noise."

"You'll have to get used to it darling," was her mother's sympathetic response.

But Margot didn't get used to it. Among the ski things in the cellar, she found some earmuffs. She put in the earplugs that she had bought with her savings, put on the earmuffs, and crammed a wool ski hat over it all. It was hot under this makeshift helmet, but the anti-noise effect was highly efficient. At dinnertime, her sister had to come and tap her on the shoulder.

Thus protected from the invasive noise of civilization, Margot set about hunting through French literature to unearth a poem twelve to sixteen lines long worthy of being recited in her French class. She borrowed the collected poetry of Éluard, Prévert, Hugo, and Apollinaire from the library. She skimmed each volume from start to finish, worried that she would not find anything she liked, which turned out to be the case. She leafed through pages of Verlaine, Baudelaire, and Rimbaud, but they didn't appeal to her. Margot made an important decision: she would write her own poem and lie to the teacher, saying she had found it in a book. She wrote:

I would like to write a poem
That is meaningful and deep.
Children everywhere would love it
It would make the whole world weep.
I would like my dad to read it—then he'd hug me
　　like a prize.
And my mother would be proud of me—I'd see it in
　　her eyes.
I would like it to be full of joy
But also somehow tragic.
I would like the world to read it
And admire its special magic. . . .
But alas! It will remain unread, unknown, and
　　unlamented.
For who cares about a poem that a mere child has
　　invented?

Perfect! Exactly twelve lines. She took out the earplugs to go recite her creation to her sister, who listened critically.

"You're crazy! He'll never believe you. Just choose a normal poem in a real book!"

Margot returned despondently to her room, picked up her books, and counted the number of lines in the poems.

"As soon as I find one with twelve to sixteen lines, that'll be it!"

In a book of verse by Raymond Queneau she found what she was looking for: "Pour un art poétique" ("The Art of Poetry").

Take one word and then take two.
Start them cooking like a stew.
Take a pinch of common sense.
Add a lump of innocence.
Heat gently on a steady flame. . . .
Good technique you need, of course.
Then pour on enigma sauce.
Sprinkle with stars—it cannot fail.
Salt and pepper and . . . set sail.

Where are you trying to go from here?
To be a writer did I hear?
A writer? Really? . . . Oh dear!

Her sister didn't seem to agree. "Everyone knows that one."

"Too bad! They'll get to know it even better!"

"It's a fifth-grade poem." Margot found this argument

convincing. By dinnertime, she still hadn't found her poem.

"Why don't you choose a song by Georges Brassens?" asked her father.

"He said *poem,* not *song.*"

"Sometimes poets write songs. You could recite that song with your name: 'Brave Margot,'" and her father began to sing it slowly by heart, pronouncing each word distinctly.

Margot was furious. "But I'd get a zero if I took that to class!" Maybe her father went wild over bawdy songs about young women nursing kittens, but she would be the laughingstock of the school.

"It'll make the class laugh," insisted her father.

"Exactly! You want them to call me busty Margot or Margot the boob? Well, if you think that sounds like fun . . ."

"It would be good to choose a funny poem."

"I just want a decent poem, an ordinary poem, a poem which might make people smile, but not too much. A twelve to sixteen line poem that'll get me a good grade. An average poem, that's all!"

The family ate dinner trying to come up with an average poem. It was no easy task, and they were relieved to finish the meal and get on with the everyday chore of clearing the table to the tune of Monsieur Melo's humming:

When Margot let her bodice down
To give little kitty her share,
All the guys from all over town
Were there, were there, were there.

How that song got on her nerves!

✳   ✳   ✳

After she had finished studying her history lesson on the Egyptians, Margot couldn't get to sleep, and when she finally did, she tossed and turned, haunted by nightmares about ghastly poetry recitals and essays full of crossed-out words.

She woke up with a start and the feeling that she had overslept. She got dressed without washing or combing her hair, and rushed to tell her mother, "Mom, the alarm didn't go off. I'm late. Please, please, drive me to school!"

Her mother roused herself like a sleepwalker, dragged a coat on over her nightie, and went out in her slippers. Margot was nearly in tears in the car at the idea of being punished, and her heart sank when she saw that the school gate was already locked. Madame Melo dropped her off and left her to her fate, "I can't come with you in my slippers and nightgown. Don't worry. Just explain that your alarm didn't go off."

Margot didn't want to be seen with her mother anyway:

the coat was okay, but the nightgown hung down to her ankles below the hem, and her mother still smelled of nighttime and sleep. But she also didn't want to face the school director all by herself. For a moment, she thought of cutting class and spending the day on the beach chatting to the seagulls. She stood paralyzed in front of the railings for a minute or two, and that's when she realized that the school looked completely dead. There was nobody around.

She wondered if she was still dreaming, and stood motionless, staring at the courtyard; not a sound, nothing stirred. In her hurry, she hadn't put on her watch, but at least fifteen minutes went by. The school janitor emerged from a door holding the huge key to the gate. "You here already? Some people are in a real hurry to get to school," he joked.

A few minutes later a handful of kids arrived. In the deserted yard, they saw a girl sleeping on a bench, like a bag lady.

*   *   *

If this day had begun badly, the rest of it was hardly any better. First of all, in physics, fate picked Margot to answer a question, which fell on her like the blade of the guillotine: "What is the difference between Roman scales and Roberval scales?" How could she have forgotten to study physics? Her brain was a total blank, empty. No message could reach her mouth, and she sat there, mute as a mummy. The panic inside her prevented the slightest murmer of an answer.

"Zero for Margot."

Zero! thought Margot. *This is it, my life is finished. A permanent black mark on my record.*

Then she became angry. Suddenly, she remembered the difference between the two scales. With Roman scales you weighed things on two pans hanging down. With Roberval scales, the pans balanced on a point below. It was the shock of being questioned unexpectedly that had made her forget the answer. The teacher had set her up to fail, leaving her helpless. Her heart filled with bitterness. Holding back her tears at the end of the class, she cried out, "It's so unfair!"

Her friends consoled her. "She's really a jerk!" agreed Denise.

"What a creep!" exclaimed Catherine.

"What kind of a teacher is she?" added Arthur. "Asking questions like that out of the blue."

It made Margot feel a bit better to know that everyone agreed with her, but she still couldn't get that zero out of her head. She felt condemned to a disastrous school career. But she had been warned: "Sixth grade is not primary school. You have to learn your lessons, and work hard."

Sixth grade is certainly not a vacation! she thought.

*   *   *

She didn't have the heart to repeat the dialogue in English along with the others:

Helen: *What is your favorite color, Kate?*
Kate: *It is green. Look! My dress is green.*
Helen: *Blue is my favorite color. Look! I have a blue skirt!*

When the English teacher asked her, "What is your favorite color?" she would have liked to reply, "Black . . . like this terrible day!" only she didn't know how to say it in English.

*   *   *

Life wasn't going to get any rosier in math; this was clear from the first words the teacher uttered: "Next week you're having a math test."

Margot's reaction was a fit of hiccups. She started hiccupping with monstrous, gigantic hiccups as if each one had individual stereo speakers. The class shook with laughter, which grew louder with each hiccup. Margot would have liked the floor to swallow her up so she could disappear from the surface of the earth and hear no more about math or hiccups for at least a hundred generations.

Everyone offered advice. The teacher sent Camille to fetch some water.

"Drink . . . and hold your breath." No effect.

"Hold the glass the wrong way, hold your nose, and drink." Useless!

"Take a deep breath." Nothing.

"Jump!" No good.

"Scream!" No.

While she was acting like a clown in front of a fascinated audience, one person shouted, "Someone, scare her!" Annick slapped her hard on both cheeks. Margot burst into tears at the shock . . . but the hiccups continued. The teacher tried to gain control of the lesson, while Margot lost control of her hiccups. She was wishing she could just die quietly on the spot and be buried without fuss, when the bell rang loudly enough to wake the dead and drowned out even the tiniest echo of a hiccup.

*   *   *

On the staircase, the stampede for the cafeteria seemed wilder than ever. Margot wasn't hungry, but she let herself be carried along. Suddenly, a boy she didn't know turned toward her, raised both hands, and smashed his schoolbag down with a resounding thump on her head. In a daze, she repeated for the nineteenth time that day: "I can't believe this! I'm dreaming! This can't be happening!" She wished she could faint there and then like the heroine of some film, but her legs didn't want to obey. She felt her head to make sure it was still in one piece, and then with her schoolbag and its eighteen pounds of books, she gave her would-be assassin what was coming to him.

∗   ∗   ∗

Things went from bad to worse, as, with a beautiful bump growing on her head, she smelled the disgusting odor of sauerkraut wafting up from the cafeteria. Margot liked food, but there were two things she couldn't stomach: beets and sauerkraut. Even though she hadn't been hungry two minutes before, she suddenly felt a craving for at least five bowls of ravioli in tomato sauce.

With difficulty she elbowed her way out of the crowd and found refuge in the telephone booth. She took her fifty centime piece from her pocket. She carried a half-franc piece everywhere with her—it was her safety net. Her mother would know how to handle everything: the sauerkraut, the hiccups, the bump on her head, and the million misfortunes of the last few hours.

"Mom!"

"Hello, darling. Everything okay?"

"Mom!"

"What is it? What's the matter with you this morning? Your alarm clock went off five minutes after we left. You were in such a rush that I didn't even think to look at my watch."

"Mom! It's sauerkraut."

Madame Melo understood the disaster. "Have you got money?"

"I think I've got five francs in my bag."

"So run to the bakery next to the school and buy yourself a quiche."

"Okay!" She hadn't thought of that. "See you later."

"Bye, darling."

Weighed down by her faithful schoolbag, Margot ran to buy her quiche. None left. No pizza either. She made do with half a baguette, which she munched in melancholy isolation on the park bench nearest the school. She had heard the word *depression,* and now she was discovering its true meaning. Gazing into the distance with her spirits close to zero and her stomach half empty, Margot caught sight of a group of girls from her gym class. They walked toward the bench. Margot was nervous. They were smoking cigarettes.

Lise took a blue pack from her jacket and held out a cigarette to Margot. "Here, have one!"

"No thanks, I don't smoke."

"Try it, you'll see. It'll make you feel good."

"No, I don't feel like it," repeated Margot, because the last thing in the world she wanted was a cigarette. In fact, the smell made her sick and the smoke hurt her eyes. No one smoked in her house except guests. Once a friend lit up a cigarette during dinner and her mother had remarked, "Does it bother you if I eat while you smoke?"

Lise kept trying to make her take a cigarette.

"Go on, you'll get used to it. We're not babies anymore."

"Have a drag, you'll see, it's great," Cathy added.

"Don't be such a baby!"

"No, really, I don't want to."

"Chicken!"

"Go on."

"Here, just a drag."

"It doesn't hurt, you'll see."

Cathy forced the cigarette into Margot's mouth. She didn't see how she could get out of the situation without looking pathetic. She took a puff, just enough to start feeling slightly sick. She was spluttering to the other girls' laughter, and she handed the cigarette back to Cathy.

"You just have to get used to it, then you'll see, it's great."

Margot had no more bread left to take away the taste

of tobacco, which was the newest member of today's club, along with the zero in physics, the bump on her head, and the stink of sauerkraut. She got up and walked with the gang of smokers toward the gym. She felt as much like doing P.E. as she did like eating sauerkraut, but she was prisoner to her school schedule, and when it said *Physical Education* you got up and jumped to it.

She liked the dance routine that they worked on every lesson. She loved jazz dancing. But today, she had leaden legs, floppy arms, and a body of foam rubber. Her feet didn't want to copy the teacher's; her brain ordered them in a different direction. And it was just at that moment that the teacher picked her to run through the whole routine in front of the class. She couldn't remember the beginning, got lost in the middle, and never reached the end. The teacher was more than surprised: she was almost insulted, angry, even furious, and she said, "You'll have to pay more attention than that my friend! Gym is no laughing matter! It's important to educate the body. And don't go thinking that you can't get zeros in gym. You have to work in gym just like in math, French, and history. You have to practice the routine at home!"

Like a zombie, Margot made her way toward the French class. Here she felt safe. She couldn't take another defeat.

"I'm going to give you back last week's test," announced Monsieur Maldonné in threatening tones. "I am disappointed. You don't have what it takes to be in sixth grade. You are immature. You're going to have to wake up! You are *no longer* in elementary school. This is your future." It was not the first time he had spoken like this, but it was the first time that these words had been accompanied by grades.

Margot was confident. Maybe she had made a few mistakes, but she was sure she had got at least half the answers right. Just in front of her desk, the paper with her name and the grade slipped from the teacher's hands and fluttered briefly like a butterfly before landing on the floor. Margot bent down to pick it up. She saw "Margot Melo: 5 = 0." A knife through her heart.

It's not possible! Is there a state of mind darker than black? Margot felt biliously black, bitter, mournful, and dead.

"I'm going to explain my marking system."

Monsieur Maldonné started writing on the appropriately colored blackboard, adding, "There were eight questions."

Margot copied the system into her notebook, trying to understand it. *I have five correct answers, so I got a zero.* The logic of it escaped her.

0 correct answers = –1 and must copy six pages out of the workbook

1 correct answer = –1 and must copy three pages out of the workbook

2 correct answers = –1 but no punishment

3 correct answers = 0

4 correct answers = 0

5 correct answers = 0

6 correct answers = +1

7 correct answers = +2

8 correct answers = +3

"The highest mark was zero with five correct answers. I'm not going to congratulate you; it's not good enough. I hope that this first test will be a warning to you all."

The best I can hope to get is a three, thought Margot. The future looked as bleak as the present. She took refuge in the memory of the golden age of fifth grade when she had been praised by a teacher who liked her. Then, outraged by this zero (her second of the day and the second in her life), she raised her hand.

"Sir, are you going to give us the tests back so we can learn from our mistakes?" She was proud of her question, a masterpiece of style. But the teacher looked furious.

"My dear girl! These tests are simply a way for me to estimate your level. I am simply taking your temperature. I do not give papers back."

He was so emphatic that Margot didn't dare ask for any further enlightenment, although she needed it badly. She hoped that her sister, with all of her experience, would be able to decipher these results.

The rest of the lesson was devoted to convincing the students that they were useless, stupid, and hopeless. The result was satisfactory.

In the history lesson, Margot had an idea. On a blank piece of paper she wrote the letters of the alphabet in a column, one letter on each line. The title was "The Mean Alphapathetic." She wrote instructions: "Fill this in with the nastiest and meanest words you know." She gave a few examples to get the ball rolling, and passed the paper from row to row.

There were stifled laughs, giggles, and smirks. The history teacher had no idea what an amazing masterpiece was being created in her class, but she complained a lot about the noise.

"It's the end of the day, and I've hardly got any voice left children. Please, be quiet." Later, she begged them, "Stop talking! Stop, for heaven's sake." Then suddenly, "I'm giving you all a punishment. Copy out the whole chapter on the Egyptians." Bam!

This plague of Egypt happened just as the alphabet arrived at its final destination on Margot's desk. By coincidence, the teacher saw it. She seized it, and read:

A asinine, awful
B bastard, buffoon, boring, BOIL, barf
C cretin, crap, caca
D dumb, dickhead, donkey, dorky, ditzy
E excrement, evil
F fool, fatso, fart, freak
G goof, goober, grump
H headcase, harlot, hormone, hippo, hyper
I idiot, imbecile
J jackass, jerk, jealous, joke
K KAKA
L liar, lecher, loser
M maniac, moron, mental case
N nitwit, nerd, nebbish, nutcase
O ozone layer, ogre
P puke, piss, pathetic
Q Quasimodo, quack, queer
R revolting, repulsive, rotten
S stupid, smug, selfish
T thug, tumor, tubercular
U ugly, upchuck
V vindictive, vulgar, vomit

W whinz̧r, wet, *wide*
X xenophobic
Y *yucky,* yeller
Z zombie, *zero*

It was Margot who added the zero. Madame Luron who was usually so nice was stunned by her students' vulgarity. "I'm going to talk to the principal. This is definitely something for the school disciplinary board. Who is responsible?"

Margot stood up without hesitating. It seemed like the perfect way to end the day—to be thrown out of school! At this point, she would have preferred to be thrown out of life.

"You realize that after three warnings, you will be suspended. I believe this will be your first."

Margot nodded her head with shame. Then, in the blink of an eye, the teacher underwent an odd transformation: a smile began to creep into her face. Rereading the alphabetical anthology, she started to laugh, and her anger subsided. "Don't do this again in class Margot, that's all. Here, I'll give it back."

Margot overflowed with gratitude for the grace and goodness of Madame Luron. She went home thinking that all life's agonies and suffering were worthwhile, because people like her history teacher existed.

In the shelter of home, she avoided her father's questioning, "How did it go today? What did you do?"

"Dad, I don't want to talk about it."

"Do you want a snack?"

"I don't want anything."

She ran into her sister who was in a good mood and smiling for a change. "Is all well, my sweet?" she chirped in sugary tones, landing two sloppy kisses on Margot's cheeks. Margot threw her a look, and Anne got out of her way.

In her room, Margot put down her schoolbag and started an alphabet dedicated to Madame Luron: "The Alphabeautiful."

A angelic
B beautiful
C cheerful
D divine
E exquisite
F fantastic
G gentle
H human
I ideal
J just
K kind
L lovable
M magnificent
N noble

O obliging
P perfect
Q quintessential, quaint
R ravishing
S splendid
T touching
U unique
V virtuous
W wonderful
X
Y
Z

X, Y, and Z always spoiled everything! She adored making up alphabets, but these wretched letters always stopped her from reaching the end. She searched the dictionary for all the words beginning with X, Y, and Z but none of them was any good. She decided to banish them from the alphabet, and crossed them out. She did her homework with the same dogged determination. At last she had found calm at the end of this terrible day.

At dinner, no longer upset, she told them all about her series of catastrophes. Her mother philosophized, "Don't worry! Some days are good and some days are bad. You'll get used to it." At that, Margot heaved a sob and burst into enough tears to set Noah's ark afloat.

Chapter

4

*M*argot stared at herself in the mirror while she was doing her hair and tried to convince herself, "It's another day. The past is past." Strangely enough, she felt full of confidence. She had a good breakfast: orange juice, cereal, a banana, a glass of milk, and a couple of slices of bread and jam. This was a kind of insurance policy in case the cafeteria let her down. She hitched her bag onto her back, like some kind of beast of burden, and set off.

In spite of the traces left on the pavement by impolite dogs, the deafening motorcycles revving past her, and the streams of cars with their stressed-out passengers, Margot's good mood remained intact. *A good mood is rare these days. I'd better take good care of it.*

In the schoolyard, Denise met Margot with three kisses: left cheek, right cheek, left cheek. Then followed the usual round of daily greetings: two cheeks for Catherine, three for Danielle, and four or five for Nicole and Esther. Some of the girls offered their cheeks to boys, but Margot's cheeks were still single sex.

Denise whispered, "Nicole's disgusting—kissing boys!"

"Oh well, whatever turns her on . . . " sighed Margot, slightly jealous.

She arrived in history class having completely forgotten what they'd be doing that day. She had even forgotten that this was the day they were going to elect the permanent class representatives. *At last I can stop being everyone's slave. I'm fed up with collecting books, giving them out, putting them away, going to get the chalk, cleaning the board.*

Madame Luron made a moving speech about liberty, fraternity, and equality. "Today we are going to elect two permanent class representatives. They will be your spokesmen. Any of you is eligible to be a candidate. We need one girl and one boy. This is an important part of your education, because it will help you to understand about democracy. We will all be helpful to the representatives any way they need."

"What do class representatives do?" asked Jacques.

"Once a term, they attend the parent-teacher meeting. They keep the administration informed of students' suggestions. Above all, the representatives defend their classmates at the meeting, and inform them of the decisions made about class members. The representatives are also responsible for the class homework record and the attendance report. Who wants to be a candidate? Girls first!"

No one moved. A tense silence fell upon the class, invading the whole room like an invisible army. Madame Luron waited, hostage to this generalized paralysis.

Margot thought rapidly. *She deserves more than this. Someone has to volunteer after all, and maybe it wouldn't be so terrible to go to the parent-teacher meeting.* These noble thoughts released a mechanism that pushed Margot's arm in an upward direction.

One second later, six more hands went up. The teacher wrote the names on the board. Now that there were other candidates, Margot could back down, but she was ashamed to chicken out. When it was their turn, seven boys volunteered. In the end, half the kids in the class were candidates!

Madame Luron gave out some scraps of paper to write their votes on. "This will be a secret ballot."

The votes were counted out aloud, while the teacher wrote the total next to each candidate's name.

Margot Melo, Margot Melo, Margot Melo, Margot Melo, Esther Triesti, Margot Melo, Catherine Laroque, Jacques Biron, Jacques Biron, Margot Melo, and so on until they reached the remarkable total of nineteen votes for Margot against a maximum of six for anyone else. Out of the boys, Jacques Biron had the most votes.

After class, Jacques and Margot were dividing the work when one of the defeated candidates, Jean, passed by.

"Hi Mom, hi Dad!" he cried.

Oh great! thought Margot.

She took her role to heart. There was no chance of her being lazy about her new job. She really wanted to contribute to the life of the class. During math (yuck!), she passed out another piece of paper. Making lists was one of her specialties. At the top of the page, she thanked all those who had elected her for their vote of confidence. "I'll do my best not to let you down. First of all I think it would be useful to get all your names, addresses, and phone numbers. I'll photocopy them and make a class directory. That will make it easier to get a hold of each other outside school. You can call me whenever you like." She added her own name, address, and phone number as an example.

The paper went around the class and finally came back to Margot. It was all filled in except for one name, whose owner had scribbled, "I don't need an extra mother."

During the next lesson, Margot had another idea. She sent around another paper, headed: "Any suggestions to improve life at school?"

After class she got the paper back with the following suggestions:

1. Change the teachers
2. Get rid of the teachers
3. Kill the teachers
4. Ban homework
5. Ban quizzes
6. Ban study hall
7. Ban lessons
8. Throw out all schoolbags
9. Throw out all books
10. Throw out pencils, pens, and notebooks
11. Put in a hamburger joint instead of the cafeteria
12. Forget gym
13. Do more gym
14. 3 days off a week
15. 4 days off a week
16. 5 DAYS OFF A WEEK
17. 7 days off a week
18. Go on trips with the class
19. Go on trips without the class
20. Fire the class representatives!

None of this bothered Margot. She sent another message: "This requires a calm discussion. Come to my house Wednesday afternoon at 2 o'clock for our first class meeting."

When she got home, Margot typed out the list of names and addresses for the directory with one finger, one letter at a time. It took her two and a half hours. Her sister couldn't resist reminding her, "When I was in sixth grade, I didn't need to work half as hard to do well."

"Good for you!" replied Margot sharply. She had hardly any time left to write her essay, which was due the next morning, so she forced herself to come up with the required amount: 150 to 300 words. Suddenly, a breath of inspiration guided her hand, and she filled the page with no trouble. She wrote the conclusion and counted the number of words: 229—just right, halfway between 150 and 300.

"Dad, where can I get photocopies?"

"At the post office they have a machine. It costs fifty centimes per copy," he replied.

Before school, she went to the post office. She stuffed her savings into the slot, and received twenty-four copies of her class directory in exchange. She would be relying on contributions to finance the operation.

Margot got eight promises to pay her back, seven immediate payments, three shrugs, and six nasty comments.

"We never asked you to do this."

"I don't want to know the addresses of these losers."

"I can't afford to throw my money away."

"Who do you think you are?"

"It's none of your business."

"I see enough of you during the day. You think I want to talk to you at night?"

Margot was surprised at such a hostile reaction. After all, she had sacrificed her own time and money. Anyway, she thought it was really a good idea to have all this vital data down in black and white.

But her enthusiasm was wounded, and she immediately decided not to go ahead with her idea of making a directory of the teachers. *We'll see about that later,* she told herself, *after the meeting.*

*   *   *

The Wednesday of the meeting, Margot went out to buy a few boxes of cookies. Ten minutes after she left, the telephone rang, and an excited voice asked Madame Melo, "Is this Margot's mother?"

Madame Melo's heart began to thump. She imagined Margot run down by a car, bitten by a dog, and attacked by a mugger all at once. She just managed to squeeze out a faint "yes."

"Oh good. I'm the mother of one of her friends, Camille."

"Oh, thank goodness. I was afraid something had happened to Margot. She just went out a few minutes ago."

"No, no. I'm sorry I scared you. You see, I have this problem, and I have an enormous favor to ask you. I don't know who to turn to, and I'm sorry to bother you like this, but it is so important, and I thought you might be able to help me."

"I hope so."

"I promise you, I'll be eternally grateful. I'll make sure you get it back in perfect condition, and that it won't be any trouble. It's just that I'm going to ask you to give me a huge helping hand."

Madame Melo was getting impatient. "Please, do go ahead."

"You see, my daughter is in a cast right up to her neck. That's why she had to repeat the year, and it's also why she's finding it hard to keep up with her schoolwork. The cast is a prison, which is stopping her from leading a normal life."

Madame Melo was upset at hearing about this woman's daughter. She was also surprised that Margot had never mentioned it.

"What can we do for you?"

"I'm sorry again to ask you this, but I assure you, it would be the most tremendous favor."

"Don't worry, it'll be a pleasure."

"You do understand, but I really have no choice."

Madame Melo wondered what this extraordinary and

incredible favor could possibly be. "No really, I assure you."

"Well, like I said, Camille can't really keep up with her classes and take all the notes. We do have private tutors to help her, but she still can't manage to do as much as she should. She would like to go to a special school for mildly disabled children, but we think it's better that she try to overcome her difficulty and be part of a normal class."

"Sure, I understand," replied the totally unsure Madame Melo.

"She's growing so quickly, her body is beginning to change. At this age, they start to think about boys! And poor Camille, she lives in this straitjacket!"

Madame Melo felt really sorry for this woman's daughter, but at the same time the smell of something burning in the kitchen was growing stronger and stronger. With no more time to wonder what supernatural favor this woman was going to ask her for, Madame Melo finally broke down. "What exactly is it that you need?"

"Well . . . I mean, I hope you understand, I wouldn't dream of asking you unless it was absolutely necessary."

"Please don't worry about it, really."

"Well!" Camille's mother took a deep breath and blurted out, "Could Margot possibly lend her physics and history notebooks to Camille? I promise you'll get them back in perfect condition just as soon as she finishes copying Margot's notes. It would be such a huge favor!"

Madame Melo couldn't believe her ears. Such a big speech for such a tiny favor! "But of course, it's no problem at all. It's our pleasure!"

"Oh, thank you so much. I won't forget how kind you have been. I hope your daughter won't mind."

"Not at all. She's already finished her homework today."

"Can I come and get them in fifteen minutes?"

"No problem." Madame Melo gave Camille's mother directions. "You should wait till Margot gets back. That way she can show you everything. She'll be back in half an hour."

"Okay then, I'll be over in half an hour. Thanks a million."

"It's a pleasure. See you later."

"Thanks again. See you later."

*   *   *

The conversation had made Madame Melo distraught. When Margot burst into the kitchen with her packets of cookies, her mother announced, "Camille's mother called. She'll be by in a minute to get your notebooks."

"Oh no!" Margot whined.

"What is it?" her mother protested. "What's going on?"

"She's already asked everyone in the class."

"And they refused?" asked her mother, astonished.

"Well, yes! You know, Camille doesn't do a thing in class. Why can't she just listen, like everybody else!"

"But with that full-body cast, it must be awful."

"What full-body cast?"

"Didn't you know that she's got a body cast from here to here?" Madame Melo gestured to show the cast stretching from waist to neck.

"Wow, she never told *us* about it," said Margot, ashamed of not wanting to lend her books. She rushed off to find them. She was holding them when the doorbell rang. Camille and her mother were in the hallway.

Margot generously offered Camille as much help as she wanted.

Camille's mother thanked her. "Essays are what she finds hardest. Apparently it's your strong point."

"Don't say that till he's given them back! Are you coming to the meeting Camille?"

"No, I have to copy out these lessons."

"We should be going, to give you more time," said Camille's mother. "Come on Camille."

"Okay, well, see you tomorrow, and ask me anytime you like."

"A million thanks," sang out Camille's relieved mother.

Margot waited till half-past four but no one came,

no one called, and no one rang the doorbell. It seemed that her ideas for improving the class spirit and life at school would be condemned to remain inside her head forever. She consoled herself with the cookies, which she stuffed into her mouth one after the other, not even noticing how they tasted.

Chapter

5

*M*argot gathered her friends' excuses like a bunch of faded flowers.

"I forgot."

"I had tennis."

"I had ballet."

"I had the dentist."

"I had accordion."

"I had housework."

"Housework?"

"Yes, every Wednesday we have to do the housework."

"Well, I went shopping with my dad."

In the bouquet of excuses, there were doctors, brothers, sisters, football, forgetfulness, grandmothers, music lessons, youth group, but above all, there was indifference. The worst were her best friend, Denise: "I couldn't be bothered," and Jacques, the other class representative: "What's the point?"

They couldn't care less, observed Margot. *I'll have to find some other way to get this class motivated.*

*　　*　　*

The French teacher served up their essays like a chef dishing out his daily special. He was obviously proud of his corrections. Margot felt terrible about all the red marks she saw all over her neat page. He had crossed out half her work with a vicious red pen. Seven diagonal lines annihilated her title, "Do You Know What It Is to Have Stage Fright?" Above these scars his suggested title gloated triumphantly, "The Competition at the Conservatory." Her large-format squared paper was transformed into a battlefield of vertical and horizontal lines, with bits of scribble like snakes and ladders in between.

Monsieur Maldonné began to tell them how he graded essays. "I would like each of you to read your essays aloud. The class will then vote for the best one. If this essay gets votes from half the class, it will receive one extra point. If the essay gets votes from three quarters of the class, it will receive another point. We will proceed in alphabetical order."

Margot found it hard to pay attention to each essay.

When her turn came, she tried to read loudly with as much expression as possible. The others read in pale monotones. Margot was used to helping her sister learn her lines for a theater group, so she had plenty of experience in drama. She knew the plays her sister had done almost by heart. Her dramatic reading woke the class out of its stupor, and her essay was voted in unanimously. Even Jean voted for her, though that didn't stop him saying sarcastically: "Are you satisfied now, Miss Teacher's Pet?"

Her final grade was therefore 16+1+1=18/20. At dinner she was beaming in front of her father, while he, with horror and disbelief, looked at the corrections. The first line, "My violin contest was about to begin. I was going from fourth grade . . ." had been crossed out and replaced in red by, "I am at the conservatory about to take my entrance test for the violin class."

"But it isn't an entrance test, it's the year's final exam," exclaimed Margot's father, scandalized.

Margot tried to divert her father's attention and take the paper away. "It doesn't matter, Dad. It isn't worth reading. Anyway, I got eighteen!"

"But what you wrote is better than what he says you should have written. Why has he crossed out, 'Suddenly, one of the jury announced the first candidate. I was shaking all over'? What gives him the right to change your ending from, 'Now you know what it's like to have fifteen minutes of stage fright' to 'the minutes I had just survived were atrocious'? I'm going to go see him!" Monsieur Melo announced.

"No, please don't!" begged Margot. "It doesn't matter. Next time I'll do it the way he wants."

"Precisely!" Monsieur Melo yelled out indignantly.

"Don't worry!" Margot said reassuringly, not too sure what her father had meant by "precisely" in that tone.

This "precisely, precisely, precisely" echoed in Margot's head when she set out to write another essay about another fifteen minutes in her life. (The French teacher gave the same assignment twice.) She wrote about the end of fifth grade, the good-byes to her teacher and the tears and sadness of the moment. But she didn't like what she had written. She began another entitled "In Search of an Idea." She paid close attention to the teacher's suggestions, and her essay turned out exactly the way he would like. Precisely!

*   *   *

Before turning in her homework, Margot was talking to Nicole. "Did you do your fifteen minutes thing?" she asked.

"No! I forgot. And it's for this afternoon! What can I do?"

"Do it at lunchtime."

"I can't. I have to go to my aunt's."

"Listen! I did two. I'll give you one of mine."

"Wow, that would be fantastic."

"But copy it out in your writing."

"Okay. Thanks!"

In the French class, Margot whispered, "Did you copy it yet?"

"No, I didn't have time. I just erased your name."

Margot was worried. What if the teacher recognized her writing, or her style?

"Too bad, we'll just see what happens."

One boy had given in his homework without writing his name. "Am I just supposed to *guess* who you are from your exquisite handwriting and your sublime style?" declared the teacher with his superior air, and handed the paper back to Pierre.

Phew! thought Margot. *It's going to be okay.*

Pierre wrote his name quickly, pressing down hard on the pen. The ink went right through the page, and Monsieur Maldonné was not smiling. "Give me that pen, young man!"

Pierre was puzzled. This was his best pen—a gift from his father, who had insisted that "Good tools do a good job." He was upset to have it confiscated. Especially since he hadn't gone through the paper on purpose.

The teacher took the pen and threw it disgustedly in the trash. Pierre could no longer concentrate and didn't take his eyes off the trash bin for the rest of the class.

After the miserable hour was over, Camille took advantage of the chaos of the bell ringing and kids leaving the classroom to rescue the pen from its fate. She caught up with Pierre, who, red-eyed, was being consoled by his friends. "What a loser!"

"A real jerk!"

Camille tapped him on the shoulder. "Here! I got it back!"

"Hey, thanks Camille." Pierre sighed with relief.

"Good job, Camille! That was really brave of you!" Margot congratulated her friend, thinking, "Maybe we're not such a bad class after all!"

*　　*　　*

"I'm having a party for my birthday next Wednesday. Can you come?" asked Danielle.

"I don't know. I may have a doctor's appointment," lied Margot. Danielle was the most popular girl with the boys. Margot was scared of the party and of the boys.

"You should go!" ordered her sister. "Those boys won't eat you. When I was your age, I was always going to parties."

"Why not go?" asked her mother. "It's a shame to turn down an invitation. You never know. You'll probably enjoy yourself."

"There's bound to be a cake!" her sister said encouragingly.

That turned out to be the most convincing argument. But still, Margot tried to find someone who would advise her not to go. "Dad, do you think I ought to go to the party?"

"Well, if you feel like going, go, if you don't, don't."

They're such a help! thought Margot, as she started to call every girl in the class. "Hi, Denise? Are you going to Danielle's party?"

"I don't know yet. My mom thinks we're too young for parties."

"You're lucky! Mine is begging me to go!"

"You're lucky."

"Yeah, but I don't want to go!"

"You're crazy!"

"Well, tell your mom that all the other parents think it's okay."

"Yeah, I'll try."

"I'm going to call Catherine to see what she's doing."

"Ciao."

"Hello, Catherine? What are you doing about the party?"

"No idea. She wants us to dance with boys."

"That's just what I was afraid of! Can you imagine dancing with Jean or Olivier or François?"

"How repulsive!" She laughed.

"I'm going to ask Annick what she's doing."

Margot did the rounds of all the girls, making a big deal about the threat of having to touch boys, and discussing what they were supposed to wear to a party.

After a week of tormenting herself thinking about it, Margot found herself right outside Danielle's front door the following Wednesday afternoon.

Danielle's room was in total darkness except for a red spotlight. The bed and other furniture had been removed to make room. Danielle put the music on very loud. The girls danced on one side, the boys on the other, like two football teams training before a game.

Margot was not unhappy. She liked to dance. Often, her sister would put a CD on and they would dance together in her room. There was the added attraction of a table piled high with cakes and cookies, potato chips, candy, and sandwiches. She helped herself to everything.

It wasn't until Danielle put on a slow song that Margot was seized with panic. One by one, her friends paired off in the arms of a boy. When Arthur tapped her on the shoulder, she was both relieved and mortified. She was pleased that someone wanted to dance with her, but worried that she had no idea how to dance to slow music. She shook her head, invented an excuse, and fled from the party.

Her sister was waiting for her. "Did you have a good time?"

"Could you teach me how to slow dance?"

"Slow dancing's not something you can learn!" her sister replied. "It just happens when it's right."

*   *   *

As the first parent-teacher meeting approached, Margot kept on trying to rally her classmates on to bigger and better things. But she had run out of ideas. It was another one of those days where the only reward for getting out of bed would be the lovely math test she was expecting first thing. Margot started getting dressed. She pulled on one sock and was about to pull on the other, when she remembered she had no underpants on. Once these were on, she started looking for the other sock, and then realized that she had nothing on under her sweater. She took it off to put on a shirt, thinking maybe she needed to start giving herself orders out loud: "Put on your pants! Brush your hair! Lace up your shoes!"

She ached all over and couldn't stop yawning. If she managed to get out of the house, it would be a miracle. To add to the situation, she had forgotten to give herself the order to brush her teeth, and her mouth felt all pasty. Each step toward the math test brought her more stomach pains. Her throat was sore and her heart was pounding.

Sitting in class, she got goose bumps. She read one question seven times without understanding a word. A quotation from one of the prophets came into her head:

"They have ears but they do not hear, they have eyes, but they do not see." *And I've got a brain but it's out of order!* thought Margot as she silently barked out a final command: *Pull yourself together! Don't give up. You're going to solve this darn problem if it kills you!*

"This is really hard," she whispered to Denise.

"No, it's not, it's easy as pie!"

She reread it and thought about it, but the only solution that came to mind was to scream out, "Help!" She read the problem over again.

Margot could not even begin to think of anything that would help her solve this problem. Not logic, knowledge, prayers, threats, bribes, promises, candy—not even chocolate. *The truth is,* she thought, *I couldn't do this problem to save my life!* So that was that.

"Can't you do it?" asked Camille, who usually copied from Margot's paper.

Margot shook her head from side to side and made a zero with her thumb and forefinger.

A sudden bitterness swept over her. *Why does everyone think that being good at math is so noble, distinguished, glamorous, important, impressive, splendid, honorable, superior, and the sign of a good family? I think it's just stupid, absurd, dumb, idiotic, ridiculous, and total lunacy!* She would have liked to continue her list of math adjectives, but she wasn't about to pull out her thesaurus right in the middle of a math test.

She continued her inner monologue, *Of course this is only my own humble opinion. I wouldn't try to stop anyone from doing math if that's truly what they enjoy. After all, France is a free country!* At least the math test had given her the opportunity to reflect on this awful subject. *There are even people who think that math contains some kind of hidden beauty.* Once, Margot had talked to a mathematician who believed that math was at least as wonderful as painting, music, history, or literature. Margot didn't find any of these subjects so wonderful either. *But if that's what he likes, good for him!*

Margot happened to turn her head toward Denise who was scribbling away. Just by chance, she glanced over at one of the numbers, and suddenly, as if by magic, she understood. Her hand came to life, and her pencil was off! As the bell rang, the answer to the problem had been miraculously transmitted from her jump-started brain to the paper.

Math isn't so impossible after all! she thought as she left the classroom smiling.

*   *   *

During French, she had an inspiration. With the parent-teacher meeting coming up, she wanted the opportunity to grade the teachers. She drew up a chart and passed it around.

Teachers' Report Card

Subject	Grade (based on 20 points)	Remarks
French	08	Obsessive (very), gives lots of punishments.
Math	12	Not bad. Makes us write a lot.
English	16	Nice.
History	14	Kind.
Physics	11	Okay.
Biology	13	Strict. Like a little kid having a meltdown.
Drawing	00	Crazy, idiotic, rude.
Industrial Arts	16	Nice.
Music	12	Tries hard.
Physical Education	15	Wants to succeed.

Do you agree? Let me know what you think.

Margot.

The paper came back to her with only one alteration:

French: -1 and must copy 6 pages out of the workbook.

*   *   *

The parent-teacher meeting was about to begin. The teachers were lined up like a jury at a trial. The parents, including Margot's father, formed a sober and serious army.

The offensive was given by the principal, Monsieur Gili: "The students in 6F are extremely lively, their energy is hard to control, and they lack concentration." Margot took down this diagnosis.

Biology teacher: "They are not a rewarding class to teach. They are always talking. Today I gave four zeros for talking in class. I am at the end of my rope. In twenty years of teaching, I have never had a class like this. They all have a smirk on their faces, which is most inappropriate for students in this grade. A few of them will definitely feel my anger before the end of the year! My job is to teach them a scientific method, not to teach them how to behave. I do not see how we are going to take 6F on our annual trip to Rome."

English teacher: "It looks like I have six students out of twenty-four who do not possess the necessary intelligence to keep up. You must check your children's homework. You have to give them help, help, help!"

Math teacher: "Sixteen students above average, and eight below average. In general, they find it hard to concentrate. They are too easily distracted, and too immature. The class is divided into two clans. Any reason is a good excuse to chat. What am I supposed to do? Have them stand in the corner? Report them to the principal? There are a certain few who could have potential, but the atmosphere of this class is not encouraging. I am supposed to be teaching them something. Have you any suggestions?"

To this appeal for help, one parent replied accusingly, "You're the teacher, not us!"

Margot started thinking with all her might. She was dying to help find a solution to the problem of this catastrophic class!

She had had no idea that the teachers were going to paint such a bleak picture. Class 6F really was the dregs of the school. What could she do?

The French teacher: "The well-behaved children have well-behaved parents! There are twelve students whose work is unsatisfactory. They must do exactly as I ask if they want to learn to write an essay correctly. They have apparently learned nothing in elementary school, and don't seem capable of keeping up. In fact, they are inept."

The drawing teacher: "They are exhausting, noisy, and rude!"

The history teacher: "I can't complain. This is a lively class where, on the whole, everyone participates. There are one or two leaders who help motivate the others."

These words were not said in vain. "Motivate the others!" Margot felt that this phrase contained the key that could save her class from sinking to the depths of disgrace.

Monsieur Gili continued his litany: "The class has a mixture of levels, with a few students at the top, but far too many lagging behind. There is a definite lack of hard work."

Nobody asked the class representatives anything, and Margot felt too unsure of herself to comment in this world of parents and teachers.

But Jacques was bursting to speak, and put his hand up. His parents were not there. His father, a locksmith, was still at work, and his mother was too busy to come.

Jacques began his speech: "I understand why we have to learn French: it's so we won't make spelling mistakes when we type letters for our boss. I understand why we have to learn math: so we won't make mistakes when we do the boss's books. But I can't understand why we have to learn history." There! He had said it. Margot admired his nerve. Jacques wanted an answer he could take home to his parents.

The teachers, caught off guard, did not really know how to answer this question. Seeing their confusion, the principal offered, "You will understand these things when you are older."

But Monsieur Melo looked Jacques in the eye and said, "You have to learn history if you ever want to understand how your boss got to be your boss!"

Apart from telling the teachers that more students would participate if classes weren't so boring, Margot really didn't see what she could suggest. She did have one argument in defense of her fellow students, though. If three-quarters of the class were below the required level, perhaps there was something wrong with the level, not with the students. Margot didn't know how to transform the long days of boredom into positive suggestions. How could they beg for a little time to do *nothing*? Just some time to daydream now and then and maybe to hang out. She had a lot to say, but she said none of it. She would simply give her classmates her version of this meeting, to go along with the principal's official report. That was all she could do.

Chapter

*J*ust as her mother had predicted, Margot was finally starting to feel like an old (very old!) sixth grader. By the time Christmas and New Year's had come and gone, she knew all the ropes, and had gotten used to everything. She was at the top of the class. She worked hard and was delighted by the portable tape recorder her parents had given her for Christmas. She used this to record herself reciting the poems she had to learn, read her history notes, and talk to herself in English. What an amazing tool! She took it to class the first day after vacation, to record the first words of the first teacher of the first class of the new year.

She wasn't the only one to arrive at school with a present. Three sixth graders sat themselves down in the corner of room 219 with their new MP3 players. The tiny headphones logged the music directly into their brains, rendering them impervious to the math lesson. They seemed to be on another planet, swaying in time to the music with silly smiles on their faces as they mouthed inaudible lyrics.

Six others had been given electronic games, which they played discreetly on their knees under the desk. A chorus of mysterious "beeps" could be heard coming from the four corners of the room. One conscientious student was doing math on a musical calculator, which from time to time surprised the class with an electronic rendition of "Happy Birthday to You." His neighbor was the proud owner of a mini–pinball machine, which he was very focused on. As for Arthur, he simply continued the project he had planned to pursue for the entire year: to saw his desk in half with a razor blade. Oblivious to his students, the teacher carried on his lesson, but Margot's recording had some pretty strange background noises!

Something seemed oddly wrong to the math teacher. It was as if there was something electric in the class atmosphere, but he couldn't quite put his finger on what had changed; he simply had a stronger impression than usual that he was barking out his sentences to an empty room. It was true that this year's class 6F was far from the best sixth-grade class he had experienced in his years of teaching, but he was beginning to feel more and more unsettled.

He thought of his mother-in-law, who had come to spend the winter in the sun of the Riviera, at his house! In his mind he went over each dead day of his spoiled holidays. He patted his stomach, rounder than usual because of all he had eaten during Christmas. He thought of how many years he had spent throwing pearls of wisdom to these monkeys who did nothing but giggle and fidget in front of him. He looked around the room. Calmly, he declared, "Tomorrow I'm punishing each and every one of you. Two hours of detention on Wednesday morning."

The shock of this shot through the class as the kids realized what it meant: no-school day was ruined! They were all staring at the teacher in silent indignation when he cried out, "Three hours detention!"

And then, "And if your parents have anything to say, they can come and say it to me!" He practically burst. "And if you have something to say, you can go and say it to the principal!" He was like one of those wind-up toys that got wound with a key, only he didn't need a key to get wound up. "Why don't you try listening sometimes? You should try doing your work properly for a change!" With his last breath he yelled, "And if you have something to say, you can leave!"

The children sat there paralyzed in bewilderment. "Yes, go, get out of here right this minute. And if you have anything to say about *that,* don't even bother coming back!"

This order was so explicit that there was no alternative but to obey. The children followed each other out like a herd of sheep, stunned by the explosion they had just heard. They didn't know where to go until the next lesson. They followed Margot, who sat on a bench in the sunny schoolyard, her elbows on her knees and her head between her hands. It was her favorite position for thinking.

After a while, she announced, "Listen, we can't go on like this." As her idea took shape she spoke her thoughts aloud. "Why can't we be more like the other sixth-grade classes that Monsieur Maldonné tells us about every day? We aren't any dumber than they are." Everyone was listening to her.

"It's true," declared Christian. "We're not as dumb as they make us out to be."

"Listen," said Margot again. "All we have to do is really settle down. All of us! We just have to decide that we're all going to work hard. We have to make a pact to become the best sixth-grade class in the school." Margot's enthusiasm was contagious.

"What we have to do is decide that we're all going to get through this together. Every one of us, or none of us at all. If a single one of us has to repeat sixth grade, then all of us will."

And as if she was reading Catherine's mind (Catherine was a good student), she went on, "The kids who are doing well will help the others catch up. We all have to get good grades somehow. We can put together study groups with one good student and two underachievers."

"Great! Fantastic!" shouted Arthur and Philippe.

"It'll never work," said Catherine and Annick.

"Oh yes it will!" protested Margot.

That evening, Margot made up a new alphabet: "The Solidarity ABC for Class 6F." It would do as their contract:

A attention
B brilliant
C courage
D discipline
E effort
F forward march
G generosity
H helping hand
I intelligence
J just do it
K knowledge
L lessons
M motivation
N never say never

O organization
P patience
Q quality
R reasoning
S success
T try hard
U up and up
V value
W willpower
X x-tra
Y yes!
Z zeal

The following day, Margot had every student in the class sign the contract. She put it away in a secret pocket in her schoolbag, and got to work immediately by helping Camille memorize the dates from the Roman history lesson. That way she would get more from the school trip to Rome in the spring.

*   *   *

"Dad, tomorrow morning I'm stuck. We have three hours detention," said Margot, shamefaced.

Monsieur Melo was astounded by the story of the class punishment. On Wednesday morning, the math teacher, victim of his own detention, was taking attendance. When he got to Margot Melo, he was surprised by the deep male voice that replied, "Present."

Raising his eyes from the attendance list, he saw a man with a beard, whom he recognized as her father, sitting in Margot's place. The teacher was speechless.

Monsieur Melo explained, "My daughter has too much homework to do, so I'm taking her place."

The presence of an adult was too much for the math teacher. He immediately freed the class from his confused clutches. This gave them time to study hard for their history test.

*　　*　　*

Margot felt strange in the history classroom. As a rule, she was not in love with the idea of people copying from her during tests. Sometimes, she was even tempted to cheat the cheat by writing a few wrong answers. But now, because of her determination to raise the level of the weakest in the class, she was happy to share her knowledge with her classmates. Instead of hiding her work with her arm, she left it unprotected for all to see. Camille and others in the vicinity had free access to her answers. They all got sixteen out of twenty on the test. For Camille, it was the highest grade she had had in her life.

Margot was delighted. "You know, Mom, it could

work. See, I helped Camille study her history lesson, and she got a good grade!"

The phone never stopped ringing at the Melos' house. "Can I speak to Margot?"

"Is Margot there?"

"I'd like to speak to Margot please." Margot's sister, who was always expecting a call from somebody or other, went crazy being her little sister's secretary. And Monsieur Melo didn't like being disturbed during meals or the news or, in fact, at any time.

Now Margot was spending most of her time explaining exercises, correcting English, and giving the homework to kids who hadn't been listening in class. She worked for everybody else as much as she worked for herself. She felt exhausted. "Mom! I've lost my history book."

"Look carefully!" Margot spent the evening looking under each pile of books, emptying her drawers, her shelves, and her schoolbag. Then she tried her sister's room. "I haven't seen it," Anne declared. Her parents helped her look, but it was nowhere.

Margot couldn't sleep. In the morning, she remembered. *What an idiot I am. I lent it to Arthur last week.* Her physics notebook was at Camille's, her math at Danielle's, while her French notebook lived at Christian's. "Solidarity 6F" was certainly going strong.

*   *   *

"Margot, can you help me with my essay? I can't think of an idea," asked Camille.

"That's exactly what my last essay was about, 'In Search of an Idea.' Why don't you do the same thing— just write down all the ideas that come into your head in one fifteen-minute period."

Margot found her essay. She read it:

Here goes. I'm sitting here thinking of a subject for my essay. My mother makes a bunch of suggestions, but none of them inspire me. I'm thinking, sitting next to the fire. . . . From time to time, my sister throws out an idea, but nothing really grabs me: my trip to America, my horse riding lessons, etc. Suddenly the fire, so bright only seconds before, goes out. My father sends me out to get some wood.

Here I am in the garden cutting up firewood, still looking for an idea, but with no inspiration. The saw moves backwards and forwards, but my brain is at a standstill. I say a little prayer:

Oh my brain, do, I pray
Find me something good to say.

I don't think it has worked. I scratch my head, rub it, tap it, but the idea is hiding, it doesn't want to come out. I put the wood into the basket, set it down next to my father, and go upstairs to my room, where I write down everything that just happened.

"Having to write an essay is a real worry," said Margot.

"Your stories are always good, but I can't write like you. It drives me crazy. Couldn't you write me one?"

It was difficult to say no, but Margot was beginning to think that helping friends didn't mean doing their work *for* them.

"You can do it, I'm sure you can. You just have to sit and think."

Camille stormed off furiously toward the group of girls on the other side of the schoolyard.

*　　*　　*

"Can you explain the math problem?" asked Danielle.

Margot showed the exercise first to Danielle and then to three others who asked the same thing.

She began to think, *Why don't they listen in class?*

"They're asking a bit much!" she told Denise.

"Can you show me your answers for English?" demanded Esther.

"Show me yours, and I'll tell you if you got them right."

"I haven't had time to do them, and we have to turn them in this afternoon."

"Oh, all right!" She didn't have the strength to refuse, but tiny doubts about her "solidarity" campaign started creeping into her head like wisps of cloud appearing in a clear blue sky. "The next one who asks me for homework is going to get a piece of my mind!"

Then Jean demanded, "Lend me your history notebook." It wasn't even a question! It was an order.

"What were you doing during the class?"

"I wasn't listening!"

"That's tough. I'm not giving you my notes."

"Well in that case, I'm not going to play this little game of yours anymore, honey bun!"

"Well neither am I, sugar plum!"

And thus it was that the plan to rescue her class from its dire reputation fell apart and disappeared without a trace. People continued to ask for Margot's help, and sometimes she gave it, but only when she could be bothered.

Jean continued to give her dirty looks. Whenever she was talking to Jacques, Jean would sneer, "So, are you going to invite me to the wedding, sweetie pie?" The more good grades Margot collected, the fewer friends she had. Even Denise kept her distance and went around with Annick and Danielle. If she had no friends left, how could she go on the trip to Rome?

"I've got no more friends. Everybody hates me," she told her sister.

"Well, you can't expect to have good grades and friends. You have to choose in life!" replied her sister with superior wisdom.

"Why?"

"That's just the way it is!"

So it looks like I'm stuck, thought Margot. *I want both!*

*　　*　　*

Luckily, things started looking up again, and the winds of change were in the air. The principal arrived in class one day saying he had an important announcement to make. As she listened, Margot could hardly contain her relief! Finally someone else was coming up with ideas.

"Dad!" she cried, slamming the door as she arrived home, "There's going to be a reform!"

"What reform?"

"A reform at school. They're going to paint the classroom walls. We'll be allowed to talk honestly to the teachers, there'll be fewer hours of class, the food's going to improve, and we get to go on trips."

"Who told you?"

"The principal asked us to come up with ways we'd

like to change the school. And next Monday, there's no class because the teachers, the parents, and the students are going to spend the whole day figuring out which suggestions they like! Will you come with me?"

"Of course I will, if I can get the time off."

*   *   *

The Monday of the "think tank," Margot and her father left for school. Margot showed her father her not-so-short shortcut across a small backstreet with no cars. The school was locked up like a tomb. They had to go the long way around to the main entrance. The schoolyard was like a desert. Monsieur Melo asked for information.

"Where is the school reform meeting?"

The guard scratched his head and thought. "Oh that. Yes, it's on the third floor." They went up and peered through the glass-paned classroom doors. There were various meetings going on. None was exactly crowded. They went into a room where they found a few people and a dog. Margot didn't see a single kid, just a few parents whom you could count on the fingers of one hand, and a few teachers whom you could count on the toes of one foot.

They were talking about the possibility, or rather the impossibility, of shortening the school day by cutting down the lunch hour or having fewer class hours.

"If the kids get out earlier, what are working parents supposed to do?"

"How will the children eat?" asked one mother.

"How will we get through the curriculum with fewer hours of lessons?" asked a teacher.

"It's all very well wanting to change everything, but we have to have time to think about it and to get it set up. Anyway, I don't see how we could possibly be ready in time for next year."

One parent interrupted shyly. "I thought that the reform was supposed to reduce the workload so the kids could do other things: go to museums, concerts, theater, have guest speakers talk to them about different jobs, take them to see their work, go on hikes. . . ."

"Oh, of course, all that's very interesting," moaned a teacher, "but who do you think is going to provide buses to take them to all these places? Where's the money coming from? Who's going to foot the bill?"

Margot couldn't sit still. She raised her hand to attract attention. "I've got an idea that costs nothing. Why don't we begin just by changing the word *school*? *School* brings out bad memories. It sounds like prison; we're stuck inside gray concrete boxes from eight in the morning till five at night, and the gate never opens except to let the prisoners come in or go out at certain times. If we change the name, we'll change the idea that we have of school, and we can start fresh."

"Changing the name is no problem," said a teacher, "but what do you suggest instead?"

"I haven't really thought about it. We could have a competition to rename school. We could give a few examples: 'the garden of knowledge,' 'the meeting of minds,' 'the field of life'; I'll ask my friends if they can think of any."

"Can you imagine? The Pine Tree Field of Life—on school stationery, in the newspapers, on the report cards?"

"While we're on the subject, will they still have report cards after the reform?" asked one mother.

"How would we manage without tests and without grades? How could we possibly know how much they know?"

An expression started going around and around in Margot's head: "The more it changes, the more it stays the same." Listening to the adults "thinking," she really didn't see how the school could change between now and next year. When she left the meeting, she realized that you can't change anything without first changing people's ideas. And that would not be easy.

She started dreaming about her field, her garden, and her meeting. In her dream, the kids would decide on the program with the teachers, and those teachers would cooperate with each other. So history would not be totally divorced from biology, which would be linked to literature and everything else. For example, in biology, the teacher had been discussing the theory of evolution. The French teacher could have had them read things from Charles Darwin's time, and in history they could learn about the century he lived in.

Her head was humming with ideas and dreams of her model school. She had read an article in a magazine about the history of schools in France. She knew that they had made a lot of progress since Charlemagne . . . and there was obviously still a long way to go. But who had the patience to wait?

Chapter

*I*n French class Monsieur Maldonné was having them read part of *Les Lettres de mon moulin (Letters from My Windmill)* by Alphonse Daudet, a collection of stories about Provence, the area where Margot lived. This was the kind of book she had no opinion about. Actually, she already knew some of it. In kindergarten, the teacher had read them one of the stories, called "Monsieur Seguin's Goat," about a foolish goat who was eaten by a wolf. There had been a girl in the class named Hélène Seguin, and all the kids made fun of her, shouting at her "Oh, Monsieur Seguin's poor little goat!" Margot felt it was dumb and babyish to read a kindergarten story in sixth grade.

The teacher had written two strange lists on the blackboard. He was more excited than usual, as if what he was about to teach them almost made him happy.

"I want you to copy down the names of the thirty-two

Provençal winds described by Daudet when he wrote about his windmill at Fontveille."

Margot set out with her best writing to write her lists:

Temps dré	(Dry wind)
Montagnero	(Black mountain wind)
Ventouresco	(Torrid wind)
Aguieloun	(North wind)
Cisampo	(Neighboring wind)
Gregau	(Greek wind)
Auro bruno	(Brown wind)
Levant	(East wind)
Auro rousso	(Red wind)
Vent blanc	(Snowy wind)
Marin blanc	(Seaspray wind)
Eissero	(Icy wind)
Auro caudo	(Hot wind)
Vent de souleu	(Sunny wind)
En bas	(Low wind)
Marin	(Sea wind)
Vent de bas	(Down wind)
Fouis	(Fouis)
Vent laro	(Seagull's wind)

Labé	(Wind of sickness)
Vent di damo	(Cursed wind)
Poumentau	(West wind)
Rousau	(Damp wind)
Narbounes	(Narbonne wind)
Traverso	(Cross wind)
Mangofango	(Mudeater)
Cers	(Strong southwester)
Mistrau	(Mistral)
Vent d'aut	(August wind)
Biso	(Biso)
Auro dreche	(Straight wind)
Tramountano	(Beyond the mountains)

She immediately tried to make an alphabet of winds, but she saw that it wouldn't work, even if she got rid of J, K, W, X, Y, Z.

But Margot was absolutely over the moon with this new supply of wonderful words. She had never learned anything so magical as the names of the winds, but she realized that she still didn't know how to tell one from another. She would have liked to be on top of the Alpille Mountains in Provence to be able to feel the winds and name them like old friends: "Hey, that's Levant the East

Wind!" or "Oh, that's Mangofango the Mudeater!" She wondered whether there were names for clouds and waves as well.

She wanted to ask, "Who named the winds?"

But just at that moment, an order came from Monsieur Maldonné: "You are to learn these by heart for tomorrow, and answer the questions on this sheet on 'Old Cornille's Secret.' The bell rang. Class was over.

*   *   *

During the break after lunch, Margot started learning the winds by heart. Her friends were laughing and shouting on the bench beside her.

"What are you doing?" she asked.

"We're making a list."

"A list of what?"

"A list of class 'mosts.'"

"Most what?"

"Here, take a look."

Margot read the list:

The most beautiful in the class: Danielle D.
The sweetest in the class: Camille L.
The ugliest in the class: Annick T.
The most idiotic in the class: Margot M.
The most conscientious in the class: Denise C.

The kindest in the class: **Catherine P.**
The smartest in the class: Nicole O.
The most gifted in the class: Esther M.
The most energetic in the class: Jacques B.
The most attractive in the class: **Arthur H.**
The funniest in the class: Dan O.
The most annoying in the class: JEAN C.
The thinnest in the class: Pierre P.
The most hard working in the class: PHILIPPE B.

"We haven't finished yet."

"Why am I the most idiotic?" complained Margot.

"Don't worry, it's just a joke."

Margot didn't find it funny to have been voted "the most idiotic," even for a joke.

So look what I get to be the most of! I'd rather be the friendliest, the smartest, the most lively, the most amazing! And what do you know? Just because I want those things, I go and get elected the queen of imbeciles.

She didn't feel like crying, but it made her feel terrible just the same. She wasn't sure how she felt about visiting Rome with these kids, but in her heart she knew she still wanted to go.

The cafeteria menu didn't help matters. It was the dish that almost beat sauerkraut at repulsiveness: Paella! A shapeless mountain of yellow rice full of nasty critters like mussels, shrimps, and other unidentifiable sea creatures. Margot didn't touch it. To avoid hurting the cook's feelings, she decided to help the kitchen aides clean up the tables. As a reward, they offered her an extra plateful of paella! She shook her head politely, saying she wasn't hungry, citing her bad appetite and low-calorie diet as excuses (all the while she was stuffing herself with leftover bread behind their backs). Her one lonely orange, a sad excuse for dessert, did nothing to make her feel any better.

She worked on memorizing her winds. Because of them, she began to find Daudet's little book more interesting.

Maybe he talks more about the winds in Letters from My Windmill. She went beyond the call of duty and read the whole book, but she was disappointed. From time to time he mentioned the wind, but there was nothing specific. Margot couldn't understand why, with the whole of the so-called wonder of French literature to choose from, they had to make her read these outdated and faded old tales. She came across a paragraph that was typical: hard to read and totally boring.

> *No one in the fields. . . . Our lovely Catholic*
> *Provence allows the earth to rest on Sundays. . . .*
> *In the distance, a cart with its tarpaulin drip-*

ping rainwater, an old woman in a hooded win-
ter coat the color of dead leaves, mules in their
blue and white draperies with red pompoms and
silver bells, taking a whole cartful of people from
their homes to mass; then farther away, through
the mist, a small boat with a fisherman casting
his line.

And blah blah blah.

Margot couldn't help feeling that all this had nothing to do with her. She lived in Provence, where the stories took place, but she preferred city life. Besides, she would rather read a love story any day—although she was going through a stage where she no longer really liked to read at all.

Totally bored, she answered the questions at the end of the story they were supposed to read, and then went to tell her mother that she wanted to go on her class trip to Rome.

"How much does it cost?"

"A thousand francs," whispered Margot, trying to make the astronomical sum seem less.

"A thousand francs! For two days in Rome? And the whole class is going? These people are crazy!"

"Not everyone's going. But it's very educational and cultural. It'll broaden my horizons."

"But only two days . . . it's like nothing!"

"Well, you paid for *her* to go to Florence!" shouted Margot accusingly, pointing at her sister.

"You really want to go?"

Margot nodded, dreaming of the sleeping compartments in the overnight train, and the picnic they would have for dinner.

"All right, I'll talk about it with your father. I don't really see how we can refuse if all your friends are going. And anyway, you deserve it."

Margot rushed to hug her mother, whose task was now simply to inform her husband of the decision.

Chapter

$\mathcal{T}$he train station started filling up with parents and children. A few of the teachers were trying to gather their groups, calling out names from the lists they were holding. Margot prayed that she wouldn't end up in the group with Jean or Annick or Camille. It was just her luck to get all three.

In the train, there were several changes of plan. First she was sitting next to Esther, but a teacher asked her if she would be kind enough to change places with Camille. In her new compartment with five strangers, she found herself in the bottom bunk, when all she wanted was to be in the top one. The other five girls didn't stop laughing all night, until around three-thirty in the morning, at which time Margot finally managed to fall asleep.

Her mother had asked her to keep a diary of her trip to Rome so that at least she would have some written record worth the thousand francs.

She wrote:

The breakfast was delicious: cake, jam, hot chocolate, bread. The teachers didn't know where we were supposed to stop, but at last we got out of the train. There was a bus waiting for us. I am in the bus now. I managed to change groups. I'm with Esther and Denise. There's a terrible traffic jam. There are trams. We're meeting up at the Vatican, but they didn't tell us who with. They told us to hold on to our bags, because there are lots of thieves around.

Here we are.

It was an incredibly boring visit, dull and never ending. The other girls accused me of making too much noise in our compartment in the train last night. I was so angry I cried. I think I'm getting a fever. I didn't like the Vatican.

Finally I'm at the hotel, which is great. I've been hanging around with Esther and Denise. I'm going to eat now. I'm happy because I managed to buy some postcards.

Lunch menu:

Pasta with tomato sauce

Meat in white wine

Fried potatoes, spinach

Ice cream (it's called "gelato" in Rome)

Everyone ate everything except the spinach

After the meal, I went up to my room, but I got the number wrong, and that's when I realized that my key opens every room on the floor. But the other keys don't open mine. Cool!

Now I'm back in the bus.

We're going to visit the Pantheon. Here we are.

The guide was explaining stuff, when suddenly a rock fell down on this guy's head.

There was blood everywhere. The ambulance and the police arrived. That was the Pantheon.

Now we're at the Trevi Fountain where you throw in a coin and make a wish. Esther has started being horrible to me. She's being nice to Camille. From four o'clock till six o'clock we were free, so I went shopping. On the way back the traffic was incredible. I'm going to eat.

Evening meal: soup, boiled potatoes, meat, salad, tart.

Esther peed in her pants. It's eight o'clock and my roommates have gone off to a party. I hope I'll be able to sleep.

They were back really fast. The party didn't exist. They went wandering around the hotel, but didn't find anything interesting.

Breakfast: bread, butter, jam, coffee. I took a whole cup of black coffee, but I only drank about an eighth of it.

We went to the Forum and it was incredibly hot. Next stop: the Colosseum.

Meal at the hotel: spaghetti Bolognese (thanks to my bad Italian the waiter gave me a double helping!), green beans, fried potatoes, gelato.

In the afternoon we visited some Roman villas. The first was gigantic and looked like a whole town: it had a theater, a circus, a guesthouse, a stadium, etc. I don't remember what it was called. The second, Villa d'Este, was magnificent, but we didn't have much time and we only saw the garden, which is mostly fountains—one fountain had 280 water jets.

It was five o'clock, and we had fifteen minutes to do some shopping. I went with Denise who bought a teddy bear, a stone, a barometer, a tie, and a box.

That's when I realized that I had hardly bought anything, and the time was about up. Denise went back to the bus, and I found the teachers in a shop where I saw a little man made of wood holding tooth-picks. I liked it so I bought it. Then the teachers told me to go back to the bus. But I was afraid of going all alone. Luckily, I met a couple of friends who wanted to go back too. We wandered around trying to find it, and we finally found the parking lot, but there were so many buses that we couldn't see which was ours. We were the last ones to arrive! A teacher asked us to tip the guide.

Dinner at the hotel. Before going to the train station, we took a little drive around Rome by night. It was fantastic.

I'm in the same compartment with the same girls as on the way here.

No one wants to give up the top bunk.

I slept till seven in the morning.

Now I'm home, back from my great expedition to a foreign land.

*   *   *

For a while now, Margot had noticed that Arthur was behaving differently. Before the trip to Rome, she had often noticed him glancing in her direction. During free time, he would play with his soccer ball right next to the bench she was sitting on. When the teacher asked who would be interested in the trip to Rome, Arthur had waited until she raised her hand before raising his own.

In Rome, she had often had the impression that he was waiting around for her. There was always an empty seat next to him in the bus, and he only gave it up once Margot had sat down somewhere else. He hung around her while the guide was explaining the Vatican, the Forum, the Colosseum, and the Villa d'Este. At mealtimes, he would shyly offer her his desserts.

After the trip, she still had the impression he was following her around. One day in French class, she read her essay to the class:

The Hailman

It hailed so hard last night that this morning all the streets are covered with thick white frosting. The huge schoolyard is covered, too, and it's very exciting. We decided to make a hailman to celebrate.

I started off by making the body, while my friends modeled a face. Little by little, our creation emerged. He must have been one meter tall by then, and that seemed big enough. We put his head on, and it fit perfectly. Three seventh-grade girls passed by and offered to help: we didn't say no. One of them found a hat which we placed onto the bald head, and another picked up some pebbles which we used for eyes. A stick

made the nose, and two branches were good for arms.
We decorated our man with yellow flowers. He looked
adorable!

We were delighted with the result, but our hail-
man looked so lonely that I hoped it would hail again
so we could make him a wife.

As usual, Margot's essay was voted best in the class. Margot heard a whispering behind her: "Love lasts no longer than ice." Turning around, she saw that the remark came straight from Arthur.

That same day, Arthur came up to her between two classes. "What are you doing after school?" he stammered.

"My homework!" answered Margot confidently.

"No, but after that?"

"Eating."

"No, but I mean in the evening after dinner?"

"I'll be going to bed."

"Oh, I see," he sighed, not knowing how to put another question.

*   *   *

In the weeks following this attempt to make contact with Margot, Arthur was to be seen, as if by pure chance, at Margot's neighborhood grocer, drug store, and bakery.

She caught sight of him just as she was paying for some bread.

"Do you live around here?" she asked, surprised to see him.

"No, but I like to try out different kinds of bread."

"Oh, I see."

*   *   *

When she found him practically outside her front door, she asked, "Do you have friends on my street?"

"No, but I like wandering around streets I don't know."

"Oh, I see."

He didn't dare say how much he would have liked having a girlfriend on her street!

*   *   *

She had no idea how he had come to choose the same swimming pool on the same day, or the same bike ride as her two days later, but it seemed to Margot that Arthur was a highly efficient spy!

Denise confided, "I think he likes you."

Margot was panic stricken. Love! That was something for the distant future, not for the present. She didn't feel even a remote connection to real-life love stories, only the ones in books. Sure, in her class there were a few girls who did nothing but chase after boys and talk about them and stare at them, but Margot had never got involved in this crazy hobby.

What was more, Margot only liked men with beards, and there was no one in sixth grade who had one. Therefore, love would have to wait. Maybe next year.

Arthur was bound to find someone else to love.

Chapter

9

$\mathcal{M}$onsieur Maldonné cleared his throat and declared, "I have just launched a poetry competition in one of the other sixth grades. The theme is 'school.' I would like some of the best students in this class to be the jury in this competition. Those of you who have an average grade of thirteen or more will be called out of class next Thursday to judge the poems and choose the winner."

Margot was delighted. Judging competitions was an ideal job. All you had to do was listen: nothing to write, nothing to do.

The next day, a girl she hardly knew brought her a small cake after lunch.

"I hope you like my poem."

Others were less subtle: "You'd better vote for me or else!"

Margot was showered with all sorts of little presents:

a key ring, a new pencil, a rubber duck. Suddenly every-body was eager to please her.

A friend asked her to vote for her cousin. Her neighbor begged her to choose her best friend's poem.

Jean accused her of doing anything for a price!

"I'll vote for the best poem!" declared Margot, "And that's all there is to it!"

*   *   *

The poetic Thursday arrived. The first girl to recite gabbled her poem through her nose:

Every morning it's a race
T-shirt, jeans and socks and shoes,
So I really cannot face
Breakfast with that orange juice.
Finally I'm nearly done
Grabbing stuff from there to here,
Off to school—or on the run?
A kid in automatic gear!

Margot gave it fifteen out of twenty. She thought it was interesting, but badly recited.

A kid's just a cake
Which like this you make:

With two cups of French
(But for math you take three)
One each for physics and for biology,
For history
Half a cupful will do.
A spoonful of English
And you're almost through.
For sports, art, and music
A pinch will suffice.
Now stir it and mix it until it looks nice.
Put it into the oven at medium heat . . .
Indigestion will follow as soon as you eat!

Margot wrote sixteen out of twenty. It was good, but too much like Raymond Queneau's.

Next came a string of poems without rhyme or reason, deadly dull to the point where Margot would have liked to fall asleep, but she forced herself to listen carefully to each one. Her friend's cousin woke her up with a poem that he sang to the guitar as he played:

I run and run
More and more and more,
From class to class
And from door to door.
I want some fun, fun, fun,

But it's a bore, bore, bore.
It breaks my head, head, head,
And at night
I sleep tight
In my bed!

The words weren't brilliant, but he sang so well, with so much rhythm and harmony, that Margot found the song moving. She thought this song could become this summer's top hit: eighteen out of twenty!

It was a hard number to follow, and unfortunately for Sylvie, it was her turn. But Sylvie managed to tune right in to the hearts of her audience, just by keeping it simple. She made the audience feel that she really believed in what she was saying. Margot had no choice but to give her twenty out of twenty, even if she herself did find the poem a bit creepy!

I like school, I love school.
A weirdo am I?
You think I'm a fool?
No, I'll show you just why.

Getting up and away
Is a pleasure for me.
I am busy all day,
Without one minute free.

Changing teachers each class
Is just my cup of tea.
What I learn is my pass
To a future, you see.

I am sure with my heart,
That school's nothing to fear.
It plays a great part
So who'll come join me here?

On second thought, Margot changed her mark: twenty out of twenty was too much. *This poem isn't realistic. School doesn't only have a good side. That's why we're discussing making changes,* she thought. As if its author had read her mind, the next poem showed the darker side of sixth grade.

In the sixth of my dreams
I'd have gotten
Chairs of cotton
Nothing rotten.
In the sixth of my dreams
There'd have been
No submission
No competition
No inhibition.

In the sixth of my dreams
We'd have had
Time to play
Every day
To be free
Just to be.

But the sixth of my dreams
Lies forsaken.
We are shaken
And mistaken
When we waken.

Margot liked this poem. She gave it eighteen out of twenty. But she was starting to feel sick of poetry: too many rhymes, too many short sentences, too much slush. She looked around the class. The judges seemed to be dying of boredom, and the audience looked like they were at a funeral. Monsieur Maldonné looked like a tourist in a seaside café, staring absently at the horizon. Instead of a glass of pastis, he was holding a bunch of lollipops, which were the prizes for the contest.

How appropriate, thought Margot, *Sugary candy for sugary poetry.* She tried to imagine the teacher sucking on a lollipop.

In between being lost in his seaside dreamland, the

teacher introduced the contestants. He practically jumped for joy when he finally got to the last poet before the jury's decision.

Was it only an accident that the last poem was Margot's favorite? Laurent threw it at the audience like a bomb. He looked the teacher and the jury straight in the eyes and declared:

So what's school for?
How does it rate?
I think the idea wasn't great.
With tons of knowledge they force-feed us,
Why? In the future who will need us?

The teacher made a face, but the poem did make the audience think. Monsieur Maldonné lectured them on how to choose the winner: "Remember to think about the tone of voice, the shape of the poem, and the words." Margot was sure that he would try to persuade them to vote for Sylvie's high-flying model of school, but in fact he kept his opinion to himself.

The discussion that followed almost reached fever pitch when it came to defending the singing poet against Sylvie with her goody-goody school. Margot was the only one to speak up for the school with no future.

Philippe favored the singer: "He's brilliant. The guitar was perfect. He's the only one who put school, music, and poetry all in one."

"But didn't you feel Sylvie's emotion: love, work?"

Margot interrupted shyly. "I like Laurent's poem, because it brings up important questions."

"Yes, but asking questions doesn't mean that it's poetry."

"Nor does music and a guitar."

"At least he didn't put us to sleep. It was the most entertaining."

"Okay," Margot admitted. It was true. The guitar had woken them up. With Margot's vote, the guitar was declared the winner.

It was only after the lollipops had been given out that Margot began to regret her decision. She thought she had been pushed into voting for the most entertaining poem, and wished she had put forward better arguments to defend the poem she liked best. Thinking about this made her write her own poem.

Can we learn to talk at school?
Have they got a golden rule?
Can they show us where to go
On life's journey? Do they know?
If they don't then how can we?
How much real life do we see?

With its secrets and much more
What is life and what is war?
School is life and war I say.
That's what school's like every day.

Margot put away her poem in her sixth-grade loose-leaf folder.

Chapter

"There's going to be a strike!" cried Jean in delight.

"Great!" shouted Christian

"No class tomorrow!" Denise announced to the others as they drifted in.

"Fantastic! How come?"

"The teachers are on strike."

"Why?"

"Because they're fed up," said Jean. "And in France, there is always someone on strike. Maybe it's their turn!"

"Are they *all* going to strike?" asked Margot.

"All except the English teacher."

"So why isn't *he* going to strike?"

"He doesn't agree."

"Well in that case, *we* should strike, just during English. We're not going to come in the middle of the day just for one class, are we?"

"Good idea for once!" added Jean.

"What if they put our names down for detention?" worried Annick.

"Tough!" answered Margot.

"Why don't we all go to the movies?" suggested Jacques.

"My parents wouldn't let me."

"Anyway, I don't have any money."

"I know, but it'd be fun."

"Haven't you got anything in your piggy bank?" asked Denise.

"I have a bank account," Dan announced proudly. "I could even take money out, and pay for everyone."

"That'd be really nice of you," said Margot. "Look, here's what we'll do. Let's meet in front of the school gate at ten o'clock. Bring something to eat, and as much money as you can. We'll see if we have enough for everybody."

The next day at ten, the joyous crowd got together. Dan had bought pizza for everyone. Denise produced a huge cake. Jacques was carrying a bottle of Orangina. As for Arthur, he had brought hard-boiled eggs, because they were all he could find at home. And on each egg he'd written someone's name, so everyone had his own personal egg.

"Where shall we go?" asked Catherine.

"Follow me!" said Philippe. "Let's take Boulevard Mendès-France as far as the sea. Then we can have a picnic on the beach."

"We can go window shopping," suggested Denise.

In front of a cool clothing shop they checked out the styles. They looked at the scuba diving equipment in a sports shop and invaded a bookstore to leaf through the comic books. They ran through every nook and cranny of the department store, where Dan was fascinated by the lingerie. He had never before set eyes on such a collection of bras and panties.

Annick and Danielle chose their favorite colors in lipsticks, nail polish, and eye shadow. Margot decided on the tableware she would have when she got married. Arthur tried on raincoats. "How does this one look?" he asked Margot.

"You look like Colombo." Arthur was delighted.

The class arrived on the beach at around twelve-thirty. Dan immediately started giving out the pizza to his friends, who were all sitting down facing the water. The midday sun was hot. Danielle took off her sweater. Others did the same. Philippe skipped rocks. Margot stretched out for a tan.

They sat in a circle to divide up the feast. Arthur handed out the eggs as if each one were made of gold. Catherine passed around a jumbo bag of potato chips. They took turns drinking from the big bottle of Orangina.

When the bottle was empty, Dan put it in the middle of the circle.

"I'm going to teach you spin-the-bottle. It's an American game. Someone spins the bottle, and they get to kiss whoever is sitting where the bottleneck points when it stops. Like this." Dan spun the bottle, which stopped with the neck pointing toward Denise. The stifled giggles turned into hilarious laughter when Dan enthusiastically kissed Denise on both cheeks.

"Now it's your turn to spin the bottle."

Denise gave it a spin, and the bottle stopped opposite Margot. The two girls kissed the air near each other's cheeks.

Margot took the fatal bottle and spun it once again. It pointed straight at Jean, who went bright red. He ran off shouting, "No way, no way! Not on your life! I'm not playing. It's a really dumb game!"

Margot spun the bottle once more. This time, it pointed at Arthur, who instantly got up and ran over to Margot. He put his arms around her and gave her a serious kiss on the forehead. Margot had to admit that the game wasn't so bad after all!

No one wanted to stop playing, but they were roasting in the sun. Christian took off his shoes and socks so he could jump around in the water, but a wave got his pants wet, so he took them off, too. Jacques did the same. Denise wanted to go in the water, too. One by one, the boys and girls got rid of their pants and strolled into the sea until the water came up to their thighs.

Thank goodness I'm not wearing the panties with the hole and the broken elastic! thought Margot.

"Try to imagine all our teachers on strike, having a meeting in a classroom, all completely naked!" said Jacques.

"Do you think school would be any different if everyone went with nothing on?" asked Denise.

"I think we'd freeze!"

"Maybe the teachers would be a bit more human with their weenies and their boobs hanging out!"

Margot burst into uncontrollable laughter at the very idea. Her friends, too.

*   *   *

"So, are we going to the movies?" said Pierre, as if he had been the one to think of the idea.

"I don't think we have enough money. Let's see."

Jacques counted the money. There wasn't enough for twenty-four places at the movies.

"Let's go there anyway," said Pierre. "We could always just look at the posters."

"Wouldn't they give us a special deal?" said Margot hopefully.

"Are you crazy or what?" retorted Jean. "The price is the price."

There were twelve movies showing at the cinema in Place Garibaldi. The children looked at the posters and chose what they wanted to see. There was no line, and the cashier looked thoroughly bored, kind of like a student in a classroom facing a teacher and the blackboard.

A customer went up to the cash desk. "One for theater four."

"Four isn't on today because there are no customers," replied the cashier mechanically.

"But there's me!"

"We can't put on a film for just one person. We have to have at least three."

The customer was furious. He threatened the cashier, waving his folded newspaper in her face. "I want to talk to the manager! I came here because in the paper you say it's showing. This is false advertising!"

The cashier called for the manager, who was about to apologize to the client when he caught sight of the group of children. This gave him an inspiration.

"What are you doing here, kids?"

Margot explained, "We wanted to see a movie, but we don't have enough money."

"Do you have enough for two seats?"

"Yes!"

"Okay, buy two tickets, and you can all go see the film in theater four."

"Oh, thank you, sir!"

Once the tickets had been bought, the whole class trooped silently into theater four where, for 127 minutes, they were thrilled by a wonderful film called *And the Ship Sails On,* directed by an Italian, Federico Fellini.

"That was great!" declared Denise. "What I liked best was when they had that singing contest for who could sing the longest in the boiler room of the boat."

"I liked the rhinoceros best," was Arthur's comment.

If only they would go on strike every day, we could learn a whole lot, thought Margot. But strikes never seemed to amount to much, just a day off here and there.

"Bye," said Margot to Arthur.

"Do you think if I brought an empty bottle to school tomorrow, we could play that game in the yard?" asked Arthur dreamily.

"We could give it a try!" proclaimed Margot, enchanted by this brilliant idea.

Chapter 11

Waiting for the final parent-teacher meeting was nerve-racking business. Margot found herself wistfully thinking of her dream scenario where her whole class finished up the year with high honors. But she knew that even for herself, honors were hardly a possibility now. She hadn't really studied this last term, and her work had been flat and uninspired. Yet the teachers continued to give her good grades, without even thinking. Sometimes she suspected they might not even be reading her work anymore, because she was sure her grades were too high. But that didn't stop her from getting furious with her math teacher who, after warning her about sloppy math work, had given her ten out of twenty for one little mistake.

* * *

"You're sure to get on the honor roll," Annick told her.

"Not sure at all, but I don't care." She was ashamed to admit it, but she was liking school less and less.

She thought of kids who went to school despite bombs falling down around their heads, and about those who couldn't go to school because they were too poor, or had a different color skin, and she felt more and more ashamed of herself. She could go to school every day under a clear blue sky in a free country. *And I have the nerve to call it a prison!*

Margot didn't feel particularly free, carrying the dead weight of her schoolbag. Somebody had told her that French schoolchildren held the world record in curvature of the spine, or scoliosis, because of the weight of their schoolbags.

In French, Monsieur Maldonné was announcing the results of his voluntary reading competition. Midyear, he had asked them to fill in an information sheet about each book they read, all except comics. At the time, the students had enthusiastically hunted down all kinds of books. Monsieur Maldonné had given them a list of long boring classics like *Moby Dick* and *Great Expectations*.

But the kids were looking for something rare and entirely different: books that were short! The shorter the books, the more quickly they could be read, so the more information sheets they could fill in. As soon as anyone heard of a mini book about this, or a micro book about that, the gold rush began. The gold was in the savings on words, sentences, and pages.

The dealings in featherweight books lasted a week—long enough to fill in one or two information sheets. After this, the competition was forgotten. When Monsieur Maldonné asked for the sheets at the end of the year, only three students had more than five sheets. Margot was among them, with the modest record of twelve sheets.

He announced the winners: Margot, Esther, and Christian. He congratulated them as if they had rowed across the Atlantic.

"Teacher's pet . . . " snarled Jean.

For the second time, Margot thought, *What do I care about stupid contests?* But she was still curious to know what the prize was. And anyway, this prize would make up for not getting on the honor roll.

Monsieur Maldonné's delight at his idea for a prize was obvious to everyone, but the prize itself was not. Had he forgotten it at the flea market or wherever he had bought it? Maybe it was in his pocket: a ring, a pen, a miniature book? Margot had a million ideas for a good prize.

He got up, ordered the three crowned heads of reading to come toward him, and announced majestically: "So, here we are! The year is finally over, and . . . I am

inviting these three lucky prizewinners to a meal . . . er
. . . to have tea . . . at . . . " He paused to increase the sus-
pense. There was silence in the room. Margot's heart
began pounding as she imagined all the amazing places
where they might be having tea: the Ice Cream Palace,
the Rotunda, the Temple des Délices. For a second she
thought, *So reading isn't an entirely useless activity.* She
pictured herself all alone at the head of a long table, dressed
in her best jeans, with a dozen waiters piling her plate high
with cakes of every color, and ice cream covered with hot
fudge. . . . The next moment, Monsieur Maldonné joyous-
ly continued the presentation and burst out, "To have tea
. . . at my house!"

"Oh great!" murmured Margot bitterly.

The others exchanged puzzled looks as if they
weren't sure whether to be excited or not.

After class, Catherine looked at Margot and sighed.
"I'd really like to go to a teacher's house, too. I wonder
what it's like. When are you going?"

"He hasn't decided yet. He told us we'd see after
the parent-teacher meeting. You know, I don't think it's
that great an idea. It'd be good if we were *all* going, but
just me and that stuck-up Esther, and Christian and
Monsieur Maldonné . . . it's not exactly the Ice Cream
Palace."

"Yes, but I'd still like to go."

"Me too!" said Annick. "I'd like to see what his wife's like."

"I'd like to see where he lives."

*   *   *

The next day Monsieur Maldonné arrived in class with three Popsicles. He handed one to each of his champion readers, muttering with embarrassment: "You see, I can't invite you home right now. We're having work done. There's too much mess. So I brought you some Popsicles instead."

Margot didn't feel like eating a Popsicle at eight o'clock in the morning, but it had started to drip, so she had to finish it before it went everywhere. It wasn't very good, but she was glad to be over with this silly episode of weird prizes, reading lists, awkward invitations, and ice cream for breakfast.

*   *   *

Today was the end-of-the-year parent-teacher meeting where the teachers decided who passed into seventh grade and who stayed back, meaning who shall live and who shall die! It took place in the French classroom: that in itself was a bad omen. The teachers' faces looked serious and Margot could definitely see the storm coming.

The principal made no introduction. He simply opened the meeting by saying, "We will proceed in alphabetical order and discuss each case in turn."

Margot was relieved that she was spared the usual litany that her class was dumb, lazy, and below level.

However, her relief was short-lived. Of the twenty-four students in her class, the teachers recommended that eight stay back. The other sixteen could go on to face seventh. Two students got honor roll: the two class representatives, including Margot.

*   *   *

Margot came out of the meeting with mixed feelings: she was happy for herself, but unhappy for the eight who might be forced to stay back, including Camille, Danielle, and Philippe. By the time she got home, however, she had decided that they should have worked harder. The idea of going into seventh grade left her cold.

After the meeting, school had even less going for it than before. Out of the eight who were told they'd be repeating the year, six sets of their parents protested. (They would have to explain their children's below-average scores and beg for mercy. Sometimes it worked.) The hours of class began to drag by. Neither the teachers nor the students cared too much anymore. Margot tried taking up time by making use of some of the entertainment that school provided: she thought about the boys in the class, and which of them she would like to kiss. She dreamed of the holidays, she dreamed of nothing at all, of writing letters to authors and film stars. She chatted with Denise, passed notes, made faces behind the teacher's back. She made lists and new alphabets, and invented extravagant menus for future picnics.

In a few days they would be giving back their books. Freedom at last!

Margot had particularly liked history class. She suggested to Denise that they write a thank-you letter to the teacher. They sat on the ground in the corner of the yard, absorbed in their hard work, all the time failing to notice Arthur watching them intently.

They wrote about how Madame Luron's class had made them interested in history, the respect for history that her class had given them, and the fact that she always gave good grades. They mentioned details from the history of the world that she had emphasized, and thanked her for the energy that had gone into her lessons.

Denise sealed the envelope and addressed it to Madame Luron.

She was holding the letter in her hand when Arthur came up.

"What have you written there?"

"Absolutely nothing to do with you," retorted Denise.

"Mind your own business," added Margot

"Oh, go on, tell me!" begged Arthur.

"No way!"

"Oh, please . . . "

"No!"

"If you show me, I'll give you my compass."

"We totally don't need your compass."

"Then I'll give you my pen."

"We don't need your pen either."

Arthur panicked. He didn't know why, but he really had to know what was in this letter. He thought it might contain mean things about him.

"I'll give you my watch!"

"Arthur, you're crazy! I mean, why would we want your watch?"

Then Arthur took hold of the handle of Margot's schoolbag and took it hostage.

"Give me back my bag!"

"Let me see your letter!"

"Don't be an idiot!"

"What have you written?"

"Arthur, what's gotten into you?"

"I want to see it!"

"But it has nothing to do with you!"

"Then go jump in a lake!"

Margot tried to get the hostage back by force, but

Arthur ran away with it, one schoolbag hanging from each arm.

"That's no way to get us to show you the letter. Give me back my bag!"

Arthur opened the hostage and took out the French notebook. He detached a few pages.

Margot, horrified, shouted, "Stop that, Arthur!"

He threw one page to the wind. Margot caught it. He threw another page and then another, faster and faster until there was a cloud of French pages flying away and floating through the air, landing in the four corners of the playground.

Everyone rushed to get the pages from the loose-leaf notebook. Some stopped to read an essay or a poem. Others threw the paper up into the wind again, and it snowed French grammar in the yard of Pine Tree Junior High. Some of Margot's friends picked up the precious pages and brought them back to her.

"Arthur, stop!"

"Show me your letter."

Arthur started on the pages of neatly written English. *Boy, girl, man, woman, mother, father, sister, brother:* into the air. *Black, blue, red, orange, green, white:* into the air. *One, two, three, four, five, six, seven, eight, nine:* into the air.

He continued with history. All the dynasties, the

kingdoms, the dictatorships, the republics floated over the heads of the students in the schoolyard.

Biology and literature, languages, history, and math took flight together toward the unknown. *Where's my history of sixth grade going to end up?* thought Margot watching in desperation, fury, and powerlessness, while her life and learning were being sucked up by an invisible vacuum cleaner.

Suddenly, without any warning, drops of rain mingled with the floating pages. The white double-spaced pages got damp, wet, trampled on, abandoned. Even if Margot felt like giving in to Arthur's irrational behavior, she didn't. It just seemed beyond her control.

By now, Arthur had calmed down. He sat on a bench with the wet and empty schoolbag on his knees. Margot took the letter from Denise's hands and went to sit beside him.

All was lost. She was holding a few escaped pages, but they had no context, no structure. The witnesses of her year in sixth grade were spread out like corpses on a battlefield, dead and almost buried. Tears of rage dried on her cheeks. The rain stopped as quickly as it had started. There was nothing more she could do, so she did nothing.

She simply unstuck the envelope, unfolded the letter, and read to Arthur:

Dear Madame Luron,

We want to write to you at the end of this year on behalf of all the students of our class to tell you how interesting we found your history lessons. We also think your grades are fair and generous. You are the only teacher who doesn't think we are total losers, and we think the same of you. Thank you for all we learned about ancient Egypt, ancient Israel, Mesopotamia, Rome and all the rest. Thank you for your dynamic way of showing us these civilizations. Thank you for everything!

Denise and Margot

Arthur listened without moving, with the schoolbag on his knees. Margot's voice, trembling with emotion, shook him to the core. He put the empty notebooks back into the empty bag. Then he handed it back to Margot. Next, he got up and ran toward the open fence at the end of the yard. He passed through the gateway and kept on running to the end of the world.

Margot lifted her bag and said, "Well, at least it won't weigh me down now!"

The catastrophe that she had just been through would certainly leave its mark on her for a long time, but it was already beginning to change into a poetic image of white pages dancing above the students' heads, each of which contained a small seed of crazy originality. Some of those seeds would develop and grow. Others would never bear fruit.

*　　*　　*

The curtain went down on one of the last days of sixth grade.

*We danced in
Bloomsbury Square*

We danced in
Bloomsbury Square

JEAN ESTORIL

Illustrated by Muriel Wood

Follett Publishing Company
Chicago

CONTENTS

* I *

The Exciting Suggestion

Debbie and I started to learn ballet soon after our eighth birthday. This happened because we went to see the Royal Ballet Company when they were dancing at the Royal Court Theatre in Liverpool. *Les Sylphides*, the second act of *Swan Lake* and *Façade* were on the programme, but this meant nothing at all to us until the curtain actually went up.

Ours was not the kind of family that went often to the theatre. In fact, until then I think that Debbie and I had only been to the Christmas pantomime. The theatre just wasn't in our scheme of things, though I know now that, to many people, going to plays, opera and ballet is an essential part of life, almost as much taken for granted as eating and sleeping.

Mother took us to see the Royal Ballet that night because our next door neighbour was taking her twelve-year-old daughter. Barbara learned dancing at a school in Liverpool, and Mrs Brown said to Mother that she thought we were old enough to start taking an interest. Mother has told us since that

I

she was really quite convinced that we'd all be bored. She thought that *she* would be, and she believed that we would wriggle and ask to be taken home before the performance was half over.

Anyway, she bought three tickets for the circle. Dad said why not do the thing properly and pointed out that if we sat at the back in cheap seats we might get someone huge in front of us and then we'd have no view at all. So our seats were in the front row of the circle; very grand.

I don't think I shall ever forget one single thing about that evening, though it is already a long time ago, and Debbie says she won't forget either. From the moment when we took our places in the warm, lighted theatre neither of us said a word. We leaned on the rail in front of us and stared down into the stalls, watching the people arrive, including a great many children who looked as though they all learned ballet. Then the members of the orchestra settled themselves and began to tune up, and presently the theatre darkened.

Since then I have been to many, many performances of ballet, often even to the Royal Opera House, Covent Garden, but that was the very first time. I remember now exactly how I felt when the curtain went up and I saw those grouped, white-clad figures in the dim light. And when they began to dance . . . well, it was like fairyland, and heaven— something quite out of this world. I don't remember even breathing for a very long time, but I do remember that during the mazurka Debbie slid her hand into mine and we held on to each other tightly.

Then, when the interval came, and the lights went up and people began to talk and offer each other chocolates, Debbie gave a huge sigh and said:

'I'm going to learn how to dance like that.'

She only just beat me to it. The words were trembling on my own tongue.

'Don't be silly, Debbie!' Mother said. 'You couldn't! A little girl of eight.'

'Barbara says she wants to be a dancer,' I pointed out. 'Why shouldn't we learn, too?'

Mother looked from Debbie to me.

'I don't know much about it, but it takes many years of training to dance like that, Dorrie. It's hard work.'

'We don't mind,' I said. 'We *will* work.'

I remember saying that, but of course I didn't understand in the least just how hard the work would be. Yet some part of my mind fully realised that those fairylike forms had been *people* and that what they could do might some day be achieved by Deborah and Doria Darke.

The second act of *Swan Lake* was another wonderful experience, but I think we were both startled by the last ballet, which was so very different. There is nothing dreamlike about *Façade*, but after a while we got the idea and even laughed. It really was funny to see dancers pretending to milk a cow, and it was all so gay.

3

We talked about what we had seen all the way home; on the bus that took us down to the Pier Head and then on the ferry-boat that took us across the River Mersey to Birkenhead. It was October then and cold on the river at night, so we had to go inside and not walk round the top deck, which we both liked far better.

By the time we reached home Mother must have known that she was beaten, for she said to Dad, who had turned off the television to listen to our story:

'These two have decided that they're going to be ballet dancers. They want to go to that place where Barbara has her classes. The Grayland School of Dance.'

They exchanged glances and I remember that my heart leaped with anxiety, because ballet lessons would cost money and, in spite of seats in the circle, we were not well off. At that time and for some years afterwards Dad managed a radio and television shop in Birkenhead.

'Maybe they'll have forgotten all about it by Monday,' Mother added, as a kind of aside, and went upstairs to make sure that our baby brother, Bim, was all right.

But we didn't forget and by the next Friday, after school, we were being interviewed by Miss Grayland at her dancing school in Mount Pleasant, Liverpool. The result was that we were going to have one ballet lesson a week. Debbie, who is much less shy than I am, was just the same then and she turned down all

4

suggestions that we might just learn tap or modern dancing. It had to be ballet or nothing.

By the time we were eleven, and at a Grammar School in Birkenhead, we were attending two ballet classes a week at the Grayland and had passed some of our exams. We always had good roles when the Grayland put on a show, too, and Miss Grayland occasionally said that it was a pity we were not identical twins, because the audience would have found that very fascinating.

But we are *not* identical. Debbie is very fair, her hair is almost silvery in some lights, and her eyes are blue. I am much darker in every way and have hazel eyes. We are not alike in character, either, for Debbie gets on much better with people, being a much more cheerful and casual kind of girl. She wasn't casual about her dancing, though; she always worked hard. Miss Grayland never said anything to make me aware of it, but by the time we were twelve I was beginning to realise—with much secret pain— that she was a better dancer than me. I had mistakes of posture that were very hard to correct; Debbie had the perfect body for a ballet dancer. I had a little trouble with my feet; Debbie never did. She got higher marks in the exams as well.

We never spoke of this to each other, and as a matter of fact I was one of the best dancers in the class. It was just that Debbie was outstanding. I hated myself for being jealous, but in my heart I would have given anything in the world to be like my twin, down to the last shining strand of hair and perfectly shaped bone.

As the years passed we saw a great many professional ballet companies, for we were lucky enough to live near a city that usually gets several visits a year. We had learned a tremendous lot by watching the Festival Ballet, the Ballet Rambert, and of course the Royal Ballet. We had seen the Lingeraux Company as well, and Cécile Barreux was one of our favourite ballerinas. We also read all the books about ballet that we could lay hands on, and were always given them for our birthday. By then Dad and Mother were quite resigned, even proud of us, but Dad sometimes said he didn't know where on earth it would lead. He didn't think the life of a ballet dancer any sort of a life at all and never missed an opportunity to point out that we'd do better to concentrate on our ordinary lessons and perhaps be teachers or something.

'Perhaps they'll join the Television Toppers or some other famous team,' Mother once said hopefully. 'There *must* be money in that.'

'Or we could put on our own act,' Debbie said facetiously. 'You know, the Darke Sisters.'

'The Darke Dancers, would be better,' I added, knowing of course that she wasn't serious, though Dad looked as though he thought it a good idea, if we had to dance at all. I knew that we didn't particularly want money. We only wanted to struggle on

6

towards our goal of being real ballet dancers, hard work, provincial digs and all.

Anyway, I had to give you our background, but this story really starts in early September, just before our thirteenth birthday. By then Barbara Brown was working in an office and had quite forgotten that she ever wanted to be a dancer. As a matter of fact she was engaged and planning to be married as soon as her parents agreed that she was old enough.

But Debbie and I sometimes told each other that we were never going to get married. Though of course lots of ballet dancers do have husbands and even children.

Well, to get back to that September day: we had just returned from our holiday in North Wales and would be back at the Grammar School in a couple of days. The Grayland had been closed during the holidays, but classes were just starting again and we were excited at the thought of dancing again. We always tried to practise wherever we might be, but our house was quite a small one, with a squashy bathroom. Towel-rails are useful things for holding while one does exercises, but there really wasn't room to do much in our bathroom in Marshland Road.

It was wonderful to get off the bus near the Adelphi Hotel and to hurry up Mount Pleasant. Wonderful to run up the steps of the Grayland and along the hall, then down into the rather dreary

7

cloakrooms. Everyone was chattering about holidays as they changed into tights and tunics and carefully tied their ballet shoes.

During the past year Miss Grayland had handed over most of the ballet classes to a Mrs Bettle, who was a very good teacher. She used to teach at the Royal Ballet School until her husband was moved to Liverpool.

So there we were back in the big studio, warming up at the *barre*, and I was very happy to be back, because those familiar exercises were the only thing in my life that seemed desperately important.

Half-way through the centre practice Miss Grayland came in and stood leaning on the piano, watching intently. Then after a few minutes she said something to Mrs Bettle and went away again. As soon as the class was over Mrs Bettle said:

'Miss Grayland wants to see the Darke twins in her office.'

Debbie and I looked at each other in a startled way, and I at once wondered if we were in some kind of trouble. But it didn't seem likely, as we hadn't been there for nearly six weeks.

'Come on, silly! Didn't you hear? We're wanted,' said Debbie. She took my hand and hauled me along to the office.

Miss Grayland was standing by the window, and when we appeared her secretary gathered up some papers and went out of the room. Miss Grayland turned round and smiled warmly at us.

8

'Sit down, girls. I want to talk to you, I've a suggestion to make.'

We obeyed, and Debbie squeezed my hand before she let go.

'You are both quite convinced that you want to be ballet dancers?' Miss Grayland began.

I nodded dumbly, and Debbie said:

'Oh, yes. But we don't know how we're to manage it. We ought to be having more than two classes a week now, oughtn't we?'

Miss Grayland nodded in her turn.

'It would be difficult here, even if I were to let you take extra classes free. You can't really spare the time to come to Liverpool more often after school, and it wouldn't be good for you. You'd be tired and would probably start skimping your meals or your school work. Besides, you ought to practise every day. Now listen. Mrs Bettle quite agrees with me in this. You are both promising dancers and we have great hopes of you. The Lingeraux School in London is offering five scholarships and ten paying places for January, and we'd like you to go up for an audition. It's on Saturday, September 15th, which leaves us very little time.'

Debbie's hair swung out in a silver curve as she turned to look at me, and my heart seemed to go down into my stomach and return slowly to place. London! The thing we had dreamed about without ever really believing it could come true. The Lingeraux!

9

'The Lingeraux is a very good school,' Miss Grayland was continuing. 'Fully educational, of course, so your dancing would simply be part of each day's time table. But they don't take boarders and I wouldn't suggest such a thing if I didn't know that you have an aunt living in London. Your mother mentioned her once, saying that she takes students. It seemed to me that, if you were successful, you could probably live with her.'

'Aunt Eileen,' Debbie said faintly, 'Dad's eldest sister. She has—has a big house in Bloomsbury. They're mostly University students or people who are at R.A.D.A.'

'But she might take the pair of you, I suppose? If your parents would agree, of course. It would be very convenient, as the main part of the Lingeraux School is in Bloomsbury Square. Anyway, I want you both to explain to your mother and ask her to telephone me as soon as possible. As a matter of fact I've already written to the Lingeraux and they are willing to let you both try for scholarship places.'

We rose to our feet, but of course it was Debbie who had enough presence of mind to say politely:

'Thank you very much, Miss Grayland. We'll explain to Mother. We—We'll do our best.'

'I should be sorry to lose you, but you really ought to go on now to somewhere where you can concentrate fully. And you'd enjoy London. It would be a very interesting life.' Then she looked at me.

'Dorrie, you don't say much. Would you like to try, dear?'

'More than anything in the world!' I cried, almost explosively. Then I blushed and felt silly, because she looked faintly surprised. I don't usually express my feelings.

'Well, I hope you won't be too disappointed if you aren't successful. I suppose there's no chance that one of you could accept a paying place?'

'None at all,' Debbie said positively. 'It must cost a terrible lot.'

'I'm afraid so. Then of course your parents might have to pay your aunt for your board during the term. I don't want,' she went on doubtfully, 'to upset your parents at all. And I don't want you to be too sad if it falls through. Just explain and then see what happens.'

Debbie and I walked out into Mount Pleasant. Grey old Liverpool looked better than usual in the brilliant sunshine, but I was already thinking of London, the city I had only visited twice. Of course it would mean leaving home—Dad and Mother, Bunty and little Bim—but heaps of rich girls went away to boarding-school and we would be home in the holidays.

'Oh, Debbie! Oh, Debbie! Oh, Debbie!' I cried, as we took our places in the bus queue.

'Shhh! People are staring.'

'But, Debbie, it couldn't come true!'

'It might,' said Debbie. 'I suppose there's a

chance. *If* they gave us scholarships. Though there would be fares and new clothes as well as all the rest. But somehow I *believe* it could happen. Something *has* to happen; I've known that for months. If we're ever going to be dancers at all we've got to get to London

We rattled and bumped down to the Pier Head and then raced for the boat, which was giving warning hoots. We dashed across the gangway and then up the stairs to the top deck. Almost at once the gangway went up and the ferry-boat moved out into the grey waters of the Mersey.

I looked at the familiar scene, at the towers of the Liver Building against the blue sky and the Cathedral rising on the hill in the distance, and knew that I was a different person from the Doria Darke who had crossed to Liverpool only two hours before. I had seen the chance of a wider life, with dancing every day. I wanted it so much that I thought I should die if we couldn't even go to the audition.

'You always look on the dark side,' said Debbie, as we ran for our bus on the Birkenhead side.

It was an old joke. 'Darke by name and dark by nature!' one of our teachers at school had once said to me in an irritated tone. That was one day when she couldn't understand me and I wasn't helping her much.

'But, Debbie, if we can't try—'

'We'll try,' said Debbie.

✳ 2 ✳

London

Marshland Road is one of those rather grim Birken-head streets with rows of almost identical houses, mostly built of red brick, with tiny gardens in front and yards behind them. But at the north end of the street there are a few semi-detached houses that are slightly bigger and slightly less ugly. We lived in one of these, No. 35. There were sooty laurel bushes at the front, but at the back there was a small garden with a rose bed and some grass. Only the grass was always rather bare because Bunty and Bim played on it so much.

But when we arrived back from Liverpool on that momentous day both the younger ones were out in the street, Bunty, who was eight then, playing ball with the children from next door, and Bim riding up and down the pavement on his shabby old tricycle.

They both shouted to us and I realised then that if the dream came true, and we *did* go to London, it was going to be awful to have to say good-bye to them and to everyone and everything familiar and dear. Bim was such a funny little boy when he was five; plump and placid and yet with an iron will. You couldn't easily make Bim do anything that didn't appeal to him.

When we went in Dad was home and was having his tea and Mother was keeping him company by drinking an extra cup of tea. We always had meals rather disjointedly on dancing days. When we were at school Debbie and I usually had a sandwich and something to drink on our way to the Grayland (we had a favourite coffee-bar near Central Station), then had our meal when we reached home.

That day Mother took one look at us and demanded:

'What's the matter, girls? Something's up, I can see that. No, wait. I'll fetch your tea first. It's sausages and chips.'

She came back with two steaming platefuls and set them before us, and I looked despairingly at Debbie. I was hungry, but I didn't think I could eat until we had told our important news.

Debbie grimaced back at me, then took up her knife and fork.

'Out with it,' Mother ordered. 'I can see that you've both got something on your minds.'

Mother is sometimes a kind of witch. She always knows. It can be very disconcerting if you are trying to keep something secret. But we weren't, that time, so Debbie explained quickly, repeating all that Miss Grayland had said. She added that we quite understood about not having much money, but if it *could* be managed —

While she talked Mother and Dad just sat looking at each other and I noticed that Mother had grown rather pale. She is like me, not Debbie, with brown hair and a good colour. But just then she wasn't as pink as usual.

When Debbie had finished there was rather a long silence, then Dad said:

'Something like this had to happen. If you're to do anything with that dancing you ought to be concentrating more. We do see that, especially after that T.V. programme you missed the other night, all about ballet training. But the first question is *would* you win scholarships?'

'We can't know till we try,' I said, speaking for the first time.

'Fair enough. But what if you fail? What's going to happen then? Won't you both be hopelessly unsettled?'

'I'm afraid we will be, anyway,' Debbie confessed. 'I mean, if we don't try at all. Miss Grayland and Mrs Bettle wouldn't recommend us to the Lingeraux if they didn't think we'd a chance.'

'And you do realise what it'd mean if you were accepted? You'd have to go two hundred miles away for three months at a time. That's supposing that Eileen would take you. Of course the whole thing would fall down if she wasn't willing. And I have the impression that you didn't like your aunt much.'

I felt myself blushing and Debbie looked rather red, too. It was two years since we had last stayed with Aunt Eileen. London had been exciting, wonderful, but even Debbie had been rather in awe of our somewhat formidable aunt.

'Dorrie was scared of her,' said Debbie unfairly.

'So were you!' I retorted, then we looked at each other and subsided. We weren't helping our case.

'We're two years older,' Debbie went on, 'We'd be thirteen and several months by January. And if she's your sister she must be all right, really.'

Dad laughed at that, a trifle ruefully.

'Eileen *is* all right. Of course she's twelve years older than me. I was the youngest of eight. I used to be a bit scared of her when I was a kid, but she means well. The trouble is that she never had any sense of humour. She's the kind who would always do more than her duty, but seemed grudging on the surface. I feel sure she'd fit you in somewhere and look after you well. In fact, she'd be sterner than we are. Not a doubt of it. Better ask your mum what she thinks.'

We turned to Mother, who said slowly:

'I'm sure I don't know what to say. I don't want to lose them, but I don't want to stand in their way.'

'I wish London was nearer,' I said, with a sigh. Two hundred miles seemed a very long way in those days.

'You'd be homesick. And it wouldn't be any good shouting that you didn't like it once you'd taken a step like that.'

16

'We aren't babies,' Debbie said, with dignity. 'Of course we'd be homesick, but we'd put up with it because it's the only way to get on with our dancing. Only what about the money? If everybody's going to be ruined because of us—'

Dad had been looking very serious.

'There's a bit put by, you know. I got that two hundred pounds when my great aunt died and I've saved another hundred or so. I was meaning to use some of it on you children as you needed it.'

'If we won scholarships we might get grants for uniforms and books,' Debbie remarked.

So, in the end, it was decided that we should go and try our luck at the audition. But this was dependent on what Aunt Eileen said, and there wasn't very much time, if it all had to be arranged with Miss Grayland. So Dad took some money and went out to telephone to London from the call-box at the end of the street. Debbie and I went as well, and we stood outside the box, staring at him through the glass. It seemed very remarkable that he was about to speak to someone so far away—to Aunt Eileen in that big Bloomsbury house that I well remembered. I even remembered that the telephone had been in her private sitting-room, with another 'public' one in the hall for the students.

Dad was talking very rapidly. We could even hear a few words when the street was quiet. Then he hung up and came out, smiling.

'That'll be O.K. Eileen seems to think you're both

mad to want to be ballet dancers, but she says she thinks you'd get a wonderful education at the Lingeraux and maybe it wouldn't be wasted. She'll expect you both, and your mother, on Friday evening, September 14th, and if you're successful she'll find you a room during term. She says it may be in the attics, but she'll take you and look after you—'

'Would you have to—pay?' I asked tentatively. Suddenly money seemed a great deal more important than I had thought. I wished that we had enough not to have to worry quite so much.

Dad laughed and, with Debbie and me on either side of him, set off towards our house.

'I didn't mention it and neither did she. She knows how we're fixed. Maybe she'd let you help a bit in your spare time; shopping on Saturday mornings and that sort of thing. I know she finds it hard to get help.'

Debbie pulled a face. She doesn't like domestic things and neither do I very much. But we were used to helping at home.

'I wonder if the others are all rich?' she said to me, when we were alone in our room.

'Not all, surely? There'd be other scholarship pupils.'

'I bet plenty of them are well off, all the same. Cécile Barreux has a niece in the School. Remember we read about it in that article?'

'She might be quite poor, even if her aunt pays

18

for her or something. And even ballerinas don't make fortunes,' I said. 'Not like film stars.'

'No, but she appears on television. That must help a lot. I expect we'll have to do the same, to step up our basic salaries as dancers.'

'Looking ahead a bit, aren't you?' I asked and she laughed, turning a pirouette that brought her up against my bed.

'Oh, bother! I would like more space.' Debbie followed the pirouette with an arabesque and the evening sun shone full on her silvery-gold hair. 'I just *know* I'm going to get there some day. We both are.'

I wished I had her certainty. Now that we were really going to have our chance I already knew that I was scared. The people at the Grayland thought that we were good, but who knew what wonderful talent might turn up at the Lingeraux on September 15th? And Debbie was a better dancer than me. *She* never said so, no one had ever said so in plain words, but I knew.

'Maybe we'll die before the 15th,' I said. 'I don't believe it will ever happen.'

We didn't die. The days passed quickly, partly, of course, because we were back at school, with almost no time for thinking. By the time we had coped with school lessons, games, homework and our extra ballet classes there was scarcely half an hour left for dreaming or even worrying. The extra ballet classes were arranged by Miss Grayland just as soon as she knew we were going to try for scholarships, and she even coached us herself when no one else at all was there.

She explained that she didn't think we would actually have to dance. It would be a matter of exercises and a medical examination. That, she believed, was what happened at the Royal Ballet School auditions and some others. She had never actually sent any pupils to a Lingeraux audition before, but, just in case we had to dance, we were to do something simple out of the last show the Grayland had given. She made us practise one or two of the dances and provided us with music. Another thing she said was that she felt sure the Lingeraux would get a report on our school work from the Grammar School. This I found alarming news, though Debbie looked complacent and remarked that she had been top five weeks running at the end of last term.

Debbie had rather thought that we would wear tutus for the audition, but Miss Grayland said not. We were to wear our Grayland tunics, which were blue.

All our friends were astonished that we were going to London on such an important mission and the *Birkenhead News* published a little paragraph about us, calling us 'The Ballet Twins'.

'Fine fools we shall feel if we don't do any good,' said Debbie. 'I can't think how on earth they heard.'

Debbie said she was nervous, but I didn't believe it. I was scared stiff. I'd wake up in the middle of the night and feel cold with terror, and then hot.

Sometimes, in the night, I thought of what it would be like to live in London. We would be able to go to Covent Garden on Saturday afternoons; in the Gallery, of course, if we saved up our pocket money. But, without paying a penny, we could wait at the stage door of the Opera House and see the great ones. We would be *there*, on the spot. We would walk along Piccadilly . . . see the spring come to the London parks . . . be able to go to places like the National Gallery whenever we liked.

If we failed, if the whole thing came to nothing, Liverpool would never be the same again. Our old life would be dust and ashes. We would probably never be real ballet dancers.

Then, unbelievably, we were in the train on our way to London, wearing our Grammar School uniforms, since they were quite our most respectable clothes. Debbie was a little annoyed about this, but Mother was adamant. I didn't mind what I wore; I was so churned up that I could hardly sit still. In fact I spent a lot of the time standing out in the corridor, watching the September dusk falling over the Midland fields and farms. It was all so dreamlike that I didn't feel like Dorrie Darke at all, though sometimes I wondered how we would return on Sunday. In triumph, or with the whole thing at an end?

It was nearly nine-thirty when we reached Euston

and the noise and the crowds added to the strange feeling of unreality that held me. But Aunt Eileen was real enough; there was no doubt about that. She was waiting for us at the end of the platform, a big, rather grim-looking woman in dowdy clothes. They were the kind of clothes you never really noticed; very drab and ordinary.

She kissed us all briskly, remarked that I looked pale (small wonder!) and bustled us off towards Gower Street, where she lived. We went by bus for just a few stops, since her house was at the bottom end near Bedford Square. I would have been glad to walk.

Even the Euston Road enchanted me and the red buses and people's alien voices. I caught a glimpse of University College under the moon. Then we had left the bus and were approaching Aunt Eileen's house. It was a very attractive place, with fresh black and white paint and a blue front door, and there were wrought iron railings that made tiny balconies at each window.

Aunt Eileen married quite well. That is, her husband had enough money to buy the London house, though she once said it was going cheaply after the war, when it was in bad condition owing to the bombing. They used to let rooms to students even when he was alive and doing his own job, which was something in a shipping firm. Then, when he died, Aunt Eileen carried on. Three of her children were married by then, but Linda was still at school. At the time of which I am writing Linda was eighteen and worked in an office in Red Lion Square.

Aunt Eileen led us into the hall, where I at once saw the telephone that I remembered and the letter-rack for the students. A huge street map of London was pinned on the wall nearby. She was talking briskly as she went towards her sitting-room.

'Linda's out. When is that girl ever in, anyhow? She's got over her beatnik phase, when she spent hours sitting in coffee-bars and never washed her hair. Now she's always experimenting with her appearance and is crazy on dancing. I can tell you, Frances,' to Mother, 'she's quite an anxiety to me. I shall be glad when she's safely married. She takes far too much interest in the students here.'

'Do they take an interest in her?' Mother asked, sounding faintly amused.

Aunt Eileen gave a kind of snort.

'Some do, but they have their own friends at the University or wherever they're studying. Linda's my own flesh and blood, but even I can't see that she has many brains. She's out of her depth in all their talk about the "bomb" and the state of the world. Linda's more interested in next week's pleasure than in starving children in China or what may happen to the world if we aren't careful. I hope yours are bright. I can't imagine that it takes many brains to be a ballet dancer yet they say that the education is first class at the Lingeraux.'

'Our brains are all right,' said Debbie, rather

23

pertly. 'And ballet does take intelligence, you know. It's not all muscle. You have to know about all kinds of things; music and art and—'

Mother gave her a quelling look and she grew silent. We stood in a little group on the hearth-rug, glad of the fire, because it had been chilly out. Aunt Eileen went on:

'Look! There's a cold supper ready. What would the girls like to drink? Better be milk as it's getting late. I've given you two the best room,' she said, in much the same tone she had used all along. 'Thought you'd like it, just for this weekend. In term-time it's let to a new student, a New Yorker who's coming over for a year. If you're coming to live with me it'll probably be a garret that you'll get.'

If we came to live with her! I remembered, sickeningly, that tomorrow would decide what was to happen to us. The dreariest garret would be heaven if it meant that we were pupils at the Lingeraux Ballet School.

I was very glad when we had finished supper and Debbie and I were alone in the best room. It had a single bed and a kind of couch that Aunt Eileen had made up for one of us, and it was a very nice room, with a gas fire and a little ring for boiling a kettle. There were also lots of book shelves, mostly empty, and I wondered what books the New Yorker would put on them, and what kind of work he would do at the little desk.

Mother looked in when we were in bed. Debbie

24

and I had tossed to see which of us should have the couch and it fell to me. I didn't mind. It was very comfortable, but I didn't think I would sleep, anyway.

'We'll go for a walk in the morning,' Mother said. 'That'll be the best thing. You aren't due at the audition until two o'clock.'

'Miss Grayland said she thought they were seeing the boys in the morning,' I said.

'Funny to be in a school with boys,' Debbie murmured, when Mother had turned out the light and gone away.

'Oh, Debbie, I don't think I shall have the courage to go, after all,' I confessed. 'To the audition, I mean.'

'We'll go,' said Debbie. '*And* do well. We've just got to.'

* 3 *

The Audition

London looked beautiful in the September sunshine. The trees in the squares were still green, but there was just a hint of coming gold and the air was mellow. Soon it would be autumn.

We took the bus to Piccadilly Circus, where Mother at once said eagerly that she would like to go into Swan and Edgar's. Mother loves big stores and we couldn't very well be selfish and make a fuss, but it was rather dreadful to have to walk through the dress department, and then look at coats, when we felt so wriggly. I knew that Debbie was tense and I felt sick. It was already nearly eleven o'clock.

It was better in St James's Park, walking beside the lake and catching glimpses of the towers of Westminster and all the big buildings in Whitehall. But in a way I should have been glad not to look at London at all, because I was so ready to love every yard of it and I longed *passionately* to be back there in January.

The Lingeraux Ballet School is in Bloomsbury

Square, only quite a short distance from Gower Street. So we returned to Aunt Eileen's for lunch and didn't have to leave until a quarter to two. I scarcely ate anything, and Debbie only made a brave try. Aunt Eileen seemed a little cross with us, but just before we left I heard her saying to Mother:

'I'm used to nerves with the students. My life is always a misery when they're taking exams. The twins will be all right when they get to the audition. It's waiting that's the trouble.'

Linda was home for lunch. She was a very glamorous girl, with her reddish hair cut in the latest style and long, vividly coloured nails. We had gathered that Aunt Eileen didn't like this much better than Linda's 'beatnik' period, when she lived in the same old sweater for weeks. But we thought she looked wonderful.

'Cheer up, kids!' Linda said to us. 'You'll be all right. Going to be future Fonteyns, I hear.'

'If we get the chance,' said Debbie. She was rather green by then and my stomach was behaving strangely. It was awful.

Yet I knew that Debbie was pretty confident. She *knew* that she was a good dancer. I wasn't nearly so sure about myself and my legs felt exactly as though they were made of cotton wool as we set off.

'I never thought,' said Mother, as we walked down Bloomsbury Street and turned into Great

Russell Street by the British Museum, 'that I'd ever be taking my twins to a London audition.'

She seemed nervous herself, which wasn't reassuring, and I gripped my little case even tighter. Very soon we reached Bloomsbury Square and there was the Lingeraux School, two big houses painted cream and black and with a board that said:

Lingeraux Ballet School for Boys and Girls
Fully Educational
Information from Madame Lingeraux or the
Headmistress

Several people were going up the steps as we approached. There was a black-haired girl of about our own age with a very pretty, stylish mother, and a little girl with a fair pony-tail who was clinging to an elderly woman's hand. It looked like her grandmother and *she* was not stylish at all. In fact, they both looked quite poor. The little girl's coat had been let down rather obviously. It was, curiously, a bit cheering.

So we walked up the steps of the Lingeraux and it was like going into the promised land, even though the entrance hall was dark and quite ordinary; shabby, really. A young woman was sitting at a table, ticking off names on a list. When it came to our turn she said:

'Oh, yes, the Darke twins from Birkenhead. Follow the others, my dears. Miss Verney is showing them where to change.'

I looked desperately at Mother, who had joined the other two adults. She looked rather lost herself.

'Everyone is waiting in the hall,' the young woman said reassuringly. 'You'll join your mothers there.'

Debbie and I went down into the cloakrooms, which were in the basement, just as they were at the Grayland. There was quite a crowd of girls of all ages, all in different stages of undress. There was something about the smell of the place that was comforting and I tried to imagine that we really were at the Grayland, just getting ready for a class. But my fingers were clumsy and fumbly and I was shivering in spite of the stuffy atmosphere.

After a few minutes, when I had managed to get into my tunic, I began to listen to scraps of conversation. A girl of about fifteen was saying loudly:

'I must say I don't think much of the *look* of the Lingeraux. Not very impressive, is it?'

'Oh, it's far bigger than it looks,' another girl assured her. 'My cousin came here. She's in the Company now. There's a hall and some studios built on at the back, and more studios in the same building as the Company rehearsal rooms just a few streets away. Then of course the Lingeraux Theatre is just off the bottom of Kingsway.'

'I *know* where the Lingeraux Theatre is,' the other one said loftily. 'Anyway, there are plenty of other ballet schools. Only my teacher at Croydon seemed to think I'd better try for the Lingeraux first. The

Company is quite a good one, though small. They do a lot of interesting experimental things.'

'I'm afraid we're pretty far from getting into the Company just at the moment.'

Another girl not much older than us was talking about Covent Garden.

'The new ballet last Saturday was marvellous. You should have heard the applause at the end and seen all the flowers. And she—Oh, she really is the most wonderful dancer in the world! I went to the stage door and got her autograph—'

'I'm going to be sick! I know I am!' a voice said frantically and I looked with sympathy at the girl nearest to me. She was brown-haired and wore a pink tunic, and, in the dim light, her face certainly looked greener than Debbie's had before we left Gower Street.

'I might be, too,' I said.

'Say we were sick right in front of *them* ... Madame Lingeraux! Fancy! Are you trying for a scholarship?'

'Yes. We can't come otherwise.'

'Neither can I. I'm Mel Forrest and I live in Campden Town. Did you say "we"?'

'Yes, my twin, Debbie. Here she is. I'm Dorrie Darke.'

Debbie finished tying her shoes and straightened herself.

'There are only five scholarship places, we were told.'

Mel Forrest groaned.

'I know. And three of them will go to boys. Will have gone already. They've seen the boys.'

Debbie and I looked at each other with dawning horror.

'Only *two*, then?'

'Well, that's what my dancing teacher said.'

'And will everyone try for them?' Debbie demanded.

'I s'pose so. Some of the better off ones will take paying places if they're offered. I can't,' said Mel sadly. 'Not a hope. My dad goes to sea and there are five of us.'

'But all these big girls . . . are *they* trying for the free places?'

'Search me! Maybe they aren't. I've heard that they prefer to take younger dancers, then they can train them in the Lingeraux way.'

'Debbie, we haven't a chance,' I whispered, as we all went up the stairs again. 'Oh, what shall we do?'

Debbie's face was set.

'We'd better pray that they all break their ankles or something!'

But no such fortunate accident was likely to happen and I felt just terrible as we were led along dim corridors and then a covered passage to a big hall. There was a stage at one end and a lot of seats scattered over the main part. The parents were sitting here and there with their daughters beside them. At first glance there seemed to be a great many girls in coloured tights and tunics. A few were wearing tutus and somehow looked unworkmanlike, out of place. Debbie whispered:

'I'm glad Miss Grayland told us. It's better to be in tunics. But, Dorrie, there are *dozens*!'

'Thirty-five,' I said, after a rapid count. 'No, thirty-six.' I felt worse than ever. Ten paying places and five scholarships, and more than half of those seemed to be going to boys.

Mother was talking to a thin, worn-looking woman with a nice face who turned out to be Mel's mother. We three sat on the edges of seats beside them, silent with fright. Every so often someone was called out or one or two new candidates appeared.

Then it got even worse, because we began to realise just what was happening as time passed. Sometimes a girl came back looking very pale, even, several times, on the verge of tears, and we heard them say to their mothers:

'We aren't to wait.'

Once or twice a girl came back looking relieved and settled down again.

It was ten thousand times worse than being in the dentist's waiting-room. It was ghastly.

It was about an hour before Mel's name was called. 'Meldreth Forrest!' She leaped up as though she had been shot and I felt sick for *her*. Yet all the time I knew that, if there really were only two scholarships, the three of us couldn't all be accepted for the Lingeraux.

32

The atmosphere grew more tense every minute. Hardly anyone was talking now. The girl who appeared just before Mel was called had departed in tears.

Mel came back at last. She actually had some colour in her cheeks. She sat down with a bump and said:

'I'm to wait.' She sounded as though she had been told that she would live after all, and I knew just how she felt.

Then Debbie was called. She didn't bounce up, but rose quite slowly, gracefully, tossing back her hair. Quite slowly she walked up the hall and disappeared, and somehow, watching her, I felt a queer little premonition. Deborah Darke, the famous dancer . . . the great ballerina. That would be Debbie one day. And I am ashamed to confess it, but I almost hated Debbie then, and I hated myself nearly as much for feeling like that. Debbie and I had always got on well together, though we had never been as intimate as twins sometimes seem to be. We usually had our own friends and didn't invariably do things together. Debbie had far more friends than I, for she was always popular. Occasionally I had minded very much when people said: 'Is that your *sister?* You're not alike, are you?' The surprise always seemed to mean that I wasn't as pretty or as clever as Debbie. But I had never before come near to hating her.

It was twenty minutes before Debbie came back.

33

She was still walking slowly and she held her head high. She no longer looked green, but unusually flushed. Her eyes were shining.

'I'm to wait,' she said, and then, to me: 'It's terrifying, Dorrie. Madame Lingeraux is there, and the Company ballet mistress, and the School's head of ballet. Oh, and Miss Sherwood, the headmistress, as well. All kinds of people. One is a doctor—a lady doctor. She looked at my feet and said they were perfect.'

I couldn't answer because just then *my* name was called. I don't really remember what happened after that. I must have got out of the hall somehow and into the big studio where the auditions were taking place. I remember a blur of faces and a voice saying very kindly:

'Just go to the *barre*, dear, and warm up.'

I know that I felt better when my cold fingers closed on the *barre* and gradually my stiff body relaxed. After a time one of the ballet mistresses made me do some centre practice, a quite difficult *enchaînement*. Then she said, 'Rest a minute, dear!' and they all went into a huddle, studying some papers and what seemed to be the medical certificate I had had to get from my own doctor. I kept my eyes on Madame Lingeraux. I knew her, because I had once seen her on television. She was a dumpy and rather ugly old woman with white hair, but I knew that once, long ago, she had been quite a famous dancer and later a respected choreographer.

34

I have very sharp ears, and though, they were speaking quietly, I caught a few phrases.

'Very good school report—'

'Not quite as good physique as the other one.'

The other one! Debbie, with her perfect body.

Then they asked me to sit down and the doctor examined my feet. She was very nice and tried to make me talk, but I couldn't.

After that Madame Lingeraux herself began to question me and I had to talk then. Suddenly it wasn't difficult, because she wanted to know what kind of music I liked. I told her I used to love Mozart and Beethoven and Chopin best, but that lately I was beginning to like some of the modern composers like Holst and William Walton and Malcolm Arnold.

'And do you have a record player?'

'Debbie and I are saving up for one,' I told her. 'We want one very much, only then records are dreadfully expensive. Some of them are *two pounds*.'

Madame disconcerted me by cackling with apparent amusement. She sounded rather like a witch, but looked quite good-humoured.

'I know. They are a dreadful price.' She had a very nice voice, just a trifle foreign. 'And what about concerts? You have a good orchestra in Liverpool.'

'We go with the school sometimes,' I said. I could feel my face flaming, but I felt much better.

Then she asked about art, remarking that we had the Walker Art Gallery in Liverpool and some good visiting exhibitions, and that was easy, too, because I love the French Impressionists and the Post Impressionists. I said that my favourite artists were Cézanne and Utrillo—and Degas, of course. I suppose all ballet dancers like Degas. Then I added that I loved some of the modern artists like Bernard Buffet, though I had never seen an original. Debbie and I collect postcard reproductions, when we can afford them, and I told Madame Lingeraux that as well. I found being able to talk quite a heady business, because usually I can't. It was like a miracle.

Finally they had another little consultation and then Madame said:

'All right, Doria—Dorrie, your twin called you. We've finished with you now. Will you wait, please?'

I tottered out somehow, remembering to shut the door quietly. Once outside I began to shiver again and the back of my neck ached with strain. I wouldn't have gone through that again for a hundred pounds.

After that everything goes all dim again. A long time passed, and eventually we were told that we could go down to the canteen if we liked and get some tea. By then there were not very many adults and dancers left. Most of the mothers ordered tea and seemed glad of it, but Mel and I said we couldn't eat or drink anything. Debbie ordered a cup of tea, but didn't finish it.

Nothing comes clear again until we were in a small office, alone with Madame Lingeraux . . . mother,

Debbie and me. But by then we knew that Mel had been offered a scholarship, and, unless she had been misinformed about the boys, that seemed to mean there was only one left. I felt worse than at any time that day and soon my fears were confirmed. Madame came to the point at once.

'Mrs Darke, we can offer your daughter Deborah a scholarship starting in January. This would cover her full tuition at the School and there would be a grant for uniform and books depending on your husband's income.' Debbie gave a stifled cry. 'We can also offer your other daughter a paying place. She has the makings of a very good dancer, and her school reports are satisfactory. We felt—'

I didn't hear what they felt. The room had gone dark and if I hadn't been sitting down I know I should have fallen. *Debbie* had got a scholarship and I hadn't! Dimly I heard Mother saying that she was afraid there was no hope of my taking up a paying place. That, in fact, she was afraid Debbie couldn't accept the offered scholarship because they wouldn't want her to be alone in London.

'I'm sorry, Madame, but I know my husband wouldn't agree. The girls have never been separated and—well, thirteen is very young to go away from home.' She wasn't looking at me, but her face was pale and her voice shaky.

Madame Lingeraux rose, holding out her hand.

'Well, don't decide now, Mrs Darke. Go home and consult your husband. We should be sorry to lose two promising dancers. I can give you a few days in which to make up your minds.' Then she turned to me, and her hand was firm and warm. 'I'm sorry, Doria. There were only two scholarships. But I hope that somehow we'll be able to welcome both of you in January. You might try appealing to your local Education Authority, Mrs Darke. In certain cases ... but time is rather short and Education Committees can never be hurried. We have to get this whole thing settled as soon as possible. You understand that?'

Then we were outside in the dark corridor. . . . We were approaching the front door. Bloomsbury Square glowed greenly in front of us, for the door was open. We were all quite silent. I stole a look at Debbie and her lips were tight and her eyes stormy.

The full meaning of the whole dreadful business rose up and swamped me. Not only had I failed, but I was also going to ruin Debbie's chances.

'I've got to be—alone!' I gasped. 'Don't come. I'll be all right, Mother. Only let me go!'

I didn't wait to hear what she said, but rushed down the steps and turned towards Southampton Row. I was on the corner of High Holborn before I got my breath and even then my chest hurt and my eyes smarted with unshed tears.

There must be somewhere in that part of London where I could be alone to cry.

* 4 *

Dorrie's Dark Hours

I am good with maps and I had spent some time after breakfast that morning looking at the one in Aunt Eileen's hall. So, even in the midst of so much suffering, I remembered Lincoln's Inn Fields.

I got myself across the top of Kingsway and then ran along High Holborn, looking for some way through. For I thought that Lincoln's Inn Fields couldn't be far away. Very soon I found a narrow passageway and beyond it were trees and grass and some quietness.

The gardens weren't empty, by any means, on that fine Saturday afternoon, but I ran into a corner amongst some bushes and sank down on the worn grass, with my face turned away from anyone who might see. And there I cried for a long time, until I felt a little better in a weak and shaky way.

When at last I looked up there was London going on just as it had before. The big square was surrounded by tall buildings . . . the sky was blue . . . children were laughing and playing. And there was an endless roar of traffic in the distance.

But, for me, it really seemed as though life was over. Debbie had won a scholarship, but she wasn't going to be able to accept it. I don't honestly know which made me feel worse; the fact that Debbie had succeeded where I had failed, or the fact that I was going to ruin Debbie's life as well as my own. I suppose most people are selfish, so after a time I didn't care so much about Debbie, but only about my own shame and bitter, bitter disappointment. All my dreams of being a dancer were in the dust, and I did care so very much about continuing my training under proper conditions.

Of course they hadn't thought me hopeless. Far from it, when one considered the matter more calmly. They didn't offer any kind of place to all and sundry. I remembered the many stricken girls who had been told not to wait. That did help my pride a little, but it helped nothing else. I dreaded facing Mother and Aunt Eileen, but most of all I dreaded facing Debbie. I remembered her angry eyes and tight lips. Debbie had a temper, in spite of her fair, calm appearance, and I was dreadfully afraid that she would say something unforgivable.

But if I didn't go back Mother would be worried and might even call the police to look for me. So eventually I rose, dusted my skirt and began to walk slowly back towards Gower Street. Mother was on the steps when I came round the corner.

'Oh, Dorrie dear! I was so worried! Oh, Dorrie,

don't look like that! I'm sorry, dear. If we could manage it we would, but—'

'You can't h-help it,' I said. 'It's me—not being good enough.'

'There were only two scholarship places. You did wonderfully well to get a place at all. I'm proud of you both, but—'

'Debbie—' I began, and she shook her head.

'I should leave Debbie alone for a while, She's very disappointed, of course. I wish Miss Grayland had never suggested coming to London—'

Aunt Eileen didn't say much. She gave me some tea and hot buttered toast and I found that I was glad of them. The worst had happened, the uncertainty was over, and I was surprised to find that I was hungry. She said, when I had finished:

'You're the quiet one. And I always say it's the quiet deep ones who suffer most. But it's not the end of the world, girl. You'll live to look back at today and think it didn't matter very much.'

'I wish I could die!' I said. For the first time I wasn't afraid of Aunt Eileen, even though her manner was so brusque.

She snorted in rather an unladylike way.

'Everyone wishes they could die some time or other. And everyone does die, sooner or later. Life's a sad business and there's no getting away from it, so never try kidding yourself. It's only the scatter-brains like my Linda who manage to enjoy themselves for long. But you've still got your father and

41

mother and your sisters and brother. You've plenty
to be thankful for, though I daresay you don't see it
at the moment.'

'Debbie will hate me,' I said. We were alone during this conversation, because Mother had gone
upstairs.

'Debbie will get over it. She's disappointed,
naturally. She was rather riding her high horse, saying that she'd done better than you and why
shouldn't she come to London alone. If I'd been her
mother I'd have given her a flea in her ear. You did
well, too. The Lingeraux won't take just anyone. It's
simply a question of money, and Miss Debbie must
realise it.'

'She realises it,' I said drearily. 'Perhaps she *could*
come alone. She isn't a baby, and in any case you'd
look after her.'

It cost me a great effort to say that. I knew
that I could never bear life if Debbie had the
Lingeraux and London and I was left in Birkenhead
to the same old round of Grammar School and the
Grayland.

'Your mother won't hear of that, and I'm sure
your father won't either. Besides, twins shouldn't be
separated so young.'

'We aren't identical in any kind of way,' I said
dully. 'Sometimes I think people talk a lot of rot
about this twin business.' Which I suppose she
might have taken as rude, but she surprised me by
giving me quite a warm smile.

42

'You and Debbie need each other more than you know.'

I didn't see Debbie for an hour after that, then I just had to go up to our room to comb my hair and make myself look tidier. She was sitting on the bed, pretending to read, but her face was all blotchy, almost as bad as mine. We looked at each other in silence, and I went to the dressing-table and began to brush my hair.

'Where d'you go?' she asked awkwardly, after a while.

'Lincoln's Inn Fields.'

'Mum thought you'd get run over or lost.'

'I don't get lost,' I said. 'I can read m-maps.'

She got up then, flung the book down and went out of the room. She didn't mention the Lingeraux for the rest of that dreadful day or during the Sunday journey home. We had been going to catch an afternoon train, but I think we were all relieved when Mother said we'd go home in the morning. I didn't want to see any more of London, though I suppose that was silly, when it might have been my last opportunity.

The train journey was slow and rather awful. Debbie scarcely spoke and Mother pretended to read the Sunday papers. Instead of returning home in triumph we were a defeated trio, with a great bursting, unspoken problem.

It didn't remain unspoken when we got home, though. Dad had to be told what had happened and after that the battle raged. Debbie found her tongue and said over and over again that she didn't see why she shouldn't go to London alone.

'I've won the scholarship, haven't I? If you turn it down I shall never forgive you. I can't be held back by Dorrie, just because she isn't as good a dancer as I am—'

'Debbie!'

'Well, it's true. It's always been true, only no one says so. She's good, but *I'm* outstanding. Miss Grayland knows it, and Madame Lingeraux knew it, too. I—'

'You'll get a smacked bottom and go to bed at once if you go on like that!' said Dad, with rare anger.

Debbie's silvery hair flew out in a cloud.

'I don't see why for speaking the truth. I'm *sorry* that Dorrie didn't win a scholarship—well, naturally I am, since I'm paying for it, too. So—'

'*Debbie!* Stop it at once, do you hear?'

'Well, I *am* suffering because Dorrie didn't do better. Why should I be held back just because—?'

I sat huddled into the oldest armchair, the one with the broken springs and squashy, comforting arms, staring at the virago that was Debbie. In a way I understood exactly how she felt and one side of me didn't blame her. She was speaking, I was sure, nothing but the painful truth. But during the last day or two we seemed to have lost each other completely. I felt as though I didn't know her, as though

44

we had never shared things and got on pretty well, on the whole. She so clearly wasn't thinking of me and how I felt.

'I don't want Debbie or Dorrie to go away!' Bunty wailed, and burst into tears. Bim, who had been playing with his train, immediately followed suit.

'Now you've started the children crying,' Mother said, in despair, and she dried their tears and sent them out to play for a little while before tea.

Long after we had gone to bed—in silence—I could hear the voices rising and falling below. When I knew that Debbie was asleep I crept out on to the landing and tried to listen. Very wrong of me, as I was well aware, but it was so dreadful not knowing.

'I won't hear of Debbie going alone, and that's flat!' Dad was saying, very loudly.

'I agree with you, Jack. But she'll be impossible to live with if we turn down that scholarship.'

'She's behaving badly. Even if the kid is disappointed she ought to think of others. It's Dorrie I'm sorry for. I only wish there was enough money to pay those whacking high fees, and uniform and books. What I've got saved wouldn't last long and we'd need most of that for fares and clothes and extras. It wouldn't end with uniform. They'd have to have plenty of other things, party frocks and such, and probably money for theatre tickets. No, it's no good. And I won't appeal to the Education Committee. Besides, as Madame Lingeraux said, it might take months. Let's make a decision now and write and say it's no go. I always knew this ballet business would do the girls no good.'

Then there was silence until the television sound suddenly came on loudly. It seemed to be the end of a play. I crept back into bed and presently music reached me through the floor. It was the Waltz of the Flowers from the ballet *Casse Noisette*. And at once I could see dancing figures and Little Clara sitting, smiling and eager, on her throne. It was almost unbearable.

One of them must have recognised the music, because it was suddenly switched off in the middle of a bar. I burrowed down, pulling the sheet almost over my head, and presently I fell asleep.

Four dreadful days followed. Mother had written to Madame Lingeraux to tell her that we would definitely not be joining the School in January. Debbie knew this and was white-faced and sulkily silent. She was off her food and complaining of headaches, and, by mutual consent, we avoided each other as much as possible.

It was during these days that the iron really entered into my soul. Life seemed so drab and dreary and it was awful to have to explain to our friends just what had happened. At least, I *suppose* Debbie explained to her friends. I told mine briefly that I had been offered a place, but that we couldn't afford to take it up. I hadn't many friends, anyway, but my two best ones were very sympathetic. They thought it romantic to want to be a ballet dancer. I knew, of course, that it wasn't. It's hardly romantic to want to launch yourself on years of hard work, with no certainty of a job at the end of them.

Mother wrote to Miss Grayland to explain, I think, but no mention was made of our going to ballet classes as usual, perhaps they were waiting for us to suggest it ourselves.

Fortunately Debbie and I didn't sit together in school, and we often did walk home separately. The worst times were in the morning and at night, when we were alone together in our room. By then I couldn't have spoken about the affair to her if my life had depended on it; my tongue felt entirely locked. I had ruined her life and mine as well. It went too deep for any words between us, though sometimes I would have given anything in the world for her to say something warm and kind, to show that we were still friends as well as twins.

By Friday I was wondering how I was going to bear it. We got up as usual and washed and dressed almost without speaking. We only made a few of the jerky, unnatural remarks that passed for conversation with us then. We went downstairs one behind the other and there was a smell of bacon and toast. Mother was just settling Bim in his place and taking the top off his boiled egg. Dad was reading a letter.

Suddenly he looked up. His face looked quite different from the strained appearance it had had since Sunday. He said, looking from Debbie to me:

'This is a letter from Madame Lingeraux.'

Debbie sent a plate flying off the table. It fell with a crash and broke. I stood frozen to the spot, with my plate of bacon burning my hand.

'You girls can relax. I suppose you'll be happy now. She offers Dorrie a scholarship, too.'

'It isn't true!' I cried. The smell of hot fat was making me feel sick. Somehow I managed to put the plate down on the table.

'True enough. It's a very nice letter. She says they've just learned that one of the present scholarship students is leaving at Christmas. Her family is emigrating to Australia. So Dorrie is offered the place.'

Debbie's face had flamed scarlet. She said, very shrilly:

'I always knew they wouldn't risk losing me. They wanted me—I know they did! So they'll take Dorrie as well.'

Dad put down the letter and stared at her, and Debbie seemed to realise what she had said. She began to dither.

'Well, but that's what it must be. Because you said neither of us could go—'

'Dorrie,' Dad said slowly and clearly, 'has been offered this scholarship because she deserves it, because they want *her*. I'm ashamed of you, Debbie.'

'Anyway, it's wonderful! So we can go, after all? Oh, Dorrie, aren't you thrilled?'

I was stunned. The nightmare misery of the last

48

few days had dropped away from me, though I knew that I would remember Debbie's words for a long time. Dad was probably right, and I had been next on the list for a scholarship, but I thought that there was always going to be a doubt in my mind. *Did* they want Debbie so much that they were willing to take me, too?

'Debbie ought to apologise to Dorrie,' said Mother. 'Really, Debbie, I don't know what's come over you lately. You want taking down a peg or two, seems to me.'

And then Debbie became much more her old self. She flung her arms round me and hugged me.

'I don't know what I said, but sorry, anyway, Dor. Who cares which of us they want, as long as we can both go? Oh, I'm so happy! So happy!'

'Well, get on with your breakfast, or you'll be late for school,' Dad said repressively.

'But aren't *you* happy, Dorrie?'

'Yes,' I said. And I *was*, because now I needn't feel guilty or ashamed, and I was going to have London and the Lingeraux.

But that week of pain and fear and misery had taught me a lot, about myself and about Debbie. I thought it would be a long time before we were really friendly again. I felt a thousand miles away from her, my 'ballet twin'.

* 5 *

A Garret in Gower Street

We settled down to our last term at the Grammar
School. . . . We went back to the Grayland. Miss
Grayland and Mrs Bettle were delighted with the
pair of us. *Two* scholarships to the Lingeraux! We
were going to be a wonderful advertisement for her
dancing school.

On the surface Debbie and I went back to our old
relationship, but underneath everything was quite
different. I wasn't sure if she knew; if she did she
made no sign. But neither of us ever once referred
to that nightmare week-end in London. Only the
memory of it was with me off and on, sometimes
when I was walking home from school alone, or in
bed at night.

It wasn't only the week-end, either; it was those
dreadful days that had followed it. Scraps of conversation kept on coming back to me. 'We can offer
your daughter Deborah a scholarship—' 'I can't be
held back by Dorrie!' 'I always knew they wouldn't
risk losing me.'

Though my dream was coming true and I was going to London to the famous Lingeraux School I seemed to have forgotten how to be happy. I knew then, more clearly than ever before, that I had always played second fiddle to Debbie. She was the prettier, the more confident, the better dancer.

I didn't always hate Debbie, of course. Even after all that had happened there were times when she won me over, made me laugh. She could be very droll and a very good companion. But all the memories were there, turning my pleasure sour. And there were times when I fully believed that the Lingeraux was taking me because it was the only way to get their future ballerina, Deborah Darke.

It was all the worse because I couldn't confide in anyone. How *could* I tell anyone in the world that I was jealous of Debbie? But it wasn't only that I was jealous; I was deeply hurt. It was as though one of the foundations of life had been removed when Debbie showed her true colours and didn't seem to like me at all. She had been upset, she had thought she was losing her big chance, but she ought to have remembered that I had feelings—so many feelings.

I tried to forget by working harder than ever before in school. I worked so hard that I even had higher marks than Debbie two weeks running. Miss Cross, our form mistress, once asked me to stay behind after school and said to me:

'I always knew you had brains, Dorrie. I wish we

weren't losing you. But what's been the matter lately? Is anything worrying you?'

'Nothing, Miss Cross,' I answered, looking at her blankly, and she sighed and said: 'Oh well, run along then.' She was the one who, in our first year, had said 'Darke by name and dark by nature.'

I worked hard at the Grayland, too, though Miss Grayland had decided, with regret, that we ought not to take part in the Christmas Show. She said we had enough to think about and what mattered was making all the progress we could before we had to face the stiff competition at the Lingeraux.

So, one way and another, the time passed quickly. November was grey and cold, with icy winds sweeping across the Pier Head. Eventually it grew so cold that we travelled to Liverpool by Underground instead of by boat, though the train cost more.

Then it was December, the big stores were gaily decorated for Christmas, the lights went on in the Birkenhead and Liverpool streets and there were brilliant Christmas trees here and there.

So that was one more thing to think about and plan for; we had all our presents to buy, never an easy business, as our pocket money didn't go very far. It took a lot of ingenuity and foresight.

By then our measurements had been sent to the big London store that made the Lingeraux uniform, but Mother said that everything else could be left until after Christmas. The new term didn't start until January 15th; it was a little later than usual because some alterations were being made at the Lingeraux and some of the studios were being painted.

Father's Christmas presents to us were both the same, lovely little blue cases for our ballet shoes and towels and things. They had silk linings and mirrors in the lids. Mother gave us each a plastic shoulder-bag in the same colour. They had safe zip pockets for money and railway tickets and other things that mustn't be lost.

Linda sent us a Christmas card—the lurid kind, simply smothered with holly and reindeers. I wished that someone would send me the kind with art reproductions on, but there is no doubt that they are the most expensive. Anyway, it was nice of Linda, and she added a message: 'Looking forward to seeing both you kids again.'

Aunt Eileen sent us plain white handkerchiefs. Her presents were always dull and useful, and now I had met her again I understood that she wasn't the kind who would ever send something pretty and use-less. But she was nice really. . . . My mind at once shied away from that bitter Saturday afternoon when she had been brusquely understanding.

Christmas was fun, mainly because Bunty and Bim were so thrilled with everything. On Boxing Day we all went to the pantomime (in quite cheap seats) and there was some rather awful ballet, but I enjoyed it all the same. I don't think I shall ever get over the breathless moment of expectation before the curtain rises.

Then our journey to London was not much more than two weeks away. I was excited and scared in about equal proportions during the first week, and then just plain scared. If Debbie was frightened she didn't say so. She was talking a lot about the Lingeraux now. Once I asked: 'Won't you be homesick?' and she was quiet for a few moments, with her head on one side. Then she said:

'Of course. I'm bound to be. I shall hate leaving them all, but we've got to, haven't we? We might have been at boarding-school for years.'

I was homesick even before I ever left. I found myself wanting to touch things like the old armchair. Yet London did beckon. I borrowed some books about it from the library and even bought a street map of my own and studied it often. I didn't want to be a country cousin; I meant to know my way about. There was a London Tube map in the new diary that Bunty had given me and I used to recite the stations on the different lines. Euston ... Warren Street ... Goodge Street ... Tottenham Court Road ... Leicester Square.

Our uniforms came in vast, impressive-looking boxes. The Lingeraux colours were grey and royal blue and there was a coat, grey with a vivid blue lining, a grey pleated skirt and a neat little jacket, several royal blue blouses and a sweater in the same colour. There was also a dark blue raincoat, a royal blue beret with a silver badge, a big, fluffy scarf and also, of course, our dancing tunics, two each. Almost everything fitted us perfectly, which Mother said was a relief. We had never had so many new clothes before and were rather overwhelmed. Even when we went to the Grammar School we got things quite gradually, starting off with a gym tunic, a blazer and a beret.

Then our shabby cases were packed and it was our last night at home. Mother had a private talk with us, telling us that she trusted us to be sensible and not cause Aunt Eileen any anxiety. We were to write as often as we could manage, at least once a week, and if we needed anything important we weren't to hesitate to explain.

'Look after each other,' she ended.

But I think I knew then that our ways were going to diverge. Debbie was all set to have a wonderful time, with hordes of new friends. I imagined myself exploring London, most probably alone. Though just occasionally I thought of Mel Forrest, who had seemed so nice. I remembered her round face and her smooth brown hair and the sound of her attractive Cockney voice. Mel was my only hope, for I expected to be very shy during the first few weeks at the Lingeraux.

So we went to sleep in our familiar beds and the next morning Mother saw us off on the London train.

The house in Gower Street seemed quite different when we arrived there on the afternoon of January

55

14th. There were letters in the rack in the hall, a pile of medical books spilling off the table by the front door, someone playing a radio very loudly near the top of the stairs.

Aunt Eileen, who had met us at the station, straightened the books.

'That's James MacDonald! He always leaves his books about. Still, I've got a warm spot for James. He comes from the Hebrides; his people are crofters. He's one of those hard-working Scots; a decent, serious young man. Or as serious as medical students ever are. That'll be Arthur Moorhead playing his radio so loudly. He says it helps him to study. The times I've told him it doesn't help *me* or anyone else. Of course a lot of their courses haven't started again yet, but they're all here. Most of them say they can work here better than at home. Good heavens, Sara! I thought it was an avalanche!' For, while she was talking and shutting the front door behind us, a girl had come rushing down the stairs. She wore jeans and a dirty fawn duffle coat and her hair was bright red.

'Sorry, Mrs Troom! I'm late.' The front door opened again and then slammed.

'When isn't she late? If she ever gets a real part she'll miss all her entrances. She's at R.A.D.A. Well, come along. I'll take you up. At the top, as I warned you, but your legs are young enough to stand it. You'll have Sara next door and Rachel at the end of the passage. Rachel's one of our future scientists.

Very much future just now,' she said grimly. 'I suppose she has brains, but she's the untidiest girl I've ever had here.'

She was beginning to pant a little as we toiled up three flights of stairs. She had insisted on carrying one of our cases.

'You'll soon get to know them all by sight. There's a Jamaican; a very nice, respectable boy. I don't object to coloured students. I wouldn't be so un-Christian. They have their way to make just like anyone else. There's Maribel Brown who's taking a commercial course and of course the New Yorker who has the room you were in, Clyde Smith. He seems very pleasant; plenty of money, anyone can see. It's a nice change. Well, here you are. No. 8.'

By then Debbie and I were puffing nearly as much as Aunt Eileen, for our luggage was heavy. The room was small and rather bare, with a sloping ceiling, and the window looked down into Gower Street. I saw the top of a bus as I went to the window. It was very cold, for it had snowed a little the night before. I began to shiver, but it was nice to glimpse Bedford Square touched with white, and the black patterns of the trees.

'I've put some money in your gas fire,' Aunt Eileen said, 'but do use it sparingly, please, girls. Gas just eats money these days. And always remember to turn it off when you go out of the room. I hope you'll be comfortable. It isn't luxury, but you'll make it more homelike when you've put out your things.'

'It's lovely!' Debbie said, with commendable enthusiasm. 'Book shelves, and a desk and a reading-lamp. We can do our homework up here.'

'The reading-lamp doesn't always work. I had to bring it out of Sara's room. She needs a good light. You'll do your homework down in my sitting-room while it's winter. In summer it may be different. Now get yourselves unpacked and take off those good uniforms and come down for something to eat. I provide supper for the students who want it at about seven o'clock and that's a busy time. You'll be able to help me when you settle down. I've got a woman in the kitchen mornings and evenings, and another one who comes in to clean the rooms, but I can always do with extra pairs of hands. Linda might as well not have hands at all for all the good they are.' Then she nodded and went away.

Debbie made straight for the box of matches on the narrow mantelpiece and lit the gas-fire. It popped a couple of times and then began to glow brightly. After that she bounced on each low bed in turn.

'Hard as iron. I s'pose it will be good for our spines. I don't like the colour scheme, do you?'

I stood still in the middle of the room, staring round me and shivering. The walls hadn't been papered for a long time, but you could see that there had once been pink flowers and blue bows. The curtains were what Mother calls 'dunducketty-mud'

and the coverlets on the beds were not much brighter.
There was a worn grey-brown carpet on the floor. It
was clearly far from being the best room; it probably
came just within the means of a very poor student,
but then we weren't paying at all. 'It's awfully
depressing,' I said, finally. 'Ours at h-home is shabby,
but—but gayer than this.' But then I saw the top of
another bus and caught another glimpse of a corner
of Bedford Square. It was a room in London and
suddenly—though I was cold, homesick and rather
frightened—it had a kind of romance.

'Well, let's cheer it up,' said Debbie, beginning to
struggle with her bigger case. 'Do you think Aunt
Eileen will mind if we stick some of our postcard
reproductions on the walls with bits of Sellotape!
It couldn't do any harm.'

'Better wait until we've asked her,' I answered
nervously.

Debbie found an old skirt and sweater and then
divested herself with obvious reluctance of her
Lingeraux uniform.

'I hope she doesn't expect us to help too much.
Do you think she regards us as free labour? Because
we're going to have quite enough to do, what with
school and homework and amusing ourselves.'

'She's taken us for nothing,' I said, and she began
to dance wildly in her vest and inelegant winter
knickers, ending by flinging herself flat on her back
on her bed. What springs there were creaked pro-
testingly.

'Well, she *is* our aunt,' she said, from that position, and began flexing her ankles and toes. 'Oh, Dorrie, I do wish we were rich! I never cared much about money until lately, but now I can see just how much it matters. But at least this will sound well when I come to write my autobiography.'

'*Are* you going to write it?' I asked, scrambling hastily into the warmest sweater I could find. In spite of the gas-fire the room still seemed terribly cold. Or perhaps it was my low spirits that were making me shiver.

'We-ell, one day. Heaps of ballerinas do. Partly because they want to, I s'pose, and partly because it brings in more money. I shall start by saying, "I came to London when I was thirteen and took up residence in a garret in Gower Street. My parents were poor but honest, and—" '

Suddenly I could stand it no longer.

'You aren't a ballerina yet, and you may never be. We may both never get any further than the *corps de ballet*, or not even that far. And if you don't hurry we won't get any tea.' I knew that my voice was sharp, but I didn't care. Debbie never used to have so many airs and graces and if she ever started an autobiography at all it ought to begin: 'My twin and I came to London when we were thirteen—'

After that we got ready and unpacked almost in silence, and then, remembering to turn off the gas-fire, started off down the flights of stairs.

We were in London and tomorrow would see us both at the Lingeraux Ballet School. But just then the biggest part of me would have been glad to be safely at home.

* 6 *

First Day at Ballet School

It was already growing dark as we went slowly down the rather bleak flights of stairs, but away from the top floor it wasn't so cold. We soon realised that there was some central heating in the house, never very effective really, and not at all effective up in our garret.

Arthur Moorhead's radio was going full blast when we reached the first floor, but all the doors were closed. I wondered if the New Yorker were in and what he thought of London. It was rather peculiar to be in a house full of strangers.

Debbie boldly turned on lights as we went and when we reached the hall there was Aunt Eileen, apparently waiting for us. She gave us a little lecture on always turning lights *off* whenever possible.

'My electricity bills are just terrible. I nearly have a heart attack every time one comes in. But leave the hall light on now. I always tell myself I'd get blamed if anyone broke their neck. That's right. Now come in and make yourselves at home. I've got you a high tea ready now, as I suppose you only had sandwiches on the train.'

Aunt Eileen's sitting-room looked quite cheerful, and there was a small ginger kitten pretending to be a tea cosy on the rug; all hunched up and fluffy. The sight of it cheered me far more than the smell of cooking. I wasn't hungry in spite of the sandwiches. I fell on my knees by the kitten, for I adore cats. I think they are almost always beautiful, whatever they are doing.

'More work!' said Aunt Eileen, with a sigh, nodding at the kitten. 'It was going to be put down, so I said I'd take it. I suppose it'll keep the mice away, though all it does at the moment is play and sleep. And eat, of course. Eats its head off.'

I was growing a little used to her gloom and somehow sensed that, in spite of the grumbling tone, she rather liked the kitten.

'What's his name?'

'Ruari. James MacDonald christened it. He says it means red or something.'

The kitten rolled over, displaying a delicious stomach and a white powder-puff of a chest.

'Get your tea,' said Aunt Eileen brusquely. 'What's that you're reading?' to Debbie, who had come down with a ballet book under her arm.

'A life of Margot Fonteyn. I got it for my birthday and I've read it three times already.'

'I suppose you think of nothing but ballet. It's not a thing I understand. Lot of silly posing. The men look just ridiculous, in my view.'

'But have you seen much ballet?' Debbie asked—

rather pertly, I thought. Aunt Eileen evidently thought so, too, for she answered tartly:

'All I want to, so don't think you're going to teach me anything, Miss. I can't think where the pair of you get it from. There's never been anyone artistic on our side of the family, and I shouldn't imagine there's anyone on your mother's side.'

'We must be changelings,' said Debbie, unabashed, and she began to eat heartily.

Linda came in when Debbie and I were washing up our dishes. She brought a wonderful touch of glamour into the rather drab scullery. High boots were fashionable that winter, and hers were scarlet and shiny. She wore a black coat and a scarlet hat, very dashing, and a great deal of vivid lipstick.

'Puts all her money on her back,' Aunt Eileen said disapprovingly, and Linda laughed.

'Where else should I put it? You must admit it works.'

'You might put some into your post office savings account for a rainy day.'

'Perhaps there won't be any rainy ones,' said Linda. 'But I sometimes think I might save a bit towards my wedding.'

Aunt Eileen grunted. Linda wasn't even engaged, though we soon learned that there were three or four young men very anxious to take her out. It seemed funny that such a gloomy woman should have a gay and frivolous daughter.

Things cheered up a lot once Linda was home.

64

She turned the television on, though she didn't pay much attention to it. She mostly chattered to us while she ate. I sat nursing the kitten, taking comfort from his warmth and grace, and Debbie did the most talking. But when Linda had gone upstairs to get ready for her 'date' Debbie sank deep into her book, slumped in her favourite attitude, with her legs hanging sideways over one arm of the chair.

There was a lot of activity out in the kitchen and scullery by then, and Aunt Eileen's help, a woman called Mrs Tonkings, kept passing to and fro on the way to the students' dining-room. Presently I began to feel guilty and asked if I could help, and she seemed grateful.

The dining-room was at the front of the house and was a big, high room that had once been elegant. Now it was rather dismal, with mud-coloured curtains and a few dark paintings, but there was a glorious great cyclamen with about a dozen cerise flowers. It looked very exotic and quite unlike Aunt Eileen, and Mrs Tonkings told me that the American student had bought it.

Aunt Eileen came out of the kitchen looking hot and discovered Debbie reclining there like a lady, though she didn't seem to think her attitude very ladylike.

'Come on, girl. It may be different when you have homework to do, but I hate to see any one wasting their time when there's work to be done. Go and bang the gong, then you can help to carry things in.'

Debbie glared, pushing back her hair. Clearly she was coming back, with the greatest reluctance, from Margot Fonteyn's exciting, successful life.

'I'm sure your mum doesn't let you be idle, and her with two young children.'

'Unpaid labour. I told you,' Debbie muttered to me, as she slipped past. She banged the gong so fiercely that it could probably be heard in Bedford Square.

The students came thundering down the stairs, with a great deal of talk and laughter. I felt very shy when I went in with the potatoes, while Debbie followed with the hot plates. All talk stopped and they stared, then most of them smiled.

'Hullo!' said the red-haired girl, Sara. 'Got you working already, has she?'

'The students get younger every term,' said a pale young man, with a floppy piece of hair. He was Arthur Moorhead, we learned later.

'Ah, but these are ballet students. Going to the Lingeraux. Debbie and Dorrie Darke, isn't it?' Sara asked. 'Mrs Doom's nieces from the darkest North.'

'Shhh, you fool!'

'Is that what you call her?' Debbie asked, giggling. 'Mrs Doom? I must say it suits her.'

'Or Mrs Gloom,' said Sara, grinning. 'Only don't you go and split on us. She isn't a bad old thing, even though she does always look on the dark side.'

'That's what someone once said of Dorrie,' said

Debbie. ' "Darke by name and dark by nature."
And Aunt Eileen was born a Darke, I s'pose.'

'She has a secret face,' said Sara, staring at me, and
I came over shyer than ever and dropped some
potato on James MacDonald's trousers. He said it
didn't matter and they were certainly very old and
rather grubby trousers. He had a lovely voice, with
a kind of singing lilt.

It was quite *extraordinary* to be there. Ballet
students . . . us! With London wrapped in winter
darkness outside and the Lingeraux in the morning.
All the unfamiliar faces swam a little and I hoped
that I wasn't going to cry.

Home seemed so dreadfully far away and the
thought suddenly swamped me that we wouldn't see
Dad or Mother, or the young ones, for three months,
And we had nowhere of our own, nowhere to hide,
except for a rather depressing garret.

I wondered if Debbie felt the same. She was
smiling at Winston Marshall, the coloured student,
and, perhaps by contrast, she looked dazzlingly fair
and delicate, striking a slight attitude.

I couldn't stay there any longer. The faces really
were swimming in a mist of tears. I bolted up the
first broad flight of stairs and locked myself in the
first lavatory I came to, where I leaned against the
door and fought my grief and homesickness. Everything, I told myself, would be all right, really thrilling, in the morning.

My bed was dreadfully hard and I was cold. Aunt

Eileen, it seemed, didn't believe in hot water bottles, but I thought perhaps I would save up for one, or ask Mother to send an old one from home. About three in the morning the wind began to howl and I heard a soft brushing sound against the window. Debbie was sleeping peacefully; I could tell by her regular breathing. I wished that I could creep in with her, but for one thing there wasn't room in those narrow beds, and for another she wouldn't welcome me.

But I suppose I must have slept, for suddenly someone was thumping on the door. It was still dark, but my watch had a luminous dial (Dad had given us both cheap watches for our twelfth birthday) and it was half-past seven. Shivering, I groped for the light and the cheerless bulb immediately showed me the garret, with our Lingeraux uniforms laid out in readiness. Debbie groaned and burrowed deeper under the bedclothes.

'Light the fire, for heaven's sake!' she implored me.

I did so, then ran to the window. Snow was piled up on the sill outside and fresh flakes spattered the panes.

'It's been snowing nearly all night,' I said, dragging on my dressing-gown. The bathroom was on the floor below and was occupied. I stood leaning against some warm pipes, trying to stop shivering, until the door opened and Rachel came out, with her mousy hair on end and looking as though she hadn't washed much. All the dearer rooms had fitted basins, but none on the top floor boasted such a luxury.

We dressed in our new clothes and went down to breakfast through the wakening house. Arthur Moorhead had his radio on; he almost always did. It was like being in a dream, I thought, and not a very nice one, with so much lying immediately ahead. But the kitten was there on the rug, playing with a feather. How lovely to be a kitten, with no worries!

'Now make sure you've got everything,' Aunt Eileen said, when we came downstairs again just after eight-thirty, wearing our raincoats over our suits. Our coats would have been warmer, but it was snowing hard and they would only have got wet. Anyway, we had our lovely big fluffy blue scarves.

Debbie checked over her case: 'Towel, house slippers, ballet shoes, pencil box, mascot—'

'Mascot? You superstitious child!'

'All ballet dancers have mascots, Aunt Eileen. Mine is a little doll wearing a silver tutu. Dorrie has a wooden elephant someone gave her once.'

'I suppose you're going to put on your gum boots? There they are behind the door. You can keep them there always, but mind you wipe your feet well when you come in. Good-bye, then. Have a good day.'

We set off into the white, cold world. Gower Street was slushy and a bus almost immediately sent up a shower of dirty snow. We shrieked and tried to avoid the splashes. But Bedford Square was white in the centre and looked nice. The British Museum was touched with snow here and there and the bare trees in Bloomsbury Square were decorated with blobs of fluffy whiteness. The wind whipped the snow in our faces as we crossed towards the Lingeraux School.

There were a lot of boys and girls in blue raincoats or grey coats converging from all directions. Some of them looked quite old, sixteen or even older, and others were quite small. Debbie marched boldly towards the steps.

'Come on, Dorrie. Don't look so scared. Our school at home was far, far bigger than this.'

'It wasn't a ballet school, though. A London ballet school,' I said.

And then we were up the steps and in the shabby hall that I well remembered from that dreadful September day. Just to be there brought it all back to me, but I reminded myself that *that* trouble was all over and must be forgotten. Though it was going to be hard to forget entirely that I had had so many doubts about whether they wanted me for myself, or simply as a kind of appendage to Debbie.

The school was lovely and warm, anyway, and the cloakrooms smelt familiarly of wet gum boots, much used ballet shoes and cheap soap. We had been told to change into our practice clothes, as ballet classes for everyone would follow General Assembly, which apparently only took place once or twice a term at nine o'clock.

The boys' cloakrooms were at the other end of the

basement and they were making an awful noise. It seemed very strange to have boys in a school.

There seemed to be no familiar faces and I stuck close to Debbie as we went up again and followed everyone towards the hall. It seemed that we were to be in Class Four and we were told to sit about half-way up the hall. The young ones were in front and the older boys and girls behind. The senior students were in the two back rows and they looked nearly grown up and very grand and remote.

Debbie began chatting to her next door neighbour, but was shushed as the staff filed on to the platform. Madame Lingeraux was not there and Assembly was taken by the headmistress, Miss Sherwood. She greeted us, with a special word to the new pupils, then she read a lot of notices and finally we sang a hymn. I tried to pay attention, but I don't think I really did. I still couldn't believe that I was at the Lingeraux, really there; Dorrie Darke, with a scholarship.

I came alive in the ballet class. It was the only thing that I enjoyed in that whole long day. Our teacher was the Miss Verney who had shown us to the cloakrooms in September, and I knew at once that she was very good. She was little and dark and decisive, and you just had to pay attention all the time. I enjoyed the *barre* work and even the centre practice. It was like arriving at something familiar and dear after wandering in the wilderness.

Miss Verney asked our names at the beginning

and after that she made no remarks to us at all. She did say some very sharp things to a few of the girls (there were no boys in the class) and I knew that if she did it to me I should shrivel up. But then the class was over and we ran away to change without a word of criticism or praise being cast in our direction.

'Funny she ignored us,' said Debbie, and I wondered rather nastily if she had fully expected to be received as the shining wonder of the Lingeraux. But the Lingeraux, of course, wasn't the Grayland. In London we were amongst dozens of dedicated students, all of whom were probably grimly set on being ballerinas.

Our classroom was on the first floor, overlooking the square. There were twenty-five of us, twelve girls and thirteen boys, and still no familiar faces. I hadn't seen Mel at all and kept on hoping she would appear. She ought to be there as she had won a scholarship.

We were given time-tables and books by a Miss Lines. Then she went away and someone else came to take English literature—*As You Like It*. It is one of my favourite Shakespeare plays, so that was something else familiar, but I didn't feel relaxed. There were going to be so many things and people to remember, and, perhaps it was the bad night I had had, but I had a headache and heartache, too, because I still felt so far from home.

It seemed awful to have got my heart's desire and to be miserable.

Really the lessons were all right, and the teachers seemed kind and pleasant, but I was shy and out of things. It was particularly noticeable in break and worse during lunch, which we had in the canteen with all the others who stayed.

We seemed to be the only new girls in our class, but I hadn't even the comfort of Debbie, because she had already made friends with a little dark girl called Claudia Wood, who turned out to be Cécile Barreux's niece, and a foreign girl called Lotti Karl. There seemed to be a great many foreigners and I thought that that was going to be interesting. There was even a coloured girl in our class, Mary Ann Schulz. She seemed a great favourite and laughed a lot, and I hoped I should get to know her. I was puzzled about what would happen to her when she was older, because it didn't seem likely that she would fit easily into any ballet company.

Quite a lot of people spoke to me, but I felt tongue-tied and stupid and they soon went away. At lunch I sat next to a boy with a Russian name, Serge Something-or-other and he asked where I came from. I told him Birkenhead in Cheshire and pointed out Debbie, sitting at the other end of the table and laughing with Lotti Karl, and he asked: 'Is that your *sister*?' in the way I most disliked. And after that he talked to the boy on his other side.

It snowed all day. Sometimes I looked out at Bloomsbury Square and was stabbed with amazement that I was in London. I wished that Mel was

73

there, as she would have made all the difference, I thought, but there was still no sign of her.

At the end of afternoon school I gathered up my courage and stayed behind to speak to Miss Lines, who was piling up books to be marked. She smiled at me quite warmly.

'Did you want something, Doria?'

'Oh, please . . . at the audition there was a girl called Meldreth Forrest. She won a scholarship, too, but she isn't here.'

She hesitated, then took up her register.

'I think she must be the one—yes, here she is. She's got measles, I'm afraid. Hard luck, isn't it? Her mother sent a note, saying she won't be able to come for two weeks.'

'Oh, dear!' I felt dreadfully dismayed.

She put her hand on my shoulder for a moment.

'Well, cheer up. Two weeks will soon pass. You're one of the ones from the North, aren't you?'

'Yes, Birkenhead.'

'And homesick, I expect? You're not like your twin, are you? When I heard that there were twins I expected to have one of those silly experiences, not being able to tell one from another.'

'We're quite different,' I said.

When I went slowly down to the cloakrooms Debbie was nearly ready to leave. She said:

'Do hurry, Dorrie!'

But by the time I was ready she'd gone. When I reached the front steps she was crossing the square,

74

going away from Gower Street with Claudia, Lotti and two boys. So I walked home alone.

I looked at London in the snow and tried to tell myself how lucky I was. I was going to get to know it all . . . some time soon I was going to the Royal Opera House and the Lingeraux Theatre. I was going to have all kinds of new experiences.

But I felt cold, lonely and hurt because Debbie had gone off without me, though really she usually had at home in Birkenhead, and it must be my own fault that I hadn't made friends.

Aunt Eileen had given me a key and I let myself in to the hall. There was no one about and I was thankful. I eased off my gum boots and put them side by side under the letter-rack, intending to move them later. I ran up the first flight of stairs in my stockinged feet, but on the landing above my spirits failed. Arthur Moorhead couldn't be in, because everywhere was very silent. I sat down on the first step of the next flight, in the shadows, and fought my desolation.

Then suddenly the door of the 'best' room opened and a flood of light came out, reaching me. Clyde Smith, the New Yorker, stood there, with some books under his arm.

'Hi Kid!' he said. 'What are you doing there?'

'Hi!' I answered hollowly and he came slowly towards me.

'What's the matter? You look kind of miserable. Homesick?'

He was so nice. He had a lovely quiet, drawly voice and crisp brown hair.

'Terribly,' I said. 'I—I—' and I burst into shameful tears.

He sat on the stair beside me. That flight was still pretty wide. And he held my hand.

'Where do you live? Is it far away?'

'T-Two hundred m-miles,' I told him, sniffing.

'Well, look! I guess it's pretty hard when you're so young, but how about me? *My* home is more than three thousand miles away.'

'But you're grown up,' I said, so surprised that I stopped crying.

He laughed.

'Don't tell me that you believe all feeling stops just because one reaches the ripe old age of twenty-one?'

I had believed it. I thought it must be lovely to be grown up and beyond suffering.

'It can't be so bad.'

'We-ell, it's just possible to feel something, you know. When one is some place far from home. I like London, but I've only been here one week. I guess I don't know many people yet.'

I thought of New York; it always looked so fabulous in pictures. High and gleaming, in clear light.

'I—I shan't see them all at home for three months.'

'And I'm not going home for a year, maybe

76

longer. Two exiles, you see. How would it be if we took a walk and explored one Saturday?'

'It would be lovely,' I said, suddenly feeling better. 'I can read a map. I've got one.'

I went up to the garret still feeling snuffly and rather damp, but not so sunk in self-pity.

* 7 *

New Friends and Covent Garden

Debbie was late for tea. She came in looking glowing, with snow all over her scarf and making her hair look even more silvery than usual.

'We thought you were lost,' Aunt Eileen said, a little tartly, and Debbie flung down her case, shook her beret and answered cheerfully:

'Oh, no. I walked some of the way home with Claudia. She lives in a flat over in Bayswater. Then I tried to get the bus back, but it was the rush hour, so I had to walk.'

'Well, I'd sooner you came straight home while it gets dark so early. After all, you're a stranger to London, and if anything happened to you ... besides, I suppose you have homework to do?'

'Yes, a horrid lot. I think it's mean on the first day.'

'Well, get your tea and then clear one end of the table. It won't be an ideal arrangement, with people in and out, but I can't have you using light and heat somewhere else.'

Debbie ate heartily, casting occasional glances at

78

me, but not asking any direct questions. She chattered to Aunt Eileen, telling her some of the happenings of the day. But when we had cleared the table as ordered, and were settling ourselves with our books, she asked:

'Where'd you get to? I waited for you on the steps.'

'You were going off with the others when I saw you,' I said, and she must have caught something in my tone because she answered rather defensively:

'I thought you were being slow on purpose. You didn't seem to want to be friendly with anyone. Why are you always so miserable?'

'I'm not. I didn't mean to be. I stayed to ask Miss Lines something. I can't help being shy.'

'Shy! You looked just awfully dumb,' she said unkindly, and I buried my face in my Shakespeare preparatory to writing an essay on my favourite character in *As You Like It*. For two pins I could have cried again, but I was determined not to. For one thing I had to get on with my work, because I didn't mean to disgrace myself at the Lingeraux that way, even if I wasn't going to turn out a popular person. Only sometimes I looked at Debbie's bent fair head and wondered how on earth we were ever going to get close to each other again. It *must* partly be my fault, I thought.

When we were getting ready for bed I said to her:

'But Debbie, didn't you feel out of things a bit, sometimes? Most of them *do* seem much better off

79

than we are, and there was such a lot of talk that was different from the Grammar School. They seem so—so much more sophisticated in some ways, and we don't really know anything about the Company and all the things that—'

'We'll soon learn,' said Debbie, diving into bed. 'Of course we'll learn. Oh, I *loved* it, all that glorious gossip, and foreigners and boys. And Claudia was so friendly, even though she's been at the Lingeraux for two years and has a lot of friends. I expect I shall meet Cécile Barreux and—'

'Was that why? I mean why you got to know *her*?'

Debbie looked at me brightly over the sheet.

'Well, no, not really. I liked her at once and she liked me. It was sheer luck. But I'd sooner know the important ones, because I mean to be an important one myself. I don't mean to be in the background.'

'You won't,' I said.

'Very catty all of a sudden, Dorrie Darke. I don't like that tone.' But she was half-laughing.

'Not really meant to be catty,' I mumbled. 'But—aren't you homesick at *all*?'

She was silent for some moments, then she said:

'I wasn't in school all day. I felt as though it was the place where I just had to be. As though it were fore-ordained. But when I'd left Claudia I felt a bit queer. It was in Oxford Street, and the snow came on again and there were such crowds, everyone pushing along with umbrellas up. And I couldn't get on a bus. To tell you the truth I wasn't even sure what bus it should be. And I felt as though I might be invisible; just a dot amongst eight million people, or however many there are in London. A man nearly knocked me down and he glared as though it was my fault. I—I did feel homesick then.'

Well, that was something. I could very easily imagine her in Oxford Street, alone and bewildered.

I snuggled down in bed, clutching the blessed comfort of a very old, rather smelly hot water bottle. For Aunt Eileen had relented and found them for us, saying that it was colder than usual and she supposed it was all right to coddle ourselves, but not to blame her if we got chilblains. As neither of us had ever had a chilblain in our lives it was a risk we were more than willing to take.

The next morning the Lingeraux did seem more familiar. We had our own pegs in the cloakroom, and we knew which studio and classroom to go to. And the ballet class was just as enjoyable as on the previous day. While I was doing those familiar exercises I felt at peace with the world and with myself.

Miss Verney still took no particular notice of us, but when I was leaving the studio—one of the last to go—she suddenly said to me, smiling:

'You've been well taught, dear. There's very little to unlearn.'

To *me* she said it, not to Debbie, and I went to the cloakroom on wings, for a time, at least, believing that they had wanted me for myself. Some of the pleasure and relief lasted until break, when I felt shy and lonely again. It was interesting to listen to the gossip, certainly, but I felt rather like Debbie in Oxford Street, almost invisible. They seemed to know a great deal about every member of the Company and names flew about. The names of senior students, too, for a lot of the girls in our class seemed to be keen on the older boys. Lotti blushed every time a certain Joseph Bartol was mentioned.

If I'd just pushed myself into a group and talked, the way Debbie did, I knew I'd probably be accepted at once, but somehow I couldn't. I had been smitten with an awful kind of tongue-tiedness.

After lunch I could stand being alone in the crowd no longer, so I slipped away from the merry groups in the canteen and the lower corridors. In fine weather, I had heard, most people strolled in Bloomsbury Square, but it was too cold to go out.

So I climbed stairs and more stairs, peeping into classrooms and an occasional studio, though most of the studios were out at the back. Once I came upon a group of little ones, all giggling and silly, and once I looked into a classroom I had thought was empty and found myself facing three big girls, sitting in earnest conversation on the hot pipes. I knew they must be senior students because their blue-lined cloaks lay over a chair. Only the senior students had them.

I fled on, climbing some more stairs that reminded me of the ones that led to our garret, and then I was up in what seemed to be storerooms. The second one

I looked into was full of music, tidily stacked on shelves, and case after case of records, all, as far as I could see, of ballet music. There were also several record players up there and I was just wondering if I dare put on a record and play it softly when someone sneezed.

The sound came from behind one of the music shelves and when I looked round the corner I was startled to discover a boy of about my own age. He looked rather red and self-conscious and I realised quite quickly that I had seen him in the classroom, but not noted him particularly.

'Hullo!' he said awkwardly, and seeing someone so obviously on the defensive helped me a great deal.

'Hullo,' I answered. 'Were you hiding?'

'We-ell, I was exploring, and then I heard you coming and didn't know who it was. Not many places where one can be alone, are there?'

When I heard his voice I knew that he was not a Londoner, but certainly from the North and quite possibly from Manchester. We had a girl from Manchester in our class at the Grammar School.

'Are you new?' I asked. It hadn't occurred to me until then to wonder about new boys.

'I am that.'

'From Manchester?'

His rather nice grey eyes flew open.

'Now that's clever, lass. How did you know?'

I laughed.

'I'm a witch. I come from Birkenhead.'

We eyed each other with growing understanding, and he said slowly:

'You're new, too. I saw you in class. You read a bit of your essay out loud this morning. It was jolly good. And at lunch you weren't talking.'

'I'm homesick and I don't know what to say to them yet. Not like Debbie, my sister. She's just— just thrown herself into it.'

'Is she in the same class?'

'Yes. She sits next to me, at the moment. Not for long, I expect. She's my twin, but we don't look alike.'

'I didn't notice her,' he said, which gave him a high mark, if only he'd known it. He was going on: 'It's pretty grim at first, isn't it? Miles from home. Do you know London well?'

'I hardly know it at all, but I mean to,' I told him. 'We've been to London two or three times. Last time was just for two nights, for the audition. The time before was quite a long time ago, one summer. It was terribly hot and Mother was tired, so we didn't see very much, just went on the river or sat in the parks. Debbie and I were upset because there wasn't any ballet on *at all*. But I do mean to make up for it.'

'I was that thrilled when I won a scholarship, even though my dad was against it. Dad says it's no life for a boy, but I've always been keen on dancing. And I tell him they gave dancers double rations in Russia during the war. They *respect* 'em in Russia. Dad says Britain's good enough for him, but he wouldn't stop me coming. The old man's not bad. Only now I'm here—'

'We'll learn to find our way about,' I said, and then I told him about Aunt Eileen's, including the students and our chilly garret. He in turn told me that he was living with his mother's first cousin up near St Pancras Station. The cousin was married and they kept a greengrocery business.

'Got to earn my keep by doing some delivering on Saturday mornings,' he was just saying when we both jumped about a foot in the air because the bell for lessons sounded far below. At the same moment there were footsteps outside our little storeroom and, horror of horrors, who should appear in the doorway but Madame Lingeraux herself.

She stood there staring at us in a very formidable way. She looked about as broad as she was long in a big fur coat and snow-boots and it was really extremely hard to imagine her as ever being quite a great dancer, though later, when I saw her moving in her quick way, I realized that she had, strangely, kept some of the grace of a dancer.

I'm sure I went pale, and the boy, whose name I still didn't know, certainly did. The bright, rather stern glance swept over us.

'Now who are you? No, don't tell me. I never forget a face. Peter Lumb. That's right, isn't it? The scholarship boy from Manchester. And Doria Darke.'

'Yes, Madame,' I said shakily, remembering the

way she had clasped my hand at that terrible interview. *She* had given me my scholarship . . . she had made it possible for me to come to London. And now I was disgraced, caught where I probably had no right to be, and late for the next lesson to boot. All my bitter uncertainty was back, because somehow my behaviour was all the worse if she had given me that scholarship because of Debbie.

But then I realised with amazement that she was smiling, not looking cross at all.'

'So you came? You and that fair sister of yours? Hum! And what are you doing up here? Looking for somewhere where you could be homesick in peace?'

Well, I'd said I was a witch, but *she* certainly was. It was a relief, anyway, that she understood and hadn't thought we were up to mischief.

'Yes, Madame. I—I—everything feels so strange, and—and I came up here and Peter was here first.'

'So you've made friends? Well, that's a start, isn't it? I suppose your sister's made plenty of friends already?'

A witch indeed, I was surprised by her accurate character reading after only meeting us once, months ago.

'She isn't shy.'

'I could see that. An extrovert type, if ever there was one. It makes life easier. Well, now you're late for afternoon school, so you'd better explain that you were talking to me. No, wait a minute. Find me the case of *Swan Lake* records, will you? You're better able to bend than I am, especially with this coat on.'

We scrabbled round helpfully for a few moments and it was Peter who found it. Then we more or less backed out, not exactly bowing, but feeling that we ought to. My face was burning by then.

'She was *nice*!' I gasped, as we hurried down the stairs.

'I thought she'd blow us sky high,' said Peter. Then, as we reached our classroom door: 'I'll walk home with you after school, if you like.'

'Oh, thank you,' I said, and we made our late entry, which was rather embarrassing as everyone looked up to stare. They stared harder than ever when we explained that we had been talking to Madame Lingeraux. Debbie looked as though she thought I'd be in trouble.

I sank down and took out my new arithmetic book, but it was a little time before I could concentrate. Debbie, an extrovert type. What on earth did it mean? I resolved to look it up in the dictionary just as soon as I had the chance.

During afternoon break, which was only five minutes, Peter came over to talk to me, and after school he was waiting in the hall, wearing his grey Lingeraux overcoat and blue scarf. He was quite a tall boy and reasonably good-looking, with curly brown hair.

Debbie was just behind with Claudia, Lottie and some others, and I waved to her casually as I went off. It was wonderful to have a friend and not to have to tag on to Debbie's companions. London looked quite different as we idled our way along Great Russell Street.

'Ever been into the British Museum?' asked Peter, as we passed that vast building, its lights shining through the snowy gloom.

'Never,' I told him.

'Never mind, lass. We'll go one day,' he said, and we grinned at each other.

It was nice to think that I had two friends with whom I might explore London.

It was certainly much better at the Lingeraux now that I had a friend. Peter and I sat together in the canteen and talked quite hard, and, hearing us, those on either side and opposite began to join in. So I was no longer dumb Dorrie Darke, though I was still often quiet and sometimes, all through that week, I was visited by dreadful homesickness and terrible doubts. I suppose I just had no confidence in myself at all.

But all the strange faces were beginning to grow clearer. I could now recognise the much admired Joseph Bartol when he walked along the hall and I knew the names of other senior students. I knew all the names in my class, too, and had learned to recognise most of the members of staff.

On Friday afternoon after school Peter and I went to look at the other studios and the Company rehearsal rooms a couple of streets away, and, as luck would have it, some of the members of the Company were just coming out. We stood in the snowy street watching them walk away or pile into cars. Cécile Barreux was there, muffled up in scarves and a huge sheepskin jacket, not very glamorous, really, but it was wonderful to see her off the stage, a real live human being. She was with the principal dancer, Michael Mann.

'Some day that might be us,' I said, but it seemed an impossibility.

We walked all the way down Kingsway in the teeth of a bitter wind. The lights were shining out, the red buses sped past, and it was London ... London. We turned into a side street and stood in front of the little Lingeraux Theatre, looking at the posters and the photographs of the dancers. But then I remembered that Aunt Eileen might be cross at my staying out, when it was so cold and already dark, and we walked back at top speed. Some of the new high buildings were a blaze of light by then and I wondered if Clyde thought that London sometimes looked a little like New York. But some of those Manhattan buildings rose seventy or even a hundred storeys; I could scarcely imagine seeing structures so high in the sky.

When I let myself into the house in Gower Street and began to climb up to the garret to leave my things I heard my name called. Clyde had evidently been on the look out for me, because his door was open and he jumped up from his desk and came out on to the landing.

89

'Hi, Dorrie! How'd you like to go to the Royal Opera House tomorrow afternoon?'

I gaped at him.

'Covent Garden? Oh, I'd love to. It's one of the dreams of my life to go there. But—But you'd never get tickets!'

He laughed, showing his good teeth.

'You underestimate Americans! I have them already. Matinées are easier than evening performances and I thought your aunt might kind of object to your being out late. It's *Coppélia*. How's that?'

'It's *wonderful*!' I gasped. 'But perhaps Aunt Eileen—'

'Now don't you worry about your aunt.' He pronounced it 'ant' as we did, though I had noticed that everyone in the South said it differently. 'She says you may go. Let me tell you something, Dorrie. She's not half as bad as she seems.'

'But Debbie—Debbie's dying to go to Covent Garden, too.'

'I asked her and she said she wasn't free. I guess she can go some other time. Is it a date for tomorrow?'

'Oh, yes!' I agreed fervently. It was only four days since I had sat on the stairs and cried and now I had two friends and was going to Covent Garden. It was a kind of cumulative thing, like those old fairy stories. Next week I might have three friends and go to the Lingeraux Theatre. It went a long way to making

90

up for homesickness and cold and not being able to stick up our art reproductions. For Aunt Eileen had said it would spoil the wallpaper.

I stumped up the rest of the stairs, humming the mechanical toys music from *Coppélia* under my breath.

* 8 *

The Arrival of Mel

Debbie was furious about Covent Garden. She stormed and almost cried, until Aunt Eileen, who witnessed the scene, spoke to her very sharply.

'It isn't poor Dorrie's fault. How can you carry on like that, a great girl of thirteen?'

Debbie calmed down a little.

'I *know* it isn't Dorrie's fault. It's all Clyde Smith's. Of course he *did* ask if I was free, but I thought he was just asking me to go exploring with him and Dorrie. Dorrie told me they were going to, one day. And Claudia *had* asked me to tea. But I could have gone another Saturday. I've been living to go to the Opera House.'

'Well,' I said slowly, and it cost me a lot, 'you'd better go instead of me. I don't suppose that Clyde will mind, and—'

But, at that, Aunt Eileen interfered, and I must admit that I was glad she did. I'm not really all that much of a martyr, and I'd been living for it, too.

'No, Dorrie, you are to go and enjoy yourself. It's only polite, anyway, when Clyde got the ticket for you. And Debbie has already accepted Claudia's invitation.'

So that was that, but it made me rather miserable and quite spoilt my keen anticipation. I didn't want any more trouble between Debbie and me.

She sulked for the rest of the evening, scarcely speaking when we went to bed, and the next morning she wasn't a bit keen on helping Aunt Eileen. I wasn't all that keen, either, but there was no escaping it and I suppose it was only fair. But it was rather hard luck when it was such a frosty, brilliant morning, with London waiting to be explored.

First of all she made us clean our own room, saying that the daily woman had enough to do, then she set Debbie to polishing some silver and brass and asked me to tidy and dust the sitting-room. Linda came down at ten o'clock, wearing a scarlet sweater, a black skirt so tight that she could hardly move, and huge ear-rings. She grinned at us and said:

'Gosh! Industrious kids! I suppose there's some coffee left?'

Aunt Eileen glared at her daughter.

'Not a drop. Everything's cleared away. I thought you were stopping there till lunchtime.'

'No, I'm going shopping,' Linda said amiably. 'Well, I suppose you'll be having elevenses soon, or I can go and get something in the nearest coffee bar.'

'Do that,' said Aunt Eileen. 'You're only in the way when there's work to be done.' And Linda laughed, patted her on the shoulder, and ran back upstairs. But she was so gay and casual that somehow one didn't resent the fact that she never helped. I didn't, anyhow, and I suspected that Aunt Eileen didn't mind all that much. It was growing increasingly evident that, in spite of the tone she sometimes took, she was secretly proud of Linda.

Aunt Eileen presently said that she was going to do some household shopping and we could go with her, if we liked, to learn just where to go, when it was our turn. Debbie said she would sooner stop at home, but I was glad to get out. There were no shops very near, but Aunt Eileen said it was cheaper, in any case, to get a bus and go to Soho.

'Of course, a lot of the things are delivered, but I like to look for bargains.'

Oxford Street was crowded with Saturday morning shoppers and pretty horrid, but very soon we were in Berwick Street and that was much nicer. I loved the whole atmosphere and was fascinated by the market stalls, but Aunt Eileen marched me firmly into a small self-service store, then into various other small shops. Clearly she was well known and was treated respectfully. She was the kind of person no one would dare to rob of as much as a halfpenny. In some of the shops she introduced me as her niece and explained that she would sometimes be sending me to buy things. One woman called me 'Ducks' and gave me a chocolate biscuit.

There were a lot of foreigners about, and a good many shops selling foreign food, but we avoided those, for Aunt Eileen said she had no time for 'fancy foreign stuff'. It was all the greatest fun and Aunt Eileen surprised me by buying me an ice cream.

'Seems absurd to me, with snow and frost on the ground, but young people have strong stomachs. Let's hope it doesn't spoil your lunch, though.

I had to have rather a hurried lunch, anyhow, because the ballet started at two. Clyde had very long legs and walked extremely fast, so it didn't take long to reach the Opera House. And, as soon as we drew near, all my vague guilt over Debbie faded away. It was so wonderful and exciting to be approaching Floral Street, breathing the smell of earth and carrots on the icy air. Later I realised that there always a country smell about Covent Garden Market and it was always bound up with ballet in my mind.

Crowds of people were hurrying along the narrow street, in the shadow of the Opera House, and suddenly I realised that we were passing the stage door. The stage door of the Royal Opera House! Often, perhaps, I could come there after a performance and see the great ones.

Then we came to the gallery entrance and I halted, but was surprised to find Clyde's hand on my elbow, steering me onwards round to the front.

'Not this time,' he said, laughing. 'I guess I thought that as it's the first time for both of us we'd do things in style.'

It was just wonderful to be with a handsome, *rich*

American, and I tried to walk with dignity as we entered the building, so warm and luxurious after the cold air outside. We went down a passage and then up some stairs, and suddenly we were in the vast, semi-circular auditorium, with its tiers rising to the high, domed roof and the great red and gold curtain.

Clyde bought two programmes and asked if I would like some candy.

'Oh, no, thank you,' I said, trying not to sound shocked, for of course he meant to be kind. But Debbie and I had long ago decided that it was terrible to eat in a theatre. We always minded when people made loud rustling sounds just at the most important moment of a ballet. But he seemed to understand, for he grinned.

'You could have eaten it during the intermission.'

Our seats were in the stalls circle, in the front row, and it seemed astonishing luxury. I stared all around, scarcely able to believe that I was really *there* at last. Then I settled down to study the programme, finding out who was dancing each rôle. It was not the first time I had seen *Coppélia*; I had once seen it in Liverpool, but it hadn't been a very good production.

Now it was marvellous. I was lost in enchantment even before the curtain rose. I sat there in the warm darkness, as the conductor took his place and the overture began. And then there was the huge brilliantly lighted stage and the village scene. Dr Coppelius's house was on the right and there was the mechanical doll, Coppélia, on the balcony, so realistic that everyone thought her a beautiful girl. A very famous ballerina was dancing Swanilda and I watched every perfect movement intently, for I had never been lucky enough to see her before.

The lively peasant dances . . . Swanilda's quarrel with Franz, because he was attracted to the unknown girl on the balcony . . . the dropping of the key to Dr Coppelius's work-shop . . . I watched it all without missing a single movement. I had forgotten Clyde beside me, everything but the ballet. Though once I smelt a cold, woody fragrance from the stage, that stage that was bigger than any I had ever seen, and I thought fleetingly: 'It's *Covent Garden*!'

In the first interval we went up into the Crush Bar, so beautiful with its chandelier and flowers and mirrors, and I found that Clyde didn't really know much about ballet. I could tell him quite a lot and he listened most respectfully and really seemed interested.

'But you must have seen some ballet in New York,' I said.

'We-ell, a little, I guess. Sometimes I go to dance companies at the State Theatre or City Centre, but I never knew the names for the movements. It's real nice to have a genuine ballet student to explain.'

That was the best thing about Clyde. He never treated me as though I were just a child.

'I'll give you a demonstration one day,' I promised. 'Then you really will know an arabesque and a fouetté.'

97

It was during the third act, while Prayer was dancing her solo, that everything suddenly fused into a huge, overpowering feeling of awareness and happiness. The misery of the past week seemed unimportant then, for it had all led to this. Watching that lovely dancing, I knew more certainly than ever before that somehow I had to be a dancer, a *good* dancer. It even seemed possible that I might turn into a ballerina, if I worked hard. Though one side of me knew, even in those exalted moments, that work alone wouldn't do it. Debbie might have that rare, precious spark, and I might not. I almost prayed that it might be in me, too, somewhere, deeply hidden.

I couldn't say much at first as we came out into the cold, dark streets. I was still remembering the clapping and the flowers, the whole atmosphere of the Opera House, and, above all, the dancing. I came to myself when I realised that we had passed Covent Garden Tube Station and were heading away along Long Acre.

'This isn't the way home.'

'No, I know. I'm taking you to have tea. Your aunt said it would be O.K.,' Clyde told me.

We went to the New Arts Theatre Club. Clyde signed the book and we climbed the stairs.

'I'm a member,' he explained. 'I joined last week.'

We had tea sitting by a window from which I could look down into Great Newport Street and over to the busy point where six streets meet. The lights glittered and everywhere looked very busy and gay.

I poured out and tried to behave in an assured, grown up way. I heard a woman say: 'That's the Lingeraux uniform. The ballet school, you know. Smart, isn't it?' And I knew she meant me.

After that afternoon, though I was still often homesick and rather unhappy, I never really wished we had stayed safely at home in Birkenhead. I had seen a wider and more satisfying world.

During the next week the Lingeraux continued to present problems and I did find life a strain. I had not quite settled down to the methods of work—school work, I mean—and there were times when I still felt shy and out of things. But having Peter for a friend did help.

Debbie seemed to feel no strain at all and it was quite clear to me that she certainly wasn't going to have to take a back seat. She was always with the most important boys and girls in the class, she laughed a lot and seemed to take part effortlessly in their conversations. When she didn't know something, or had to confess that she had never been abroad, she said casually: 'Poor me, I'm from the darkest North and we haven't much money.' And she smiled in her winning way, tossing her pale, shining hair.

I wished I could behave just the way she did, for it obviously worked. It wasn't that I wanted to hide the fact that we were quite poor, but I *was* sometimes burningly conscious that we had missed things, that we came from a dreadfully narrow world. It was obvious, even in the things that were discussed casually and sensibly. Dad and Mother would have been shocked. Yet I could see already that that was a wrong attitude.

Peter felt much the same, I knew. Our backgrounds were similar. The point was that Debbie was totally unself-conscious and she was much quicker than me at adapting herself to the new atmosphere.

Yet, curiously, I was much happier at Aunt Eileen's than she was. I was finding that I *liked* the house in Gower Street, even the garret, though it continued to be cold and rather cheerless. I found the students absolutely fascinating and was surprised that they were so nice to me.

Sara asked me to her room, which was hung with pictures of famous actors and actresses, and the book shelves held many plays. We made coffee on her gas-ring and she told me about R.A.D.A. and her hopes for the future. Of course her fears were something like mine; of not being good enough, of not being able to make a living at the end of her training. She acted bits of plays for me and I sat on a cushion, entranced by Lady Macbeth, Ophelia and Puck. When I was leaving she said I could borrow all the plays I wanted, as long as I was sure to return them.

Rachel was nice to me, too. We got friendly during the second week in rather an odd way. Because I found *her* crying on the stairs—a future scientist and almost grown up, fancy!—and I sat beside her, not quite knowing what to say or do. But I soon found, when we had moved to the privacy of her room, that all I needed to do was listen. Her boy friend had deserted her for a girl who worked in a big store.

'And she hasn't any *brains*, Dorrie. I know that; I met her once. But she's terribly smart and pretty. Anyhow, I suppose men don't like women with brains. Oh, I wish I were dead!' But she did cheer up a little when we had made some coffee on *her* gas-ring and she told me about her home in Birmingham and her brothers and sisters and her dog called Dash.

Gradually I learned bits about the other students. Maribel Brown, who was studying commercial subjects, was mad keen on photography and had taken some lovely London pictures. Winston Marshall told me about his home in Jamaica, and perhaps best of all I liked to hear about the remote Hebridean island, Barra, where James MacDonald lived. It sounded so alien and beautiful and wild and I quite forgot London while he talked in his soft, sing-song voice. I had met him in Bloomsbury Street and we walked along together.

The nicest thing about *all* of them was that they didn't treat me as a child, but as a fellow student who had her way to make. Just being with them, and listening to them, taught me an enormous lot.

Linda was always fun. She often said very droll things and the constant procession of boy friends made each evening interesting. We never knew which one would turn up to take her out and I always hoped that two wouldn't arrive at the same time and perhaps fight it out in our presence. Linda was certainly frivolous, and of course hadn't the brains of the students, but she had what Aunt Eileen once called 'native wit' and was really no fool. She was just determined to enjoy herself.

'All this talk about atom bombs and world troubles makes me sick,' she said once. 'I'm alive now, aren't I? And young and pretty. It's really all that matters. Of course I *hate* to think of starving children, or what might happen after an atomic war, so I *don't* think about them. I can't do anything, anyway. Can you see *me* sitting down in Trafalgar Square, or taking part in one of those protest marches?'

'No, I can't, Miss,' said Aunt Eileen, overhearing the end of this speech. 'Not in those shoes, *or* in your lack of sensible underclothes. You'd get your death if you sat down for five minutes.'

'I mean to stay alive,' retorted her daughter and executed quite a good arabesque. She was wearing jeans that time, not a tight skirt. 'I could even be a ballet dancer if I tried.'

'You stick to earning your living in a sensible way,' said her mother. 'There are enough actresses and dancers in this house.'

I liked Aunt Eileen more and more. She certainly deserved her nicknames of 'Mrs Gloom' and 'Mrs Doom', for if there was a dark side she would certainly look on it, but even that was rather amusing and endearing, especially in contrast to Linda. The students played a game of what they called 'Doomisms', in which they tried to see who could make the most miserable and hopeless remark, but they didn't really mean to be unkind. They were all fond of her.

She was really very good to them, and when Arthur Moorhead was ill after having some teeth out she looked after him like a mother.

The only thing that Aunt Eileen and I had trouble about was Ruari. I just loved that kitten and we hadn't been in the house a week before he was finding his way up to our garret and sleeping on my bed. Sometimes *in* my bed, as the nights were still bitterly cold. Aunt Eileen found out and threatened dire things to me and Ruari if it happened again. But you can't keep a clever, comfort-loving kitten away from a nice warm bed in winter, and in the end she turned a blind eye, after saying:

'Well, if you want to catch some unpleasant disease you're going the right way about it, girl. I heard of someone once who developed terrible skin trouble after letting her cat sleep on her bed.'

A typical 'Doomism', but as though I could catch anything, when Ruari was such a delicious, clean kitten, who washed himself all over about twenty times a day. He was growing and looked perfectly enchanting, with quite a thick bush of a tail that he always carried high, proudly.

Debbie got on with the students all right—they

obviously liked her—but she and Aunt Eileen just
didn't hit it off. Debbie was always fighting her and
trying to get out of things, with the result that Aunt
Eileen probably gave her more tasks than she would
have done otherwise and there was a constant
atmosphere of sulks and argument.

'I wish you didn't suck up to her so,' she said
crossly, one night.

'I don't,' I said, distressed. 'I don't mean to,
Debbie. I like her, and she's really awfully good to us.'

Debbie grunted and burrowed down in bed. Bed-
times were never chatty affairs; never had been since
we came to London, or really long before that.

Sometimes I lay awake feeling dreadfully miserable because Debbie and I were still so far from each
other. I missed the old days still, when we had been
friends and could say things to each other. But I
couldn't think of anything that would help matters,
and in my heart I hadn't really forgiven Debbie for
all the awful things she had said in September.

Debbie was near the top of the class at the end of
the second week at the Lingeraux and her eyes
sparkled with triumph.

'Soon I'll be first, you'll see, Dorrie.'

I was tenth, which I suppose wasn't bad, but all
the same I felt depressed. I had one of my familiar
moods, when I decided that it wasn't worth trying to
compete with Debbie. I'd always played second
fiddle, anyway.

On Saturday afternoon the whole of our class went to the Lingeraux Theatre to see *Checkmate, L'Après-Midi d'un Faune*, and the revival of a ballet choreographed by Madame Lingeraux. Peter and I sat together and we both liked *Checkmate* best. Cécile Barreux was the Black Queen and the Bliss music was very exciting. The Lingeraux was a beautiful little red and gold theatre, very tiny after the Opera House, and I wondered if I should ever dance on that stage.

Suddenly, right in the middle of *L'Après-Midi*, I went cold with horror, as I thought of Debbie being accepted as a member of the Company and me not. It would be ten times worse than that business of the audition. It would be unbearable, for what *else* could I do with my life if I couldn't dance? The old, old problem of the young ballet student, as I knew even then, but it didn't help to think of all the people before me who had had to face and conquer rejection.

Something of that horror remained with me all through Sunday, which was too windy and snowy to go out, and when I got up on the Monday morning I wasn't greatly looking forward to the coming week, But I had forgotten about Mel.

She came into the cloakroom when I had just tied my ballet shoes. She was flushed from the cold, her hair was in a short, tidy pony-tail and she looked shy and hesitant. When she saw me her face broke into a wide smile.

'Oh, thank heaven! Dorrie, isn't it? I hoped and hoped you'd be here to hold my hand. Wasn't it awful getting measles so near the beginning of term? I cried like anything because fate had been so unkind.'

'I missed you,' I told her, realising, with a rush of wild relief, that she was just as nice as I remembered. 'I asked about you on the first day.'

'And what's it like? Have you made hordes of friends? Can you keep up with the dancing and the school work? Is it very terrifying?' She was changing rapidly as she fired off these questions.

I told her what I could as we went up the stairs, and on our way to the studio we met Peter, so I introduced them, hoping that they would like each other. I had already told Peter all I remembered about Mel.

Mel's presence made the most astonishing difference. Debbie had moved to sit with Lotti, so Mel was able to sit next to me and I was told to help her to try and catch up with the work. She was shy at first, though not, of course, with me or Peter, and before three days had passed I knew that she was going to make the most satisfactory of friends. She was so warm-hearted and understanding; funny, too. She was also a Londoner and could tell Peter and me a great deal. She promised to go around with us at week-ends or in the evenings, just as soon as it was light enough.

For a start she asked both of us to go to tea with

her on Saturday, but before that, on the Friday after school, I went with her to the top of one of those high, new buildings. It happened unexpectedly because I had said how much they fascinated me and she explained that she had an aunt who was an office cleaner and who had just got a new job cleaning the top floor of the Dunthorp Building, near Haymarket.

Peter couldn't go, because he had to hurry home to help in the shop, so Mel and I had tea, a sandwich and a bun in a coffee bar (Aunt Eileen had grumbled that she didn't know why I wanted to stay out in that bitter weather, but she supposed it was an opportunity, so long as the lift didn't stick or something worse) and then we walked through the rush-hour crowds.

It was frosty and stars glittered above the lighted streets. The endless traffic whirled around Piccadilly Circus, and I suppose I must have begun to identify myself with Londoners, because I didn't feel in the least alien in those hurrying crowds. I felt as though I belonged, had a right to be there.

The Dunthorp Building, every huge window a blaze of light, towered high above the lesser buildings.

'Twenty-four storeys,' said Mel, craning her neck and then promptly banging into a man with a briefcase and a rolled umbrella. She recoiled, with apologies, and, giggling slightly, I said:

'Clyde Smith laughs at our skyscrapers.'

'Still, we'll get a lovely view, and we can't all be New Yorkers.'

She led the way through the swing doors and we stared up the huge, modern entrance hall—the lobby, Clyde would have called it. It was after half-past five and most of the office workers had gone. Cleaners were already hurrying on their way and Mel's aunt arrived a few minutes after us; a small, dumpy woman, with a good-humoured face and a cheerful Cockney voice.

'There you are, ducks! This your friend? Well, let's get on up. Only, mind you, you'll have to behave or I'll get shot. No poking into things as don't concern you.'

'We always behave,' said Mel demurely. 'We just want to see the view. Dorrie does, particularly. She comes from the North.'

Mrs Forrest clicked her tongue.

'I don't hold with building up to the sky, but there's no doubt these modern places make less work. In there, ducks. Press 24.'

The lift rose smoothly, silently, up and up. It was very exciting, I thought. And then we emerged into a long, gleaming corridor, with offices on either side. Mrs Forrest went off to find her brushes and cleaning materials, but before she went she said:

'I start in No. 1 and work my way along. You can go and look from that window at the end. It's a door really and opens on to a terrace. If you go out there be sure and close it after you. Only don't stay out there long, or you'll freeze your noses off and maybe get me into a row as well.'

We walked away along the corridor towards the glass door. Beyond it lights glittered, the lights of London.

* 9 *

Debbie Determined to be Noticed

We pushed open the door and went out on to the high terrace of the Dunthorp Building, and, the moment we saw the view, I quite forgot the intense cold.

'Oh, Mel! Mel!' I cried.

We were looking east and south and it was wonderful, beautiful. It was all outspread; Trafalgar Square ... the Mall ... Whitehall ... all picked out with lights. We could see the Embankment and the river, with the Shell Building rising, flood-lit, beyond. Then Waterloo Bridge, and far away, St Paul's.

It was a dream city on that frosty winter night and I loved it with all my heart.

'Not bad,' said Mel, with the calm of one who has always known it. 'But then we haven't seen New York or even Paris.'

'We might—if we ever become real dancers,' and then, perhaps because we were all alone, and staring at that view of London, I went on: 'Oh, I could be so happy if only—if only—'

'If only what?' asked Mel, not looking at me. 'I knew there was something. You may as well tell me.'

'And you won't tell a living soul? Not Peter, not anyone?'

''Course I won't. Cross my heart.'

So then I told her the whole story, standing there high on the Dunthorp Building. There was no wind and we were warmly wrapped up; I was glad she didn't suggest going in. Light spilled through the glass door and from a window near by, but we seemed very much alone.

I told her all about Debbie and me and how I had felt for a long time that Debbie was the better looking and far the better dancer, the one who was going to go far. And about what happened at the audition after she had left, the awful time that followed. I told her how mean Debbie had been and how jealous I felt of her, though I had tried and tried to conquer it. And how, at the same time, I hated being far away from her, that it seemed to be going on forever, and might be my fault. She listened in silence, only about half-way through she put out her gloved hand and held mine.

'I never expected to tell anyone,' I ended, rather shakily. 'Is it awful of me to be jealous? *She* can talk to anyone; you've seen what she's like at school. She's always gay, and she's so dazzlingly pretty, and she's going to be top of the class. She's going to be a ballerina, too, she's quite certain, and I-I'm not sure of anything.'

III

'Well,' said Mel forthrightly, 'one thing she *can't* be sure of is being a ballerina. We all know it will only be one in several hundred, or even one in several thousand. Just now she's only in a class of ordinary thirteen-year-olds, and—Does Miss Verney praise her dancing much?'

'No, that's a funny thing,' I said slowly. 'She doesn't seem to have said a word. But she doesn't criticize her much, either.' I paused, then added: 'She told *me* I'd been well taught and hadn't much to unlearn.'

Mel frowned.

'I'm not really the one to tell. P'rhaps I'm not old enough to give you good advice. But I think you're being a bit silly.' I jumped and she clutched my hand again. 'No, don't get shirty. I'll tell you what I mean. *I* don't think she's better looking than you, for a start.'

'But she *must* be. She's so striking, with all that silvery gold hair and her interesting pale face.'

'She's pretty, but so are you. You have lovely colouring, too. It was the first thing I noticed about you. Your hair is bright and your eyes are lovely, and you've got those rosy cheeks. And your face is a lot more thoughtful than hers; it has far more character.'

'Goodness!' I said, feeling very shy; embarrassed, really, but very comforted. No one had ever talked about my looks before.

'And then *is* she cleverer than you? Can't *you* be top of the class?'

'I was at school in Birkenhead, once or twice. I beat her because I *meant* to work. Only here she seems to have got into the new methods quicker and I thought perhaps it wasn't worth bothering.'

'Well, it jolly well is. I s'pose rivalry is awful, but my old dancing teacher says there's bound to be extra special rivalry in ballet schools. She hates it, but says it's quite inevitable. If I were you I'd work as hard as you can, and if you're top sometimes and Debbie's top others she can't really mind. If she does she not a nice person.'

'She's nice really,' I said defensively. 'It's only sometimes that she—that she—'

'Well, I'd get it out of your head that she's better at things than you. She may not even be a better dancer. Did anyone ever tell you so? Say so?'

'Only Debbie herself,' I confessed, feeling startled. 'But she did get higher marks in the exams, and I used to have a little trouble with my feet. It seems to be over now—'

'I bet all dancers have trouble with their feet some time in their lives. That's nothing, especially if it's gone.'

'But, Mel, you're forgetting the scholarship. *She* was given one and I—'

'Well, there *was* only one place. They had to give it to one of you. How do you know they didn't have a fierce argument as to which of you should have it?

It may not have been a foregone conclusion. Daft, you are. How could you tell? They offered you a place and then gave you the first chance of a scholarship.'

'But—perhaps because they wanted Debbie. That's the thing that—'

Mel snorted.

'You *are* daft, if you can believe that. What would be the good of them taking you if you were going to be a dead loss? Debbie wouldn't have balanced out, seems to me.'

'Oh, Mel, you *do* talk sense. I've been an idiot. I *will* work and try and believe in myself. Debbie has so much confidence.'

'Over-confidence, maybe,' Mel said sagely. 'She's very full of herself and no one seems to mind, I suppose because, as you say, she's always friendly and gay. Look here! We'll *both* work like anything. We always do at dancing and we'll go all out at lessons, too. We'll show 'em. Debbie isn't the only future ballerina. We've all got equal chances—'

'Not really. Don't you think that some people have the—the spark?'

Mel looked sober, tossing her pony-tail; when she moved the lights behind us shone on her thoughtful profile. I knew that she, too, sometimes felt doubts of the future.

'Perhaps they have, but we don't *know*. So we'll try and believe it might be us.'

'Yes,' I agreed fervently. Then: 'You've helped an

114

awful lot, Mel. But there's still the fact that Debbie
and I don't seem to have any—any point of contact
now.'

'Well, it's her fault, whether she knows it or
not.'

'She *was* pretty horrid, and she isn't being very
nice now. But I miss her very much, in a queer kind
of way.'

'I should wait. Maybe she'll come round. Maybe
something will happen. I quarrel with my sister
sometimes. Once we didn't speak for a month.'

'But we never actually quarrelled, so it's harder to
make it up. It's so—so subtle—'

The door behind us opened and Mrs Forrest's
voice cried:

'Well, blimey! You kids still out here? Bin here
twenty minutes. You'll catch your deaths and get me
into trouble as well. Don't you want to come and see
another view?'

We spun round and followed her into the light and
warmth and the subject of Debbie and me wasn't
mentioned again. But I felt ten times better and full
of resolution. Mel was right, I had been silly to suffer
so much. I was never going to let myself feel jealous
or lacking in confidence again.

I was very grateful to Mel, for I was sure she really
had talked sense. She seemed to me rather an unusual
person and there was no doubt that she was clever.
She was soon very near the top of the class.

When she was eleven she had passed to quite a

famous London day school and she had been there for two years before coming to the Lingeraux.

'We don't know where she gets her brains,' her mother said once, giving Mel a proud glance. 'We're ordinary folk, as you can see.'

They were, too, though very nice. I soon felt as though the overcrowded terrace house in Campden Town was a second home. Mel had an older sister, Cherry, and three brothers, and about the only thing that wasn't ordinary was their names. Cherry was Cherry Hinton Forrest, and the boys were Milton, Barton and Drayton, but always called Mill, Bartie and Dray. They were places near Cambridge, for Mrs Forrest had been born in the little village of Meldreth and had met her husband when she went to live and work in Portsmouth.

'Don't know what I should have done if I'd had another girl,' she said, laughing.

'You'd have called the poor child Cambridge, Mum,' said Mel.

Mr Forrest was usually away, but he was home for a few days early in February and Peter and I met him then. He was quite a good-looking man, with a nice smile, and he entertained us with stories of his experiences at sea.

Anyway, after that long talk with Mel I did begin to find things much easier at the Lingeraux. I continued to enjoy every moment of the ballet classes, and I liked the 'character' classes as well. At school lessons I worked harder than ever before and at the end of the second week in February I was second, with Mel top. Debbie was fourth and seemed surprised, but not really annoyed. She grinned and shrugged.

'I could work better if we didn't have to do our homework in that awful sitting-room.'

It wasn't really easy to work there, especially when Linda had the television on, but it was still far too cold for us to work upstairs. In fact it was bitter, with snowstorms every few days and a lot of frost. But the afternoons were growing much lighter, and sometimes Mel, Peter and I could snatch an hour to go exploring after school.

We had quite a varied life at the Lingeraux, for we were taken to concerts at the Royal Festival Hall, to the National Gallery and the Wallace Collection, and there were quite often lectures on a variety of subjects; the art of make-up, stage design, the history of dance and so on.

The man who gave the history of dance lecture was very famous indeed as a ballet critic and writer on the theatre and I had known his name for years. The whole school crowded into the hall and somehow I found Debbie next to me. She looked around and said:

'Such a lot of us! Do you know, sometimes I *hate* being one of a crowd. It makes me feel invisible.'

She had made quite a few remarks of that nature lately and I understand her well enough to know exactly how she was feeling. *I* was rather glad, just then, to be safely anonymous, but Debbie liked to stand out.

'You're far from invisible,' I said, thinking how pretty she looked. It really wasn't any good Mel telling me I was as nice-looking as Debbie. I thought it far more romantic to have fair hair and not much colour. She wasn't in the least insipid, because her eyes were so bright and her lips so red.

'I *mean* to be noticed,' said Debbie, in quite a low voice, so that her next door neighbour couldn't hear. 'My hopes are pinned on the Spring Show. They'll be starting to plan for it in March, Claudia says. It's held in the Lingeraux Theatre on the day we break up for Easter and there are always at least three ballets. One for the little ones, one for the middles and one for the boys and girls in Classes Five and Six. The senior students don't have anything to do with it. They have their own matinée before Christmas, when they do something grand like the whole of *Swan Lake*, with a few to help out from the Company.'

'But we haven't a hope of getting a part, even a small one,' I said, rather startled. I had already heard about the Spring Show, of course; *everyone* hoped for a chance to dance. It was the great event of the term, or even the year.

'Well, Claudia says they often give new students a chance. It's rather a policy of the School. And I simply don't see why *I* shouldn't get a part. I always danced the main rôle at the Grayland Show.'

Well, the Grayland wasn't the Lingeraux, as Debbie must really know very well, but her words gave me a sudden, springing hope. How *wonderful* if I could get a part, too, even if only a tiny one. Aunt Eileen and Linda could come and watch, and maybe Clyde. And to dance on the Lingeraux stage would be the most exciting thing that had ever happened.

Then I forgot all about Debbie beside me, and even, for the time being, the Spring Show, because the lecturer appeared on the platform and was introduced by Miss Sherwood. He was a very handsome man, tall and commanding, with a ringing voice. And of course I found every word that he said interesting. I knew quite a lot of it from my wide reading of ballet books and magazines, but some things were absolutely new to me.

Debbie was still near me when, after the lecture, we all streamed out into the entrance hall, and the great man was standing there talking to Miss Sherwood. We had been kept behind for a few minutes because the principal ballet mistress had something to say to us, and then we had to move our chairs to the side.

Debbie said in my ear:

'One way to get some notice would be to fall in a dead faint at his feet!'

'Oh, you wouldn't!' I gasped, not at all sure that she was joking.

'Well, I bet I could do it convincingly. And he'd

say: "Who is this beautiful young girl? So fair, so pale!" And maybe he'd write a piece about me for *Ballet Monthly.*'

'And maybe he'd say: "This one obviously isn't strong enough to be a dancer. Why on earth did you accept her?" ' I retorted tartly, and then saw that she was grinning mischievously. She went off with Claudia.

A few days later our class was taken to the Tate Gallery one afternoon. It was a dark, bitterly cold day and the wind swept icily off the river as we climbed out of the special bus on Millbank. The Tate loomed above us, very impressive, and I was thrilled, because I hadn't yet had a chance to go there and see the collection of French Impressionist and Post Impressionist paintings.

It was very exciting to go up the steps and into the entrance hall, which was very warm and bright. Beyond stretched the huge main hall, with modern sculptures here and there.

Miss Jacks, the art mistress, waited until we had left our coats in the cloakroom and then gave us a brief lecture on behaving well.

'Because' she said, 'a special exhibition is opening this afternoon in one of the rooms. Some important people will be there and I don't want the School disgraced if they chance to see any of us.' And she looked rather fixedly at the Russian boy, Serge, who was a bit of a clown. Surprising, I had thought it at first; I always believed Russians to be rather solemn and tragic.

She then led us from room to room, spending much too long on the Turners and Pre-Raphaelites, I thought. I was dying to get to the French rooms, and I particularly wanted to see the Utrillos. I knew they had his *Place du Tertre*, one of my favourite pictures.

We did get there in the end and I was very happy, not really listening to Miss Jacks, but taking my own pleasure in the paintings. Then she said that we were free to go and look again at any pictures we had liked particularly, and to meet by the main door in twenty minutes.

I stayed behind to look again at the four Utrillos and Debbie was there, too, for a time. Then gradually everyone wandered away. I followed them slowly, last of all to mount the stairs from the lower rooms, and the bigger rooms seemed very empty. Of course it was winter and a horrid day, so perhaps people hadn't been in the mood for making the journey to Millbank.

Eventually I wandered out into the long, tremendously high main hall. A little way away a smartly dressed party was emerging from the special exhibition and heading towards the exit. One man with a camera over his shoulder turned the other way and stood looking thoughtfully at a very peculiar piece of statuary.

I stood in the shadow of a pillar, thinking how

wonderful it was to have places like the Tate almost on our very doorstep, and how especially nice it was to see it almost empty, with no jostling crowd.

Then suddenly I saw Debbie near the far end of the hall. She was by herself; in fact there was no one else in sight from where I stood, except for the man with the camera, who had wandered in Debbie's direction, and a very bored-looking attendant who was standing just within a doorway on my left.

Debbie was walking slowly, almost on tip-toe, with her hands clapsed behind her back, sometimes stopping to look at a piece of sculpture. I wondered why she had left her friends, but then Debbie really did like art and was far more knowledgeable than I was about sculpture. She had several pictures of famous sculptures in her postcard collection.

Debbie glanced vaguely up the hall, then unclasped her hands. She was almost dancing now . . . she *was* dancing. She suddenly did a series of pirouettes round the plinth on which the statue stood. She was wearing her Lingeraux suit and outdoor shoes, but somehow that didn't seem to matter. Her hair caught the light as she spun round. It seemed rather an odd thing to do, to turn pirouettes in the great hall of the Tate Gallery, yet I thought I knew how she felt. Such a lovely empty floor; so much space.

Then my heart leaped, for of course Debbie *shouldn't* dance in an art gallery. It might be against the law or something. My heart leaped even more when I saw the man stop looking vague and whip out his camera. He took a picture of the last pirouette and then walked quickly towards Debbie, who had her hands behind her back again, and was staring fixedly at a big block of stone.

'Debbie, you idiot!' I said to myself, starting towards her. But I was quite a long way away and the man had reached her. They were talking . . . he had taken out a notebook and Debbie was smiling up at him, telling him something that he apparently wrote down.

Then he put the notebook away, said: 'Well, good-bye, kiddie. Thanks!' and strode away towards the exit, passing me without taking any notice of me. I rushed to Debbie's side.

'Did he take your picture? Oh, Debbie!'

Debbie grinned at my dismayed tone.

'Why so shocked?'

'But—But perhaps you shouldn't dance here and —and what's he going to do with the photograph?'

'Put it in his paper, I hope,' said Debbie cheerfully, and just then Lotti and Claudia bore down on us.

'Come on, you two! Miss Jacks is waiting.'

I thought that that might be the end of it, so I didn't mention the odd little affair to anyone. But the next day when I got home from school Debbie was already there, with her nose in a London newspaper, and Aunt Eileen was crying:

'Well, I never! Just fancy that young man happening to see you dance! I must say it's a good picture. I asked Mrs Tonkings to buy a few more copies. You'll want to send one to your mother and dad.'

The picture really was awfully good. He had caught Debbie just as she whirled into sight round the statue. Underneath was printed: 'Young Dancer in the Tate Gallery. Miss Deborah Darke of the Lingeraux Ballet School dances a series of pirouettes in a most unusual place. Miss Darke is thirteen and came to London in September.'

Debbie was in bubbling spirits all evening.

'Well, at any rate I've come out of the crowd at last!' she said triumphantly.

When we arrived at school the next morning she was immediately besieged by her friends, most of whom had seen the picture.

'But when did you dance, Debbie? None of *us* saw you.'

They obviously thought she had done a very clever thing in getting her picture in the paper, but the school authorities took quite a different view. Debbie was sent for after the ballet class and remained in Miss Sherwood's room for some time. She looked rather subdued when she finally appeared in the classroom, but we couldn't question her until break. Then she said crossly:

'What a stuffy lot they are! I gave the school some nice publicity, I thought, but they aren't a bit grateful. In fact they're mad with me. Miss Jacks was there, too, and she seemed really annoyed. I wasn't doing any *harm*.'

'They are rather stuffy,' Claudia agreed. 'They won't let us accept any kind of professional engagement while we're here. It's not like a stage school, where kids get licences when they're twelve and go into pantomime and so on. All our parents had to sign that they agreed to the conditions.'

'I didn't know that,' said Debbie. 'But I don't suppose it matters.'

The affair didn't die down then because Debbie, amazingly, had several offers on the strength of that photograph. A film company offered her a test, a famous theatrical agent wanted to put her on his books, and a well-known management wanted her to audition for a West End play, in which they needed a young, fair girl.

All the offers had to be refused and Debbie was both thrilled and disgruntled. Then finally resigned.

'What I really want,' she said, as we went to bed one night, 'is to be a ballerina, so I suppose I've got to stick to the Lingeraux and work hard for years and years. But gosh! I should have *loved* to try for films. And the play would have been fun, too.'

'And never be a dancer?' I said.

She frowned.

'I know. The Lingeraux would have turned me out. They made that quite clear.'

'How very, very strange it is that all this happened

just because you felt like dancing in the Tate. Such a coincidence that that photographer was there.'

Debbie stared at me. She was just ready to leap into bed. Her striped pyjamas were washed out and rather too small for her.

'Oh, Dorrie, you idiot!'

'Why?' I asked, puzzled.

'Well, dumb Dorrie Darke. I *knew* he was there, of course. I saw him much earlier, going into that special opening, and I spied him just as soon as he walked back into the hall. I *told* you I wasn't going to stay invisible.'

'Well,' I said to myself, 'I *am* dumb Dorrie Darke and no mistake.' Because I had never guessed.

* 10 *

The Spring Dance

On the whole the weeks of term passed very quickly and it seemed as though we had always been in London. Home seemed far away, and there were certainly still times when I missed it fiercely, but Easter would come and, meanwhile, life was terribly busy.

The evenings were much lighter, but there were not many signs of spring. Mel, Peter and I searched for buds in the parks, but there was nothing but a few spears of crocus, pushing up in the still frozen ground.

One Saturday the three of us went to Hampton Court, which I just loved, as the Tudor period had always interested me particularly and we were doing it in class just then, too. Another time we went to Epping Forest, but it was bitterly cold and bleak and we came home early.

'If only it were summer and we could lie in the sun!' I said wistfully. I did long for heat and blue skies.

At the Lingeraux, when March came, most of the

talk was about the coming Spring Show. Madame Lingeraux called the whole school together one afternoon (apart from the senior students) and told us about the different ballets. The junior one was to be a flower ballet, *The Magic Garden*, ours was to be one that had apparently been danced a couple of years before, *The Princess in the Secret Wood*, and the one for the older pupils *Moon in a Net*.

I listened breathlessly to the story of *The Princess*. It was about a Princess and her young lady-in-waiting, Amanda, who decided to go adventuring in the secret wood and all the things that happened to them there. The main part was, of course, the Princess, and Amanda had quite a lot of dancing, too. Then there were the Spirits of the Wood, the Green Witch, the Trees and quite a number of village children. The leader of the village children was called Betty and she had a very short solo dance.

'You see that there are a good many parts,' Madame Lingeraux said, smiling down at us from the stage. 'But even so only about one-third of the pupils will be able to dance. This, as I say every year, is quite inevitable, and I do ask you not to be too downcast if you aren't chosen. It need not be any reflection on your dancing. The lists will go up about the middle of the month, and from then onwards there will be intensive rehearsals, but we always try not to take too much time from your school lessons.'

Madame Lingeraux could talk until she was black

in the face, but of course every single boy and girl hoped for a part. One could see it in the bemused faces as we all dispersed.

'I do wish that Dad and Mother could come south to see me dance,' Debbie said that evening, looking up from her homework.

'To see *you* dance?' Aunt Eileen asked. 'I thought you didn't know yet who's going to get the parts.'

'Well, we don't. But somehow I feel it in my bones that I'll be chosen. I can't *imagine* not being chosen.'

'And what about Dorrie? What makes you think she won't be chosen, too?'

'Well, of course she may be. I didn't say she wouldn't. Only Dorrie has no push. She doesn't make people notice her.'

'She'll get along all right without that,' Aunt Eileen said tartly. 'It will just serve you right, Miss, if you get passed over.'

'I'll never be passed over,' said Debbie, with such calm certainty that, in a curious way, it wasn't really offensive. Oh, how I envied her that wonderful self-confidence!

Would I get a part? Oh, even a tree or the humblest village child would be enough, because it would mean being made-up in a real dressing-room and dancing on the Lingeraux stage. Debbie was quite right; I didn't push myself, but I seemed to have done well during the past few weeks. I had worked just as hard as I could, to the limit of my ability, and I was never very far from the top of the class at lessons. I felt all right in the ballet classes, too. My body seemed to obey me effortlessly and I was always happy. The constant repetition of those familiar exercises was no drudgery to me.

Just a little part ... just any part. But in my imagination it didn't stop there. I began to day-dream about being chosen to dance the Princess, or at least Amanda, the young lady-in-waiting. Debbie would probably be the Princess, for she certainly looked the part. Well, Amanda would be lovely; Amanda in the secret wood, a wood that would, of course, only be painted scenery. Beyond the foot-lights would be the Lingeraux orchestra and then the blurred faces of the enraptured audience.

I could see us taking many calls at the end; the Princess, Amanda, and the handsome village youth, William, who rescued us from the clutches of the Green Witch. We would be given flowers, perhaps, and Dad and Mother would be there and would come behind afterwards to shower us with congratulations. I could actually hear Dad's voice saying:

'I'm proud of my ballet twins.'

Not that he would quite say that, of course. He had never called us his 'ballet twins'. It was the local newspaper that had used the term.

It didn't stop with day-dreaming. One night I dreamed that I was dancing the Princess on a stage far bigger than the Lingeraux one. It was a huge stage ... Covent Garden, of course. And I wasn't, I suddenly realised, the Princess in that unimportant little children's ballet. I was Aurora in *The Sleeping Beauty*, and I was dancing the *Rose Adagio*. Each of the four Princes came to me in turn, as I balanced delicately *en pointe* . . . the music rose to that wonderful crescendo at the end. The applause rang out . . . the cheering . . . the wild thunder of clapping.

Then, of course, I awoke and it wasn't clapping, but the sound of Linda thumping on our door.

'Seven o'clock, kids! Rise and shine!'

But somehow the dream stayed with me and made me strangely, unexpectedly happy. I was, secretly, filled with almost as much confidence as Debbie, sure that I couldn't be passed over. Not the Princess, of course, maybe not even Amanda, but Madame had said that the Trees had a delightful little dance. I would settle joyfully for being a tree.

To add to my sudden flood of happiness and certainty of success, spring suddenly decided to show itself a little. There came a day, the thirteenth of March, when the sun was almost warm, and when we walked in Bloomsbury Square after lunch, the crocuses were making vivid pools of purple and gold in the beds. Even in London it seemed that one could smell spring in the air and it was intoxicating to feel the warm touch of the sun on my face.

We all went indoors somewhat reluctantly for afternoon school, and when I entered the class room Miss Lines asked me if I would take a message to Miss Verney, whom she thought was in the Green Studio with some of the senior students.

The Green Studio was one apart, reached by way of the big hall, and I went cheerfully, glad to have that much respite from lessons. The hall was quite empty and filled with sunlight, and suddenly I couldn't resist that lovely bare stretch of floor, for all the chairs were piled up at the sides.

I began to dance, and in an odd way I was suddenly possessed, inspired, as I had never been before. The memory of the sunlight and the crocuses and that nameless feeling of spring in the square all fused into movement. I think I had never been so happy in my life as I leaped and whirled, interpreting my feelings in conventional ballet movements and many that were not.

'The Spring Dance!' I thought. 'I'm a choreographer.' But mostly I didn't think at all, just let myself go to the faint music that was coming from the Green Studio. It was, I dimly realised, the rather wild, strange music that a modern composer had created for one of Madame Lingeraux's ballets.

It was glorious while it lasted, but suddenly the mood was gone and I remembered the message and the fact that someone might come in at any moment. I tried to tidy my hair with my hand, and, a little breathless, opened the studio door. Miss Verney didn't notice me at once, so I was able to watch the six senior students for a few moments. It must be wonderful to be a senior student, I thought; it meant that admission to the Company was almost certain, and, even while still in the School, they had walk-on parts or even filled in if the *corps de ballet* needed a few extra members.

When I returned to the hall Madame Lingeraux herself was standing in the middle of the floor, apparently lost in thought. Though she had been nice to me the very few times I had had contact with her I was still, in company with most people, very much in awe of her. I tried to get past her with only a mumbled 'Good afternoon, Madame!', but she fixed me with her bright, almost black eyes and said:

'And how are *you* these days? Settled down, have you?'

'I—I think so, thank you, Madame.'

'You've a good colour, not like some of these pasty London children.'

I could feel my face immediately flaming, so that my colour was greatly improved.

'I—I often wish I were pale and interesting.'

She cackled at that, rather alarmingly. She often looked and sounded a bit like a witch, a plump witch.

'You wouldn't like it if you were anaemic. It can be a perfect nuisance and not at all interesting. Well, get along, child. Oughtn't you to be working? I suppose you're as idle as the rest of them.'

'Idle!' I said to myself, as I dashed away. 'None of us get the chance to be idle in this school.'

I hoped very much that she didn't really believe I was lazy. I wondered if she ever saw the class lists, or was that only Miss Sherwood's business? Yet

133

people said that Madame had a finger on every aspect of the School and I was fully prepared to believe it.

Excitement mounted and mounted, as the days passed. The lists for the Spring Show might go up any day, any hour. Even people like Claudia or Serge, who had been at the Lingeraux for quite a long time, were restless and unsettled, and everyone made excuses to walk past the big notice-board in the entrance hall. But the fourteenth of March passed and nothing had happened.

'It will be today,' said Lotti, the next morning. 'I know it will be today.'

And my spine tingled with excitement and dread. Oh, just a tree, if I couldn't be Amanda! I must, must, must get something. I didn't know how I would live if I were left out.

Lunch was delayed that day owing to some mishap in the kitchen and by the time we were drinking our milky coffee it was almost time for the bell to ring for afternoon school. Suddenly a very small junior dashed into the canteen.

'I say, everyone! The lists are up! The lists are up!' she cried.

Peter knocked over his cup, but fortunately there wasn't much in it. Debbie, Lottie and Claudia had already gone and the others were following quickly. Mel said:

'Are you coming. Dorrie?'

'In a minute,' I said, trying to make my voice

sound calm. 'You and Peter go on. I'll—just finish this.'

Mel and Peter gave me understanding looks and went away, and I finished my coffee—pretty nasty it was, at the best of times—and rose slowly. I *couldn't* hurry. Suddenly I knew that I couldn't see those lists in the company of all the others. Not even, really, with Mel and Peter.

So I went along to the cloakroom and washed my hands and combed my hair. The looking-glass was spotted with damp and it was a constant joke that it made one look terrible. I certainly looked most unusually pale and I felt sick. But it was mostly excitement. I was fairly sure that it would be all right, that I would have got something.

Finally, still very slowly, I went up the stairs. The bell had gone a few moments before and by the time I neared the top of the stairs the hall was almost empty. Mel and Peter were just being ordered up the stairs by one of the big girls.

I ducked back until everyone had gone. My friends had obviously wanted to wait. They must know I hadn't seen the lists yet. And if I didn't hurry I'd be in trouble over being late for class.

I took a deep breath and walked across the hall towards the notice-board.

Dorrie Alone

It was always rather dark in the hall, even when the sun was shining, and at first I couldn't clearly see the various lists and notices that hung on the board. Then I found them on the right-hand side. There was a special strip heading, saying 'Spring Show', and then three separate lists.

I ignored *The Magic Garden* and *Moon in a Net*, for they couldn't possibly concern me. The only ballet that mattered was *The Princess in the Secret Wood*. My hands felt damp and I could hear my heart thudding.

The Princess in the Secret Wood! Claudia was the Princess, a girl called Caroline Best from the class below was Amanda ... Serge was William, the village youth ... Lotti the Green Witch. Debbie was Betty, the leader of the village children.

My heart was thudding louder than ever and I could hardly breathe. I blinked to try and clear my sight. I looked down the rest of the list, right to the bottom of the Trees, but my name was not there.

At first I couldn't believe it. My happiness and certainty must have gone quite deep, because it was the most appalling shock. I had worked so hard, hoped so much, and I had got nothing. I wasn't even the humblest tree or village child.

I didn't know what to do or where to go to be alone. I *couldn't* go upstairs as though nothing had happened and face their possible pity and commiseration. Debbie would be so thrilled at being chosen to be Betty, for she would have that little solo dance. It wasn't the Princess, but it was quite a lot, all the same, for a new girl. Mel and Peter, I had dimly noticed, were both trees.

No, I couldn't face it. I couldn't bear it. I had to get away. It wasn't even any good hiding in the cloakroom, because I would probably be discovered.

I don't really think my mind was working at all clearly. I only had that overpowering urge to get away, to be alone to face my desperate diappointment.

I bolted down to the cloakroom, and, with fumbling, ice-cold fingers (though it was warm down there), I put on my coat, beret and scarf, changed my shoes. Then, taking my case, I went upstairs again, not even trying to be cautious, but there was still no one at all about in the hall. It was silent and offered escape. The front door was not far away.

I pulled it open and heard it shut with a snap behind me. I almost fell down the steps.

The springlike weather had lasted. It was sunny and almost warm out of doors, but I scarcely noticed. I turned north and soon came to Russell

Square, then Woburn Square . . . Gordon Square. It helped me just to keep moving, but I nearly got run over on more than one occasion.

I hopped out of the way of a swooping taxi in Gordon Square and the driver leaned out to swear at me. But I crossed Euston Road safely. I never thought at all about what I was doing . . . that I had simply walked out of the Lingeraux and might get into trouble. I only wanted to get away, preferably out of London. I had a desperate, only half-formed need for open spaces.

I plunged down into the Tube at Euston and, almost at random, took a ticket for Highgate. Mel, Peter and I had been there one Saturday afternoon and walked to Ken Wood House. It was lucky that I had some money with me; Dad had sent us both postal orders for five shillings only the day before and I still had most of it left.

The train roared and rattled northwards and still I didn't think. Once or twice tears welled up in my eyes and I blinked them back fiercely, because I couldn't cry in public. I thought if I once started I should never stop. I must have looked a little strange, for a fat, motherly woman suddenly leaned forward and asked:

'Are you all right, dear?'

I nodded and said, 'Yes, thank you.' I didn't want her sympathy, *any* sympathy. I was much relieved when she left the train at Archway.

It was better in Highgate. I walked very fast along

quiet, sometimes tree-arched streets. There were big, peaceful houses and the sound of bird-song. The smell of earth and the soft blaze of crocuses reminded me forcibly of my joy on that day when I had danced. Only two days ago! I couldn't bear to think about it and I walked even faster. I couldn't cry in Highgate, either, for there were a few people about.

Presently I reached Ken Wood House, but I didn't go into the building. I cut away across the gardens and into the woods. It was very quiet there and I met almost no one. The paths were a little muddy, but I found a dry and secret corner and flung myself down on some old leaves. And then I *did* cry, for a long, long time.

I am almost ashamed to have to explain all this, but it is part of the story and has to be told. I cried and sobbed and shook, burrowing down into the leaves. Madame Lingeraux, as I remembered even in the midst of my shame and disappointment, had expressly said that we weren't to mind if we weren't chosen. She had said that only about a third of the pupils in the school could hope to be in the ballets. I was not the only one to be left out.

But other people didn't have a sister called Debbie, or know how awful it was to be the one who always came second. *Debbie* would dance on the Lingeraux stage; Aunt Eileen, Linda and maybe Clyde would go to watch her, and I would only be in the audience, playing second fiddle as always.

It wouldn't have mattered nearly as much if I

hadn't worked so hard, and if I hadn't felt so much unusual hope and confidence.

I cried until I was exhausted and then I realized that the leaves were damp, after all. I'd probably get rheumatism if I stayed there. So I mopped myself up as best I could, horrified by the look of my face in the little mirror in the lid of my case. I brushed my coat, straightened my stockings and set off again.

I wandered for a long time, somewhere on Hampstead Heath. There was still almost no one about and gradually the sunny silence, the suggestion of green buds in hollows, soothed and comforted me. At last I began to think more coherently, and it was then that shame really started. For of course I had definitely done something awful when I ran away from school like a baby. I was sure to be missed and everyone would know why I had gone.

It had been a cowardly, stupid thing to do and I would never live it down. I should probably go down in the annals of the Lingeraux School as the girl who ran away because she didn't get a part in the Spring Show.

Debbie would laugh at me, perhaps, and Aunt Eileen would be angry. Or she might very well be worried as well. Perhaps, when I was discovered to be missing, they would telephone her. She and everyone would soon know that Doria Drake was a spineless girl, with not enough character to face up to a disappointing situation. I suddenly heard Mel's voice saying, 'Your face has far more character.'

Well, she had been wrong. Spineless, soggy, feeble Dorrie Darke.

I sat down again under a gorse bush and tried to think, that time really constructively.

It had happened; I hadn't been chosen and I had run away. Nothing could wipe out either of those facts. So somehow I had to set my chin and face the thing. I had to go back to the Lingeraux . . . But not that day. A glance at my watch, the first time I had looked at it, told me that it was already nearly four o'clock. And I was somewhere in the heart of Hampstead Heath, not even on a main path. I hadn't the remotest idea where I was, in fact. Earlier I had been able to hear distant traffic, but now all I could hear was an aeroplane somewhere far overhead.

Aunt Eileen would be horrified if she could see me. She was always rather nervous about us and often prophesied dire things. 'Doomisms', naturally, but she would have thought it most dangerous for me to be in the middle of the Heath alone. Not that there seemed to be any danger. There wasn't a soul anywhere. It might have been the heart of the real country.

All right, so I had missed the whole afternoon at school. I was certainly in trouble, but I would have to face it. And of course it wasn't the end of the world because I wasn't in the ballet. There would be other Spring Shows, and I had no choice but to go on working and hoping. Not unless I wanted to give up all idea of being a dancer, and that was unthinkable.

I suddenly saw my behaviour as absolutely silly as well as shameful. The fact that I had acted on the spur of the moment, entirely without conscious thought, was no excuse at all. In an obscure way it made it worse.

I got up again and began to walk rapidly out of the hollow where I had been sitting. The path was narrow and uneven and I was walking very fast. Suddenly I tripped over a stone and wrenched my ankle so painfully that for a moment everything went black.

I sank down again and waited for the agony to pass, which eventually it did, but walking was painful and difficult. I heard children's voices in the distance and even thought of calling for help. But what could they do? They couldn't carry me to the nearest bus stop or Tube station.

I could hear traffic now and suddenly, to my great relief, I emerged on to a broad path. There were quite a lot of people in sight and, when I struggled up the rise, I could see buildings to the left and a red London bus passing along a road quite near. It really was a tremendous relief, as it was by then after five o'clock and all I really wanted was to get to a telephone.

On the road I asked a passing woman if I was near a Tube station and she told me that Hampstead Station wasn't far away.

But first a telephone. . . . When I found a booth I had to wait for five awful minutes while a woman chatted to a friend. I could hear snatches of her conversation when there wasn't too much traffic and it seemed dreadfully trivial.

I must have looked desperate, for eventually she opened the door and asked:

'You want to come in, ducks?'

'Please! It's terribly urgent,' I said. So then she talked for another minute or two and hung up.

I already had the money in my hand and I wasted no time. Aunt Eileen's voice spoke almost at once and I gasped with relief.

'Hullo! Who is it? Dorrie? Is it you, dear? Speak up; I can't hear you!'

'I—I—I—Aunt Eileen, I'm at Hampstead.'

'At *Hampstead*? What on earth are you doing there? I've been frantic with worry. They rang up at two-thirty from the Lingeraux to ask if you were here, and of course you weren't. And I've been having visions of every sort of terrible thing. I was just going to telephone the police—'

'Oh, don't! I'm all right, honestly. I—I'm sorry. I ran away. I know now that I was silly.'

'Ran away? Why? Debbie says she knows of nothing that could have upset you. Well, listen . . . Just where are you in Hampstead?'

'Not far from the Tube station and I've got money. I'll be back as quickly as I can. And, Aunt Eileen, I—I'm terribly sorry.'

'I shan't have an easy moment until you're back,' she said. 'The rush hour, too . . . still it'll be going the other way. Except that most probably you won't be able to get on a bus at Euston. Listen, Dorrie, are you still there?'

'Yes,' I said faintly. If I couldn't get on a bus I was going to have to walk, and my ankle still ached. I might really damage it.

'Take a taxi when you get to Euston. You sound done in. Tell the man I'll pay when you get here.'

'Yes, all right,' I said.

It was wonderful to be on the way home, but when at last I sat in the taxi, being driven rather slowly in the rush hour traffic down Gower Street, I wasn't looking forward to my reception. To facing Debbie . . . to facing the whole result of my behaviour. But I had to and I was going to. I was going to explain honestly, and apologise to everyone, and never be such a fool again. Only it really was awful of Debbie to say she didn't know why I had been upset; I couldn't understand that.

I could see faces at the upper windows of the house when the taxi stopped, so the students must know all about it. Aunt Eileen and Debbie were on the doorstep, and Debbie's eyes were red, as I noticed with amazement. She couldn't have been *crying*! Debbie, who never cried.

Aunt Eileen paid the man, then led me indoors, making clucking noises.

'Child, you look terrible! Your face . . . your coat! What are all those marks on the back of your coat?

Your face is filthy and you look. . . . Have you hurt yourself?'

'Only my ankle a bit. I ricked it. I—I'm all right.'

'You don't look it. Get your things off and I'll just telephone Madame Lingeraux to tell her you're here. I rang after I'd spoken to you, and she seemed much relieved, but she asked me to let her know when you got here. You're shivering, child. It's gone cold. Keep close to the fire.'

'M-Madame!' I stammered, in horror. 'Oh, does *she* know? Is she mad with me?'

'Of course she knows. They told her, naturally. I expect she is angry with you; who wouldn't be? But she was worried, too, None of us understands what happened; why you ran away.' She was dialling the number as she spoke.

'Madame Lingeraux?' she said, into the telephone. 'She's here. Says she's ricked her ankle and she looks all in. No, I haven't had time to get anything out of her. I will, yes. I'll ask my own doctor to look at her foot. In the morning, yes, if she's able to go to school. I'll tell her.'

'Oh, dear! Oh, how awful!' I thought, as the blessed warmth of the fire began to reach me. Debbie stood on one foot near by; silent and oddly subdued.

Aunt Eileen hung up and then turned to me.

'You must have a hot drink at once. Your tea's ready. So get your coat off and never mind anything else for the moment. Debbie, where are her slippers?

145

Her ankle *is* quite puffy. Everything else can wait till afterwards.'

It was nice to be fussed over, but I wasn't looking forward to 'afterwards'. I was just dreading it.

12

Debbie and Dorrie

I was going to argue that I couldn't eat a thing, though I longed for a cup of tea, but the moment Aunt Eileen put a plate of food in front of me I knew that I was ravenous, in spite of what might come afterwards.

'Get on with your homework, Debbie.' Aunt Eileen said, in the kind of tone one couldn't ignore. Debbie gave us both doubtful glances and then, without a word, moved to the cleared space at the end of the table, took out her books and began, very slowly, to write.

Aunt Eileen then went back to the telephone and called the doctor.

'I'd be glad if you'd look at her foot, Dr Thompson. A dancer you know; can't have anything wrong with it. Yes, at the end of surgery. Thank you.' Then she turned back to me. 'You can leave your homework tonight, Dorrie. You don't look in any shape to tackle it.'

'But—But I ought—I must—'

'Finish your tea,' she ordered, and I obeyed, but by

the end of it, though feeling better physically, I was boiling up into really awful anxiety. I pushed the plates aside and looked at her desperately.

'But are they really terribly mad with me? Is Madame?'

'Well, you can't expect them to be delighted when you gave everyone a most anxious afternoon. I should think that girls have been expelled for less, you silly child. Anyway, if the doctor'll let you go, you'll have to face Madame at ten o'clock tomorrow morning. In her office.'

'Oh, *no*!' I groaned, dreadfully frightened. Miss Sherwood wouldn't have been half as bad.

Aunt Eileen gave me a look in which pity and annoyance were mingled.

'Well, come and sit by the fire and put that foot up on the buffet. The doctor won't be here for some time yet and by then you'd better be in bed. Best place for you. Debbie's lit the fire, so it'll be warm up there. Now, Miss, let's have the whole story. What on earth possessed you to behave in that stupid way? Debbie says that the last she saw of you you were sitting in the canteen with your friends and apparently perfectly all right. So—'

'I was all right then,' I said, in a muffled voice. But I had made up my mind to face it all bravely, so I gulped and went on: 'That was before I saw the lists—the lists for the Spring Show, you know. I'd worked so hard and h-hoped so much, and then, when I didn't get a part, not even a tiny one, I—I

148

just had to get away. I know now it was an awful thing to do. I knew it about half-way through the afternoon, but then it was too late.'

Just then Linda came in, ready for her evening date. She said in her usual breezy way:

'I saw the return of the prodigal from my window. Are you all right, Dorrie? What got you?'

'She's all right and we're talking,' Aunt Eileen said, still in that tone that brooked no nonsense. Linda flashed me a commiserating look and shrugged.

'O.K., I'll make myself scarce. I think I hear Derek, anyway. 'Bye, everyone! You'll survive, Dorrie.' And she was gone to open the front door.

During this exchange Debbie had pushed back her books and was staring at me with wide, startled eyes.

'Didn't get a part?' she said now. 'But—'

'But Debbie said—' Aunt Eileen began, looking bewildered.

'I looked at the list for *The Princess in the Secret Wood* and my name wasn't there. I saw that Debbie was Betty and—and so I ran away. I *know* I was childish. I know—'

'Dorrie, will you listen?' Debbie almost shouted. '*You* are Betty, you silly, great, lunatic chump!'

'*Debbie!*'

'Well, Aunt Eileen, she is. A daft, idiotic—'

'Debbie, if you can only call your sister names please be quiet.'

'I *know* it said "Betty, Deborah Darke",' I said, staring at both of them. My heart was leaping and I was wishing I hadn't eaten all those sausages.

'It said "Betty, D. Darke",' Debbie told me.

'But—But—Well, that must have been you. There weren't *two* Darkes down.' I was still gasping. 'You *can't* mean you didn't get a part?' I added faintly. I couldn't believe any of it.

'Oh, I got one. Of course I did. If you'd looked at the other lists you'd have seen. I'm the New Moon in *Moon in a Net*. It's quite a small rôle—the Full Moon is the chief one—but I do get a tiny solo dance. It said "Deborah Darke" on *that* list, so I suppose the secretary thought "D. Darke" was enough for the other one, though it was rather careless of her. When Claudia, Lotti and I went up to look Miss Verney was there, and she explained that they needed someone young and very fair for the New Moon and it was better to have me than someone in a wig. She asked if I minded very much not being in our own ballet, and of course I don't, so long as I'm in something. None of us *dreamed* you'd read it wrongly. I thought you'd be quite thrilled to get Betty. And—And—It was all so awful, and now you've made everyone mad, you idiot, and—'

I sank down into silence. *I* had been chosen to be Betty, and Debbie was quite right. I'd made everyone angry as well as worried, and Madame would almost certainly say that a girl who behaved so badly must be deprived of her part as a punishment.

Aunt Eileen glanced at me quickly and said:

'Well, I suppose it will work out somehow. It's all been most unfortunate, and I must say you were rather silly, Dorrie. Get upstairs now and have a hot bath. Go with her, Debbie, and see she's all right. I'll have to get on with the students' supper.'

I dragged myself weakly up the first flight of stairs. My ankle didn't feel too bad, it had almost stopped hurting, but my knees felt wobbly. Debbie hovered anxiously behind.

'Are you all right? Shall I ask someone to help?'

'No, I'm all right. I—I must just go slowly.'

Clyde's door opened as we gained the first landing.

'Well, hi! You're back O.K. What's the matter?'

'She's hurt her ankle,' said Debbie.

'Well, I guess I can manage to carry you to the top.'

'No, you can't. I'm heavy,' I protested.

'Heavy! A little slim girl like you? Mean to say you think I'm a weakling?' And he seized me in his arms and carried me firmly up the remaining flights. Rachel and Sara both came out to see what was happening.

'What's up with her? Can we help? Where did you get to, Dorrie?'

'She's fine. Just tired and hurt her foot a little.'

'She's going to have a bath and go to bed,' said Debbie, still close behind.

'Well, we'll come and see you later. Was Mrs Doom mad?'

'Not very p-pleased,' I said.

Debbie went down again to run the hot water in the bathroom on the floor below and Clyde dumped me gently on my bed.

'O.K. now? Shall I come back and carry you down when you've got your robe on?'

'No, thank you. I can manage all right,' I told him, and he said:

'Well, cheer up, kid. You're home all in one piece.' Then he went away and I undressed, put on my dressing-gown and slippers and went slowly down into a comforting cloud of steam. I *was* home all in one piece, but that was about all. My thoughts were still whirling. Oh, what had I done? What was going to happen to me at the Lingeraux *now*? Betty, oh, Betty! I had been given Betty when Mel was only a tree. And now I was going to lose it.

Debbie seated herself on the stool and surveyed me through the steam. She looked rather odd still, though her eyes had almost stopped being red. For some reason I felt quite shy with her, but I soon began to relax in the lovely hot water. It felt wonderful, only—

'Oh, I have made a mess of things!' I wailed.

'You certainly have,' Debbie retorted, in more her usual tone. Then she said in a burst: 'Oh, Dorrie, I'm so *glad* you're back safely! You've no idea how awful it was. Everyone questioning me, as though I'd murdered you and hidden the body. Even Madame. She was in the building, and they told her, and she asked to see me. . . . I was shattered. And then, when I came h-home, Aunt Eileen started dreadful Doomisms and I was sure you'd never be found again. Or only your d-dead body. And then I knew—well, I'd have missed—I couldn't imagine life without you.'

'Goodness!' I cried, genuinely astonished and then moved. This was Debbie come back, not the rather hard and remote sister I had known for so long.

'Why "goodness"? We're twins, aren't we? You don't think I want a *dead* twin, do you?'

'I don't know what you want,' I said slowly. 'You have so many friends, and you haven't been a bit nice—'

'Well, neither have you. You've seemed a thousand miles away for a long time. There didn't seem anything I could do, so I didn't try. Just let you go your own way.'

'You mean you think that I—I haven't been n-nice?'

'Well, have you? You didn't talk, and you seemed to disapprove of me. I didn't know what I'd *done*—'

The steam was clearing and I stared at her as though I had never seen her before. She didn't understand. She didn't know what she'd done. I think I realised then that Debbie just wasn't sensitive and I would have to come to terms with the fact. She wouldn't change.

'But, Debbie, don't you remember? It all started during that awful week-end in September. You were so horrid, and then, when they gave me a scholarship after all, you said—'

Debbie gaped at me.

'You mean you still hold that against me? I say a lot of things I don't mean. My reckless tongue. But it wasn't important. I can't even remember a word of what I said. I was just cross and disappointed—'

'Yes, I see,' I said slowly, tenderly soaping my slightly puffy ankle. 'But didn't you think I might be hurt? I was minding awfully badly about everything.'

'But so was I. We were both in a jam. You *can't* hold that against me, it wouldn't be reasonable. Let's be jolly again, Dor. Let's be as we used to be.'

'All right,' I agreed, and she heaved a big sigh of relief.

'Well, *that's* all right, anyway. One thing out of the way. We've still got Madame to worry about, and Betty—'

'Yes.' I didn't want to stay in the bath any longer. I felt sick with regret for the loss of Betty. For I was convinced that I was going to lose that part.

Soon after I was in bed Aunt Eileen came up with the doctor, who was quite young and very nice. He examined my ankle, took my temperature and said:

'Not very much wrong with her. Tired and upset, that's all. A good night's sleep will put most of that right. The ankle . . . well, I'm going to put an elastic bandage on it, just for extra support. She ought to

154

stay off it as much as possible for day or two. Certainly no dancing. If she stays in bed tomorrow—'

'Oh, doctor, I can't! Honestly I can't! I'm in trouble and I've got to go to school and face it. I shall *die* if I'm stuck here!'

'The Lingeraux?' he said. 'Not far, is it? Well, I suppose you won't do yourself much good if you lie here worrying. Go to school then, but don't move about any more than necessary, and go straight to bed when you come home,'

'Oh, thank you!' *Anything* was better than staying at home with my thoughts.

'I'll give you a note for the school. They'll probably want their own doctor to look at your foot. Not that it's much to worry about.'

No, there were worse things. I lay alone and squirmed, while Debbie finished her homework below. Yet there was a small core of inner peace, because Debbie and I might be happier together in future. I still felt that there was quite a lot of thinking to do on that score, but not just at the moment.

I was glad when Sara came bouncing up after supper. She brought me the latest Terence Rattigan play and some peppermints, and stayed to chatter about her day at R.A.D.A. She didn't ask any questions about my escapade and I was grateful. Sara had scarcely gone when Rachel came in, bringing some chocolate and a pile of magazines. She was very happy, because she had got her boy friend back.

'I don't really think he's much good, Dorrie. He's too much of a ditherer. But I *did* miss him, and at least it means I can't be as unattractive as I thought.'

Rachel was still there when Clyde arrived with a box of candy, followed closely by Winston Marshall with more sweets and magazines. Then came Arthur Moorhead with nothing, but being kind enough to want to know how I was, and finally Melinda arrived with a bunch of violets, which we put in my tooth-glass. They all sat on Debbie's bed and Aunt Eileen looked rather scandalised when she came up to see how I was.

'My goodness! Gentlemen in your bedroom, Dorrie!' But she smiled at all of them. 'She's a lucky girl to have so many good friends, but I think you'd better go now. She must have plenty of sleep, if she really means to go to school tomorrow.' When they had departed she went on: 'Two of your friends telephoned; Mel and Peter. Mel seemed really upset. I said you were home and quite all right and that they might see you in the morning.'

I didn't sleep much. After Debbie came up we talked for quite a long time, and even when I settled down my thoughts were whirling so much that I couldn't relax. I couldn't forget that I had to face Madame at ten o'clock the next morning. I couldn't forget that I might lose Betty, and now I longed more violently than ever to dance on the Lingeraux stage.

About two o'clock I went cold all over, wondering

if the very worst would happen and they would ask me to leave. About four I fell into an exhausted sleep, from which Linda's usual thumping on the door awakened me.

* 13 *

Facing Madame Lingeraux

Needless to say I didn't feel too good, but I was determined to go to school. Aunt Eileen shook her head and said I was a silly girl not to stay in bed, but, after eating the minimum of breakfast, I set off with Debbie. Debbie was being her very nicest, which was some comfort, but nothing could alter the fact that I had to face Madame as well as all the rest.

Mel and Peter were just crossing the square as we approached and they turned and saw us, then came running back.

'Oh, *Dorrie*, you've come!' Mel cried. 'Your aunt said last night that you might, if your ankle wasn't too bad.'

'We're right glad to see you,' said Peter, beaming at me.

Debbie tactfully melted away, and I was left with my friends on either side of me, both looking at me rather anxiously. Of course they probably knew nothing beyond the fact that I had run away and hurt my foot.

As we approached the school I told them a little.

'I *know* I was a fool and a coward, but I really did think it was Debbie who was Betty. Mel understands; you don't, quite, Peter. But Debbie always seems to come first, and I—I thought she had again, that I'd got nothing. And now I have to face Madame, and she'll be mad, and I shan't be able to keep Betty.'

'Oh, I do hope you can keep her!' cried Mel, very generously, because she would probably have loved to dance Betty herself.

'I may even be expelled.'

'Oh, they wouldn't do that. Don't be daft, lass. Not just for missing afternoon school,' Peter protested, his nice face very troubled.

'And upsetting everyone and wasting their time. They may think I'm not a stable type—'

'Maybe they'll put it down to your artistic temperament,' Mel suggested hopefully.

'Are we allowed to have one, at thirteen? They're much more likely to think it was just sheer naughtiness. Oh, I wish I'd stayed in bed today, as the doctor wanted,' I groaned.

It was pretty awful meeting all the others, because they did stare at me, and several asked if I was all right. Most of them were nice to me, really, and not inquisitive, and Claudia even came up especially to say:

'Debbie says you've got to see Madame. Don't be too scared. She isn't so bad, really. She'll understand.'

But I couldn't imagine *explaining* to Madame. I thought I should be completely tongue-tied and that would make everything worse.

I didn't have to change, of course, as I wasn't to dance, but I went along to the studio and gave the doctor's note to Miss Verney. She asked about my ankle and said she would pass the note on to Miss Sherwood. The school doctor would be in later to see one of the juniors and could have a look at my foot.

She didn't ask any questions, or seem angry with me, but I felt wretched as I trailed upstairs to the classroom. It was quite empty and I knew that I should try to do some of my untouched homework, but I couldn't settle down. I walked round the big room, looking at the modern reproductions on the walls, then stood at the window, looking out across Bloomsbury Square. It wasn't a very nice day, rather grey and blustery, but the crocuses were still bright.

My stomach was behaving strangely and I felt cold, in spite of the central heating. I wished that it were ten o'clock, so that I could get the dreaded interview over. Yet the other side of me would have given anything to avoid it.

About twenty-five past nine I sat down at my desk and opened my books, and it was just as well because Miss Lines came in. She went briskly to her desk, then turned and saw me.

'Oh, you're there, Dorrie? Someone said you'd hurt your foot.'

'It's not much, Miss Lines. Just—Just ricked a bit.'

I felt bad enough facing her, but to my amazement she didn't ask any questions either. She just smiled at me and said:

'Well, I suppose you've some work to get on with?'

'Yes. I—I didn't do my homework last night. I—I've to see Madame at ten.'

She merely nodded and absorbed herself in some books she took out of her case.

It was twenty to ten, a quarter to. . . . I heard footsteps and voices below as everyone began to come out of the ballet classes. Just after five to ten the members of my class began to troop in and I put away my books and rose. I felt so terrible that I thought I might be sick on the way to Madame's office.

I met Mel in the corridor and she took one look at my probably white face and said:

'Oh, Dorrie, it's rotten! I'm so sorry. But she may be all right.'

'I'm scared to death of her,' I answered. My lips felt stiff and my teeth actually chattered as I went downstairs. It was just no good telling myself that Madame had always been quite nice to me. She wouldn't be nice now, when I had behaved so badly.

I half-expected that Miss Sherwood, the principal ballet mistress and perhaps half a dozen other august people would be there, but when I knocked and

161

timidly opened the office door Madame was alone, writing at her desk. She looked up briefly, said: 'Good morning, Doria. Sit down, will you?' and continued to write.

I sat down on the edge of a chair facing her, wishing wildly that I had gone and been sick while I had the chance. The office was rather well furnished, with a thick grey carpet. If I were sick on that carpet that would just put paid to everything.

Madame Lingeraux looked to me much more formidable than usual. Small and fat she might be, but she couldn't have looked more awe-inspiring if she had been ten feet high. I jumped and nearly fell off the chair when she looked up. The bright black eyes surveyed me and then she put out her hand to the telephone. I thought that she was going to send for Miss Sherwood. but, amazingly, she asked for the canteen and then said:

'Madame Lingeraux speaking. Send me up a pot of *strong* coffee, please. Really strong, not that dishwater you give the students. And two cups.'

She replaced the receiver and said to me: 'You look as though you need it.'

'M-Madame,' I stuttered desperately, 'I think I'm going to be s-sick on the carpet.' It felt like a nightmare.

'Rubbish!' she said promptly. 'Don't you dare! What's there to be sick about? Go and sit in that other chair. It's more comfortable, so relax that tense stomach. How's the foot this morning?'

'Oh, it's nearly—nearly all right.' I practically fell into the lower chair. 'But—'

'I want to hear the whole story, of course. You must have had a reason for running away in that precipitate fashion. Someone unkind to you?'

'Oh, *no*, Madame!'

'Well, that's good. We don't get much unkindness here, but I suppose one never knows. Your sister said she could think of no reason for your being upset.'

'D-Debbie didn't know.'

The coffee came then, brought by a girl from the canteen. Madame poured out two cups and handed one to me.

'Put it on that little table and stop shaking, child. Take plenty of sugar. Now drink some.' I obeyed, burning my throat, but it was wonderful coffee. Quite different from our 'dishwater'. It made me feel better almost at once.

'Now let me hear your story.'

I looked at her helplessly. She just didn't talk like a famous figure, someone who was often in the limelight. Why, only the other day she had been on television.

'Something to do with that twin of yours, was it?'

And then I started to talk. I had never, never imagined telling Madame, but gradually I told her the same story that I had told Mel, only of course adding the end part. How I had though it was Debbie who was Betty and all the rest, including the way I had realised that, even without a part, I must face the situation.

'And—And I've had such a terrible night, thinking I was going to be expelled, or of course lose Betty—'

Madame Lingeraux silently poured second cups of coffee and handed mine back to me. My hand had stopped shaking, that was something. Then she said, in quite a gentle voice:

'I see. I thought it might be something like that, though none of us realised about the "D. Darke". You really saw it as Deborah?'

'I—well, I suppose I must have done. It seems silly now. But even if—I would still have thought that "D. Darke" was Debbie.'

'Well, your friend Mel seems to have talked sense to you and there's not much I can add, except to tell you straight from the horse's mouth—' and she gave her characteristic cackle—'that *I* wanted you to have the scholarship. There wasn't much in it, but I look for character as well as for good technique.'

'You wanted *me*?'

'Yes. As I say, there was very little in it and we had to give the scholarship to one of you. I am the owner and head of this school, but I have advisers, and those advisers slightly preferred Debbie. Only slightly; she has a beautiful body and excellent technique for her age. But you, to my mind, had something more and since then you have proved it. *I* gave you Betty, but this time everyone agreed.'

'*You* gave me Betty, Madame?' I wished I wasn't behaving like a parrot, but I had to say something.

She gave me a quick, bright glance, then shot at me:

'What did you call that dance you made up in the hall the other day?'

I gasped.

'But no one saw! I *know* there was no one there. You only came afterwards.'

'Child, I was up on the stage, looking at a rent in the curtain. They were slightly across the stage, you know. And so I watched you, and I was—more than interested. It was a good little dance and full of feeling.'

I said with difficulty, for I was so moved, so amazed:

'It—It was a Spring Dance. There were crocuses out in Bloomsbury Square and—and the sun was warm and I could smell spring coming.'

'Yes, and you interpreted it well. Now I'm glad we understand each other and you had better go back to your lessons now, and in future try and forget this inferiority complex over your sister.'

I rose. Was that *all* she was going to say?

'But, Madame, Betty—'

'What about Betty?'

'I—I thought—I was quite sure that you'd take her away from me.'

She cackled again.

'Wrong again, Doria Darke. You may keep Betty and mind you dance well. Off you go now.'

'Oh, *thank* you, Madame!' And then I fled. I raced up the stairs, quite forgetting my ankle.

I was going to dance on the Lingeraux stage! I was, perhaps for the first time for years, really sure of my own important identity. Doria Darke of the Lingeraux Ballet School.

* 14 *

The Princess in the Secret Wood

After that the last weeks of term simply flew. There were school examinations to occupy us, for one thing, and then, of course, there were rehearsals.

I loved *The Princess in the Secret Wood* from the start. The music was sometimes gay and sometimes almost eerie and I soon knew it off by heart. I had learned to whistle and I whistled those dances so endlessly that Aunt Eileen vowed that, if I didn't stop, she wouldn't come to see us dance. But, though I did try to stop, or at least to whistle something else, the others had caught it and could often be heard dashing up or downstairs whistling Betty's dance or bits from the rest of the ballet.

Debbie loved *Moon in a Net*, too. I think she particularly enjoyed rehearsing with the older ones, and Lotti and Claudia seemed to envy her.

Debbie and I had gone back to our old happier relationship. We had our ups and downs, of course, but now we could talk again nothing mattered very much. Whenever I was tempted to think that she was prettier, or cleverer, or a better dancer, I remembered some of the things Madame had said and at once felt better and more confident.

Spring had really come at last. There were daffodils out in the parks and delicate sprays of blossom. In St James's Park the willows were brilliantly green and all the other London trees were covered with a soft, shrill fuzz of bright buds.

Peter, Mel and I were very happy. We made a spendid trio, sometimes increased to a quartette by the presence of another boy called Denny Grenville, a small, cheerful Londoner who had been at the Lingeraux for just one term longer than we had. Sometimes Peter and I talked of the joys of being home at Easter, but I think he had quite settled down above the shop in St Pancras. His relatives were quite nice, though a bit rough and ready and not greatly in sympathy with a boy who wanted to be a ballet dancer. They would have understood it far better if he had wanted to be a professional footballer. All the same, his uncle and aunt had promised to come to the Spring Show.

Aunt Eileen would come, we knew, in spite of her remarks, and Linda had promised to be there, too. Clyde Smith took two tickets and said he was bringing Rachel. They were growing very friendly, which pleased me enormously, for I liked them both so much. I even hoped that their friendship would grow into something more. Rachel could probably be a scientist in America just as well, if not better, than in Britain.

The one thing that saddened Debbie and me a little was that Mother had written to say that she didn't think they could make the expensive journey south, though maybe they would another year. It would have made everything just perfect to have them there, but, in any case, we would be going home the very day after the Show. It was quite strange to think of seeing Birkenhead again and all our old friends. I longed to see Bunty and Bim, especially Bim, for three months can make such a difference to a little boy.

Easter was so late that the holidays were going to be unusually short, but we planned to make the best of the time at home.

Our costumes for the ballet were made in the Lingeraux workrooms, and we all had to go for fittings, which was very exciting. Debbie's moon dress was a silvery tunic, and she was to wear silver ballet shoes and a silver band on her hair. I, as Betty, was to wear a soft, short dress in a vivid rose pink. The other village girls were to be in yellow, blue or paler pink; Betty had to stand out.

The costumes were deliberately kept simple and as cheap as possible, but I was rather conscious that it was another expense. We didn't get them under our scholarships, but had to pay for them.

So the April days passed, the exams came and went and I hoped that I had done well. I was only really afraid of the maths papers, for figures were not my strong point. The ballets—our ballet, anyway—was almost ready and the dress rehearsal loomed ahead. I was thrilled, but, as the Show drew nearer, I was also nervous. For it would be terrible if I didn't dance well, after all. Madame Lingeraux had given me the part and she believed in me. I just had to justify her trust.

'I feel terrified, though,' I said to Mel, as we walked along Great Russell Street, just the two of us for once, on the afternoon before the dress rehearsal. 'Debbie's hardly ever nervous, but I always used to be before the Grayland shows, and they didn't matter nearly as much as this one.'

Mel nodded.

'I know. I'm almost glad now that I'm only a tree. We get some nice dances, anyway. Think if we ever become real dancers; we'll have to face it all the time, and critics as well.'

'Some ballerinas are always nervous before a performance, they say,' I remarked. 'They never grow out of it.'

All the same, though I was all fluttery with excitement and fright, the dress rehearsal went off well. It was glorious to be behind the scenes in the Lingeraux Theatre; it got into my blood and I knew that I was going to want it often. Though of course it might not happen again for years. Our ballet, that had started off as a series of apparently unconnected dances, seemed like a kind of miracle in its entirety, and the music sounded quite different when played by the

Lingeraux orchestra. Madame sat unnervingly in a box, and the principal ballet mistress sat out in front with most of the other ballet teachers. It was a relief when we could take our places in the circle and watch the other two ballets.

We broke up on the morning of the Spring Show and were then told to go home and rest. But 'resting' was just about the last thing we wanted to do, and Mel, Peter, Denny and I went to the Zoo. It was a curiously soothing place, especially watching the snakes, which always fascinated and slightly repelled me.

When I went home to tea I met Debbie in Gower Street; she had been out with Claudia and Lotti. Our tea was ready, but Aunt Eileen seemed a little remote and absent-minded. She wasn't very busy just then, because most of the students had gone home. Rachel had stayed for an extra night or two because of coming to the Show, and Clyde was off to spend Easter week-end with some American friends, leaving the next morning.

We had to be at the theatre early and Aunt Eileen seemed to be in a hurry to push us off.

'Get along, the pair of you. I have things to do. And stop looking so green, Dorrie; you'll be all right when the curtain goes up. What a child you are for showing emotion. Debbie is quite calm.'

Debbie grinned at her.

'I'm a bit fluttery, too, but I'm looking forward to it. You will come, Auntie? You and Linda?'

'Of course we'll come. It will be quite something for me to go anywhere with Linda. But it doesn't start until seven-thirty. I have to get into my best clothes before that.'

Her 'best clothes' were a dismal brown coat and a mud-coloured hat, once bought in a sale at Selfridge's. She had just no dress sense at all, but I felt very fond of her as she saw us off.

'You're sure you've got everything?'

'Everything, including our mascots,' Debbie assured her.

'Oh, those mascots! You ought to be ashamed of being so superstitious. What I say is—'

We didn't wait to hear her words of wisdom and she didn't seem to expect us to. We smiled and waved and set off through Bedford Square.

It was a dream of an evening, luminous and still, and I felt full of love for London, dear London. The high buildings shone in the lowering rays of the sun and the trees had that soft spring green that almost stops the heart. But then, when we reached the theatre, and walked in importantly at the stage door, I forgot everything but what was to come. I sniffed the stuffy, exciting atmosphere backstage and knew that it was my world, the world I wanted above all others.

Oh, it was so very thrilling, even though I was still terribly nervous. There was an air of controlled bustle, such as there might before a real professional performance. Electricians hurrying about, calling to each other, the Lingeraux stage manager in command.

Our ballet was first, then the junior one and finally *Moon in a Net*. So Debbie had to wait longer than me, but it had been decided that everyone was to get ready at once and then occupy themselves quietly in the dressing-rooms, taking turns to stand in the wings, if they were very quiet indeed. There were plenty of people in charge to see that we behaved. but Debbie was one who managed to slip on to the stage as the audience was arriving.

She came dashing back to me, where I was warming up with others in the first ballet. She looked most unusually startled; her eyes were big and full of news.

'Dorrie! Dorrie! I think I'm seeing things! Do come and look!'

'Everyone off stage in a few moments, except for the beginners in *The Princess*,' said Miss Verney, frowning at her.

'But please, Miss Verney, she *must* see! It's so extraordinary. Our father and mother are sitting in the third row, with Aunt Eileen and Linda, and they weren't coming. *We* didn't get the tickets.'

'They can't be!' I cried, and darted after her. 'They're two hundred miles away.'

The stage manager frowned at us from the prompt side, but we were already peering through the tiny gap in the curtains. Beyond was the lovely little red and gold auditorium, brilliantly lighted, and the seats were already almost full. It took me several

173

moments to train my eyes on the middle of the third row, where—incredibly—sat Dad and Mother. Mother was reading the programme; I could just see her face. She was wearing a new hat, blue with a small blue flower. It gave me the most extraordinary feeling to see them there; real again at last. It was like a miracle, for we had been told so emphatically, three weeks earlier, that they wouldn't be coming. It explained Aunt Eileen's preoccupied air and the way she had wanted to get rid of us.

'Isn't it wonderful? *Now* we'll have to dance superbly,' Debbie cried.

Debbie was then swept away by the stage manager and I continued to warm up, my thoughts whirling. But I knew I only had to think of Betty, of the coming ballet, and I did my best to concentrate on the secret wood.

'Overture and beginners. . . .' We heard the music of the overture beyond the thick curtains. My mouth was dry and my knees felt weak. The village children opened the ballet.

And then the curtain rose, the auditorium was a dark blur, and we were dancing against our background of painted scenery. And suddenly I was no longer nervous, but very happy. I was Betty, a village child, surrounded by trees and meeting a Princess for the first time. I was frightened of the Green Witch . . . I was lost in the atmosphere of the ballet.

When my own little solo came part of my mind seemed to stand apart, as though I were someone else, sitting out in the audience. And that other person could see the bright stage and the solitary, pink-clad figure that was me.

It was my night of nights ... my dream world come true, if only briefly in one little ballet. It seemed to be over so quickly; the curtain came swishing down and the applause rang out behind the heavy folds.

Then the curtain rose again for all the dancers to be seen, and after that Claudia, Caroline and Serge went out in front, to bow and smile and to have their extra rounds of applause. Then the Green Witch alone and finally me. Claudia and Caroline were presented with flowers, but I had not expected any. However, two bouquets were handed to me and I stood there in the blaze of light, blinking and almost overcome. Not important ... the real thing still unimaginably far away ... but then, just for those moments, it seemed real.

I found myself back in the wings, back in the dressing-room I was sharing with a number of others Debbie was there and took the flowers.

'I say! From Clyde and Rachel! And from Dad and Mother, Aunt Eileen and Linda. And a note from Mother. Can I read it?'

'Do,' I said. Somehow I couldn't see properly.

Mother's note said: 'We are here, after all, and will come round after the show. Best love.'

Debbie had her little triumph, too. I watched from the O.P. corner throughout *Moon in a Net*. She looked lovely in her silvery costume, with her flying silvery hair. A little New Moon, enchantingly fair. And Debbie had two bouquets as well and was starry-eyed with happiness.

'Oh, Dorrie,' she said, clutching her flowers, 'if this is what it feels like I'll work until I drop!'

They all came behind as they had promised. By then I was in my ordinary clothes and had taken off my make-up, but Debbie was still in her moon-tunic. Mother looked very slightly red-eyed, but said she had enjoyed every moment.

'I had to pinch myself to make myself believe you were my twins. Oh, Dorrie! Oh, Debbie!'

We hugged Dad and Mother unashamedly. No one was noticing, anyway. There was a terrific mob.

'But why did you come? It's wonderful, but we thought—'

'We changed our plans. Something came up. You'll hear in time. It's a secret and a surprise.'

'But Bunty and Bim?'

'Mrs Brown has taken them. We're all staying in London until the day after tomorrow.'

They would say no more, and neither would Aunt Eileen or Linda. We all went home in a taxi—great luxury—and there was a real new moon shining down over London. I couldn't imagine what the second surprise might be.

＊15＊

The Second Surprise

No one would tell us anything. That night we were sent up to bed just as soon as we had had some milk and biscuits. Mother came to see us in our garret when we were in bed and I thought she looked round critically, but she made no comment.

'We like it,' I said defensively. 'It was terribly cold in the winter, in spite of the fire, but we've grown very fond of it.'

Mother just said 'Hum!' and went to look out of the window, drawing back the curtains to see the moonlit, lamplit view.

'You both like London?' she asked, after a few moments.

'We *love* it!' said Debbie. 'There's no place like it.'

Mother laughed, then tucked us in and kissed us as she used to do when we were little.

'Try to go to sleep at once. I know it has been a very thrilling evening.'

'But we won't sleep unless we know about the surprise,' I said coaxingly.

She just laughed and went away.

No one would tell us in the morning, either, but Aunt Eileen said we were all going out together. It all seemed extremely mysterious, but we obediently went upstairs to get ready. It wasn't like Aunt Eileen to take jaunts in the morning, but when we came down she was waiting with Dad and Mother. Mother looked pink and pretty, and Dad looked rather handsome, too.

'And you won't tell us where we're going?' I asked, and they all laughed and shook their heads.

Well, it was really rather nice to have a surprise coming, for otherwise it might have been rather an anti-climax, with the Spring Show over for a whole year. By then I was familiar with many parts of London, for we had wandered quite widely during the past weeks, and also I never ceased to enjoy my London street map. But in any case we didn't go far, though we travelled on three buses. The third bus we took for just a few stops down Vauxhall Bridge Road. Debbie kept catching my eye and once she shook her head. It was all very strange, but interesting, even exciting. We sensed that the three adults were also rather excited, even Aunt Eileen.

Vauxhall Bridge Road is by no means beautiful, but after we left the bus we soon turned off it, heading towards the south end of Vincent Square, which is a simply huge green stretch given over to the playing-fields of Westminster School. I named it before we quite got there and Aunt Eileen said:

'She's a real Londoner already.'

We were soon in a quiet, old-fashioned street. It had a few shops and some rows of small, ordinary houses, fronting straight on to the pavement.

'Between here and the Tate there are mostly new blocks of flats,' Aunt Eileen remarked.

'Are we going to the Tate Gallery then?' Debbie demanded. But Aunt Eileen had stopped outside one of the houses and was taking a key from her purse. I noticed then that the house was empty. It was quite newly painted, with a yellow front door.

Aunt Eileen opened the door, and, silent and puzzled, Debbie and I followed them into a small, cream-painted hall. All the doors were open, showing empty rooms, very scrubbed and clean.

'But why have we come?' Debbie asked, standing on one foot and staring into the neat little kitchen. It was modern, though the house must be quite old. 'Whose house is it? Why—?'

'All in good time,' said Aunt Eileen and began to show the house to Dad and Mother. They went from room to room, exclaiming over cupboard space and electric light fittings, the number and size of the bedrooms. Debbie and I trailed behind, grimacing at each other.

'It's really rather nice,' Mother was saying. 'Quite a big yard, almost a garden, with that flower-bed and the plane tree. And it isn't far from the bus.'

'Is Aunt Eileen going to move here, do you think?' Debbie hissed at me.

179

A wild suspicion was starting in my mind, but I couldn't really believe it.

'Do you think *we* are?' I hissed back, and she looked startled, tossing back her hair.

'How could we? Dad works in Birkenhead.'

'Just for the next two weeks,' Dad said suddenly. 'After that I shall be working in London.'

We shrieked and the sound echoed through the empty house.

'But how . . . why? You can't mean it! You mean we'll live with you and not in Gower Street? That—'

'I believe they'll miss your house,' Mother said, laughing. 'Oh, we came up quite early yesterday and your dad had an interview. He got the job and is to start in two weeks' time, so we shall have to buckle to when we get home. There'll be a lot to do. He will be working in the radio and television department of one of the big stores. Not as manager—just yet, anyway—but the money is more than he's getting now. And your aunt had promised that, if he got the job, she could find us a house. It belongs to her husband's brother, who owns quite a lot of property in these parts and he's willing to rent it to us. Otherwise we'd hardly have managed, as houses or flats are so difficult to get in London.'

'We hope you're pleased,' Dad said, and we both hugged him at once and talked loudly, trying to drown each other.

Then we looked at the house more carefully, since

it was going to be home. It was certainly small, perhaps too small for six of us, but I thought how glorious it was going to be to be so near the Tate and the river.

'But I hope you'll often come and see me,' Aunt Eileen said, as we walked back to the bus stop. 'I shall miss the pair of you.' She even looked quite fondly at Debbie, and Debbie actually blushed.

'Oh, of *course* we will,' I promised. 'We'll miss you, too, and all the students and dear, dear Ruari.'

I felt just a little sad as we went back to Gower Street for lunch. It would be wonderful to have Dad and Mother, Bunty and Bim in London, and not far away; to go home every evening from the Lingeraux and to be able to see Mel in the holidays as well as in term-time. Yet I should miss our strangely romantic garret in Gower Street and all the excitements of the students' lives.

'I shall miss it, too,' Debbie agreed, when we were back in the garret. She turned a couple of pirouettes, then took my hand. We danced a wild *pas de deux*, leaping and twirling in what space there was.

'The Darke dancers!' Debbie gasped, just as the door opened and Aunt Eileen came in.

'Good heavens, girls! You'll have the ceiling down in the room below. This is no place for your capers. Lunch is ready.'

We followed her meekly down the stairs; those

familiar stairs that had seen so much of my suffering. Our first term at ballet school was over, but next term we would dance again in Bloomsbury Square.